D1796196

First published by Maria Lewis in 2017
This edition published in 2018 by Maria Lewis
Copyright © Maria Lewis 2017
marialewis.com.au
The moral right of the author has been asserted.
It Came From The Deep
EPUB: 9781925579871
Cover design by Maria Lewis and Samuel Spettigue
Map illustration by Allison Tyree

❀ Created with Vellum

IT CAME FROM THE DEEP

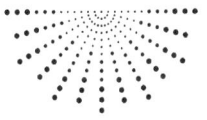

MARIA LEWIS

ALSO BY MARIA LEWIS

Novels
Who's Afraid?
Who's Afraid Too?

Anthologies
Doing It: A Sex Positive Anthology
Hot Stuff: Surfing Love

PRAISE FOR WHO'S AFRAID?

"Gripping, fast-paced, and completely unexpected, Who's Afraid? has more twists than a tornado. I loved this story!" – NY Times best-selling author Darynda Jones

"The next True Blood." – NW Magazine

"If you love a strong female lead, then Who's Afraid? by Maria Lewis is a must-read." - BuzzFeed

"It's about time we had another kick-arse werewolf heroine - can't wait to find out what happens next!" – NY Times best-selling author Keri Arthur

"Journalist Maria Lewis grabs the paranormal fiction genre by the scruff of its neck to give it a shake with her debut novel Who's Afraid?" – The West Australian"

"It's Underworld meets Animal Kingdom." – ALPHA Reader

"Truly one of the best in the genre I have ever read." – Oscar-nominated filmmaker Lexi Alexander (Green Street Hooligans, Punisher: War Zone)

"Lewis creates an intriguing world that's just begging to be fleshed out in further books." –APN

"If you haven't heard about Maria Lewis, you must have been living under a rock." - Good Reading Magazine

"Lovers of werewolves and paranormal fiction take note: Who's Afraid? isn't your typical urban fantasy." – Geek Bomb

"Really, really refreshing." – ABC Radio

"The Sydney-based author takes the reader somewhere they've never been before." - Daily Record

"We can't wait to see where she goes next as this series continues to go from strength-to-strength." – SciFi Now Magazine

"How long until we see Tommi Grayson on the big screen?" - AusRomToday

"In a world filled with daily anxiety Maria's series is a respite and a haven." - Teri Hatcher (Lois & Clark, Desperate Housewives)

"This is an excellent sequel in a series written by a supernatural genre lover for genre fans." – APN

"Maria Lewis is definitely one to watch." – NY Times best-selling author Darynda Jones"

"The concept is so original that I had to know where this story came from." - Handbag Mafia

"It's about mermaids and mermen, with a murder mystery, and the procedural elements are her experience as a journalist coming out." - 2SER 107.3FM

DEDICATION

To sea men everywhere.

MAP

PROLOGUE

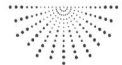

The police found his body exactly the way it had been left: face-down, spread-eagle, and lying in a pool of his own blood as it oozed across the pearl-white tiles. Professor Viktor Waldman had lived in a quiet, up-market suburb that consisted mostly of small mansions and elaborate houses positioned around a sprawling freshwater lake. It was aptly titled The Lakes, although there was only one lake to speak of. Neighbours had heard – and some had seen – an SUV charge down the Professor's gate. Although none of them left the safety of their homes to investigate, they *had* called the police.

A three-car accident on the highway had kept officers longer than expected. Long enough for the murderers to escape and for snoopy Mrs Petsch across the way to get a glimpse at the carnage left behind. Detectives were on the scene in just under an hour though, and that wasn't bad for a Thursday night in Australia's fastest growing city. Senior Constable Robert Housego ducked under the police tape that had cordoned off the property from curious passers-by and – he was displeased to see – the press. He nodded at a few familiar faces before stepping into the house. If you could call it a house.

It had probably been your typical lakeside mansion in the eighties – cream carpeted steps leading upstairs, soft pink walls and a completely white tiled floor. But the house had since been converted into something else entirely. Two steps through the entranceway and it was no longer a home, it was a laboratory. The kitchen was barely visible behind a large fish tank, just one of dozens in the space that looked more like an aquarium than the dining room it had been converted from. Tanks lined every wall, most of them full of water and an assortment of sea creatures: fish, a few stingrays, starfish, seahorses, eels, and Lord knows what else.

A cleared area near the entrance housed several computers, with a workspace and smaller tanks positioned next to that. Tidal charts and sheets of figures Senior Constable Housego had no hope of understanding were pinned and highlighted on corkboards above. The interior had been added to at some point to make what had once been an outdoor lap pool into an indoor lap pool. It was now empty, along with a huge tank on the opposite side of the room big enough to fit a shark. Or three.

In the centre of it all lay a man, quite old and quite dead. Senior Constable Housego took a step towards the body and paused as broken glass cracked under his feet. The man's blood had mixed with puddles of water and spread in inconceivable patterns throughout the room. A woman in navy overalls looked up from her position next to the body.

'Senior Constable Housego,' she said, formally.

'What have we got, Lenny?' If the informal use of Chief Forensic Officer Luyen Chan's nickname annoyed her, she didn't show it.

'Helluva mess, apparently.'

'You're not bloody kidding,' he replied, taking in the state of the room and some of its still-smoking contents.

'This here is Doctor Viktor Waldman.' She gestured to the body. 'Award-winning marine biologist who works over at Hodgkins University.'

'Worked,' corrected Senior Constable Housego. 'You got all that from the body?'

'The neighbour,' she said, nodding at a heavy woman dressed in pyjamas who was being comforted by a junior officer.

'What I got from the body is your standard execution-style kill. One to the knee cap for emphasis and a short time later, another to the skull.'

'Only two bullets fired?'

'Only two bullets.'

'Hmph. Professionals then. Last month there was a bikie hit a few suburbs over from here. Any chance this could be related?'

'I don't see how an esteemed academic could have any ties to an outlaw motorcycle gang. Also, different weapons, different style, different MO. This doesn't feel like that.'

'You've been wrong before,' he muttered, stepping carefully around the body.

'Once,' Chan snapped.

He sniffed, taking a whiff of the burnt plastic. An officer stepped out of his way as he examined several ruined computers.

'Hydrofluoric acid,' Chan said from behind him. 'A quick way to destroy a computer when you don't have much time.'

'Is any of this retrievable?' he asked, looking around for a tech specialist. One was hovering nearby, clearly anticipating the question.

'Afraid not, the acid did its job,' she answered. 'Any information that was on there is lost forever, unless it was backed up via an online storage system. The security footage is gone too.'

'Security footage?'

'That was destroyed as well. Smashed.'

'No acid?'

The tech girl shook her head.

'You have the acid out, why not destroy the security hard drive at the same time? Unless ... one was done by the victim, and the other by the killers trying to cover their tracks,' mused Senior Constable Housego.

'Why would the victim destroy his own files? That doesn't make any sense.'

'Look at this room, Lenny, we're practically in Atlantis. None of this makes any sense. Where's the security monitor?'

The tech pointed as the detective went to investigate. They were right, the monitor and hard drive had been completely smashed and ... shot?

'Lenny, I think we may have had some more shots fired over here. See if there are any bullets embedded in the wall behind the monitor or in the wreckage.'

'Aye aye, captain.'

His gloved hand slipped into his pocket, where he retrieved a pair of tweezers. Grabbing the flashlight holstered to his utility belt, he crouched down as his eyes ran over the pieces of broken plastic and glass that acted like a mosaic layer across the tiled floor. As his light swept the area, a metallic glint caught his attention. Slowly, carefully, he leaned forward and used the tweezers to retrieve a golden bullet casing.

'9mm,' Senior Constable Housego said, holding it up for inspection.

Chan paused what she was doing, looking back at him. 'Same as what I took from the body.'

'Not the bikie ammunition of choice.'

Glancing around, Senior Constable Housego fished five more casings from the debris and sealed them each in evidence baggies.

'So he gets two, one to the knee and one to the head. Then it looks like they emptied almost an entire round into the security system. That's a lot of noise and a lot of bang.'

'We've got two sets of footprints coming in and going out,' Chan added, indicating an area on the floor that had been highlighted with bright yellow markers.

'But only one gun used?' Senior Constable Housego asked, speaking mainly to himself. 'The other person was there for … what? Moral support?'

His gaze fell on a familiar logo just over Chan's shoulder: Seeing All Security. A small ping of excitement shot through him.

'Constable Mead,' he shouted, calling to the younger officer who had been getting a statement from the neighbour.

'Yes, sir?'

'Get in touch with Seeing All Security. These assholes might have destroyed the physical backups, but everything that's caught on camera is recorded and saved directly into their system at the Southport head office. We need the footage for the last, say, twelve hours. Account holder is a Doctor Viktor Waldman, 83 Rio Vista Boulevard, The Lakes.'

'I'm on it, sir.'

'And Mead?'

'Yes?'

'We need that footage ASAP. We'll get a warrant if we have to, but explain the situation and they should be accommodating.'

'Yes, sir.'

Senior Constable Housego hoped this was just the first stroke of luck he'd have with what was quickly turning out to be a very weird case. He turned to survey the room once more. It was cloaked in shadow, with the only visible light coming from police lamps and the eerie reflection of the tanks. The glow of heaters and filters inside the enclosures made shades of blue and green project around the room. The tanks' occupants were silhouetted and the area felt almost alive. He didn't like it.

'Can we get some proper light in here?' he yelled. Various shouts of confirmation were given in response.

'Power was cut. They've been working to get it back up since I got here,' Chan said.

'The tanks are still working,' he noted.

'They run off a separate generator.'

'Lot of effort for some fish.'

'He *was* a marine biologist,' she said, dryly.

The detective's attention was drawn back to the huge, empty tank at the edge of the room. Being careful not to step in the puddles of blood and water, he examined the interior of the bare space through the glass. A single object lay at the bottom of the tank: a squeaky toy shaped like a conch shell. He frowned.

'What do you 'spose was in there?' he asked.

'Don't know,' Chan replied, approaching behind him. 'Something.'

They looked thoughtfully at the tank for another long moment.

'Something big.'

CHAPTER ONE

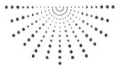

I n a country famed for its natural beauty, Surfers Paradise beach was one of the most iconic in Australia. It was towards the northern tip of a flawless length of golden sand that spanned some fifty kilometres. It also happened to be the unofficial capital within the burgeoning coastal community of the Gold Coast. The sand was barely visible as thousands of bodies packed on to every spare inch of space on the beach for the Australian Surf Live Saving Titles. Kaia Craig was one of those bodies, but she was blocking everyone else out as she kept her eyes focused on what was in front of her.

Surf.

Surf rolling in massive, frothy mounds of eight to ten feet. If it got much bigger they were going to have to cancel the event. But there was only one day left of the six-day competition and it was doubtful officials would call off the race now. She was standing on top of the starting platform, just minutes out from the beginning of the Open Ironwoman race – the shiny crown of Surf Life Saving. Arguably the more important title was the Energen X Ironman Series (which she had taken out three weeks previously) or perhaps the notorious endurance race, the Coolangatta Gold (another win, albeit by a slim margin at the start of the season). Both of those titles brought money, prestige and press to the winner. The Aussie title gave you nothing – nothing except the knowledge that you had taken out the three most important events in the sport: the trifecta.

And Kaia wanted it. At the age of eighteen she'd spent more time doing this sport than anything else. It felt as if every moment had been leading up to this one. Every hour spent body surfing with her brother, every wave break she smashed through racing her father, every mouthful of water she'd swallowed after a wipe out … it had all been leading up to this. She shook out her legs and arms to calm her nerves, all the while keeping her eyes on the surf. The sets were big, and getting bigger. The waves were coming in groups of seven to eight, followed by a tiny lull of no more than thirty seconds or so. She'd been out in much worse than this. From the green looks on the faces of her competitors, they hadn't. She told herself that all she had to do was be the fastest to the drop zone, time her breakthrough perfectly and she'd have this in the bag. A deep crackle rang out over the PA system marking the beginning of the pre-race commentary

'Thanks, Jimbo. Yes, that's right, folks – we have the final event of the day with the fight for the coveted Open Ironwoman Australian Title. For spectators joining us for the first time, the race is held over three legs: board, swim and ski, with the order being exactly that for today's race. The ladies here will paddle out through the particularly brutal break on their boards and around three apex cans, before returning to the shore and running around the marked flags. They'll head out again, this time swimming around the string of buoys before once more running around the flags and heading out for the final leg: the surf ski. The first girl to cross the finish line will claim the title.'

'I think it's gonna be a tough race for the gals, Tony. As we saw, the men's race earlier took 20 minutes longer than it usually would, which is testament to the trying conditions.'

'It's certainly the roughest swell we've seen this season. Let's talk favourites: who's your pick?'

'I think that's a no-brainer: the defending champ Kaia Craig. She been in impeccable form this season and we just saw her dominate the Energen X Ironman Series. She's got the Cooly Gold, she's got the series, I think she has her sights firmly aimed at the title and these are certainly her kind of conditions.'

'Yes, you're on the money there. Kaia is, of course, the daughter of Aussie legend and three-time world champion surfer Ken "KC" Craig, who I believe was down on the beach giving her a pep talk in the marshalling arena.'

'Her older brother, Storm, has a few Aussie board titles under his belt too from back in the day, and there's no doubting the Craigs shine in tricky conditions like this.'

'They're a talented family and old man KC has certainly passed on his uncanny ability to read the surf to his daughter, who has been racing for Middle Beach Surf Life Saving Club since she was a nipper. But I think there may be more out there today than even she has bargained for – something lurking under the water, perhaps?'

'You're not wrong, Jimbo, you're not wrong. Another one to watch has to be Amy Perkins from the Maroubra Surf Life Saving Club down in New South Wales. She's certainly a strong competitor on the craft and—'

'Ah, it looks like the starter has them lined up and they're ready to go, Tony. Let's get this race underway.'

The gun fired and Kaia was off, sprinting to her board and wading through the shallows as she tugged it along behind her. It was too windy to tuck it under her arm – like some of the other girls had unsuccessfully tried – and given how far in front she was already, it seemed she had made the right decision. But she knew she couldn't think about a lead now. All it took was an unlucky knock from one ill-timed wave and she could be back in the middle of the pack.

Never waste an opportunity, she thought, repeating her father's favourite catchphrase in her head. Ever since she could walk, KC had been teaching her and Storm how to read the surf, how to take advantage of the unnoticed currents and the unexpected openings. She did this now as she popped over a broken wave and angled herself in the direction of a small, but significant rip that would help drag her beyond the break quicker.

Suddenly she was heading back to shore, uncertain of how she had got around the course so quickly. The rip hadn't moved *that* fast, yet Kaia didn't remember paddling around the cans, in fact, she didn't remember the rest of the board leg at all. Now wasn't the time to focus on that, Kaia reasoned, shaking her head as she copped a splash of water to the face. Blinking the salt out of her eyes, she hardly felt the sting any more. Her arse was sky-bound as she bent down on her knees and extended her arms to push the water and propel herself forward as she paddled. There was no one around her, yet Kaia urged herself to go faster, to dig deeper as she rose and fell with the movement of the ocean. She was heading into the break zone when she lurched forward and her board came to a dead halt.

Impossible.

It felt as if the fin had run aground on a sand bar, yet she was still a solid 100 metres from the shore. She looked behind her to see what it could have been caught on. Nothing. There was nothing there. She could see her rival competitors quickly approaching and behind that a monstrous blue set of waves looming. She needed to get out of there and fast. Wiggling into position on her stomach, she began paddling frantically. Yet she wasn't going anywhere. What in the hell was holding her up? Propping her legs over each side of the board, she swivelled again to look behind her. She felt the water drawing back as the first of the set waves started sucking up. Her heartbeat quickened as she realised she was in the drop zone. A sudden splash near her ankle had her looking down. There was a shadow, a round, dark shadow getting bigger and bigger as it moved closer to the surface. A hand shot out of the water and grabbed Kaia's calf tightly in its grip. It was a human hand, but it was an off-green colour, and slimy. A piece of seaweed was caught around one of the fingers. She didn't scream, didn't shout, didn't do anything but stare in abject horror as the owner of the hand slowly emerged from the water.

She had been young, barely seventeen when she died. Whatever afterlife she'd had hadn't been kind to her. Her flesh was puffy and bloated from being underwater so long. Cuts lined her arms and her face: a mixture of decomposition and other animals taking a nibble here and there. Her once-vibrant red hair was now the colour of rust, like the hull of a sunken ship. She drew herself closer, towards Kaia, and up onto the board. Kaia was frozen in shock and fear. It wasn't until she was inches from her face that the creature smiled, an evil and toothless grin. As her lips extended, a small crab scuttled out of her mouth and down her neck.

'Remember me, Kaia?' she whispered.

With surprising strength, the *thing* yanked her off the board and into the water. Kaia twisted her body at the last minute in an attempt to grab something, anything. She managed to clutch the back strap of the board and held onto it for dear life. The girl might be strong, Kaia thought, but she wasn't strong enough to pull her and the weight of the craft down under. All she had to do was not let go of the strap and she'd be—

A loss of pressure reverberated through her as the handle snapped free of the screws that had been holding it in place. Kaia had a second to stare at the broken handle in her hand before water rushed over her face as she was pulled down, down, down into the depths. She screamed a soundless scream that was lost to the never-ending abyss of the ocean.

Kaia woke shouting and thrashing, as was her habit. Jerking upright, it was a good ten seconds before she seemed to realise that she was wet with sweat and not, as she feared, seawater. The sheets were also not trying to 'get' her. She stilled her movements and hung her head between her knees. Her shoulders heaved in time with her heavy, forced breathing as she tried to adjust to the reality of it being *just* a nightmare. A horrific nightmare, sure, but she had those most nights.

This was nothing unusual.

Placing a hand on her chest, she tried to still her rapidly beating heart as it did its best to escape from the confines of her chest. A whimper made her raise her head and look around the room for the source of the noise.

'Quint?' she whispered. 'Here, boy.'

It took another moment before she realised the sound was coming from her. Sweeping back the hair that was hanging over her face, she wiped the tears from her cheeks and let out a ragged breath. She let her eyes adjust to the darkness as she took in the comforting sight of her room. Another deep breath. Then she rolled over to her bedside table, pulled open one of the drawers and retrieved a bottle that rattled as she moved it. It was too dark for her to read the dosage instructions, but she already knew what they said. Benzodiazepines, prescribed to her seven months ago to help battle night terrors. She cradled the cool plastic in the palm of her hand for several long minutes before tossing the bottle back in the drawer and slamming it shut. A bright light illuminated the room as she pressed several buttons on her digital wristwatch. It was 4.27AM.

'Son of a bitch,' she groaned.

There were exactly three more minutes until she had to be up. Kaia threw the damp sheets off her body, slid to the side of the bed and stood up to stretch. The tiles beneath her feet were cool, but she welcomed the change in temperature to help wake her up. Pulling her loose-fitting flannel pyjama pants down the significant length of her legs, she felt like she barely had time to wriggle into a Speedo swimsuit before her alarm was buzzing at 4.30AM. She flicked the button off and didn't examine her darkened reflection in the mirror. She didn't need the lights to see what was there: it was the same thing every morning when she rose at this hour.

She tugged on a pair of tracksuit pants and her favourite hoodie, then tucked her hair under the hood. In a daze, she padded out to the kitchen and grabbed a container of water from the fridge. She dumped several spoonfuls of protein powder into it before heading out to her car. The only sound that followed her was the soft sloshing as she shook the ingredients together. Sitting for a moment in the front seat, she reluctantly looked up at her reflection in the rear-view vision mirror. Kaia Craig was a girl in serious need of an uninterrupted night's sleep. She pulled herself away from morbid thoughts and glanced at the clock as she began reversing down the driveway. Not even 4.45AM. It was early August so it wouldn't get light until at least 6.30AM. She flicked on the headlights of her silver Honda CRV and began the drive to the swimming pool.

The mellow sounds of Angus and Julia Stone played through her speakers, but she barely registered the music.

Even with the seat pushed back as far as possible, her long limbs still felt cramped as her feet tapped the gear pedal and moved the car into third gear. At six foot one, Kaia was tall enough to be a runway model – or so her mother, Leah, had always told her. She could even hear the exact words her mother would have used playing in her head. It always started like 'with your height, sweetie' followed by 'you wouldn't have to waste your years with centrefolds'. The concluding remarks tended to be a variation on 'of course you'd need a nose job to get rid of the lump, but everyone gets those these days'. All of this would have been said from the other side of a martini glass, which would be getting drained quickly.

Kaia's mum had been an American swimsuit model in her prime, which was when her dad had met and married her in the early nineties. They divorced when Kaia was six and Leah Craig moved to Hawaii, leaving her son and daughter behind. She called on birthdays. Sometimes. What she may have neglected to give Kaia in motherly tendencies, she had certainly made up for in physicality. Both Kaia and her brother sported the impossibly long, lean and lanky bodies courtesy of Leah's genetic blessings. Their hair, however, was entirely their father's fault. It was so blond it was almost white, which probably wasn't helped by constant exposure to the sun and ocean. Unlike Storm, Kaia had also received a visible ridge in the centre of her nose from her dad's genetic pool: something that made him look masculine and she felt made her look like Owen Wilson on a bad day.

Pulling to a stop at a traffic light, Kaia couldn't help but let her mind wander as she thought about her dad. Ken Craig had been the first Aussie to win back-to-back surfing world titles – three in total – and had only retired from the world tour six years ago at the age of forty-five. Now he spent his time chasing storms with his buddies in search of the biggest surfable wave on the planet. He also mentored a handful of grommets on the Silver Swell Quest. Needless to say, he wasn't home a lot. At least he hadn't been since …

Shaking her head slightly, Kaia told herself she didn't have time to think about this now. She tried to wipe the thoughts from her mind like an Etch-A-Sketch. Her psychiatrist – the same one who had prescribed her the pills – discouraged her from reflecting on childhood, saying that she had enough to deal with in the present. So that's where Kaia tried to drag herself back to, her eyes flicking over the dark, empty road. A reflective light flashed ahead of her as she neared a group of cyclists in high-visibility clothing.

By the time she made it to the pool, she was desperate to get in the water and drown her thoughts.

───────

'Hi Kaia!'

She glanced at the kid who had called her name, nodding in response as the girl leapt out of her parents' car. A bleary-eyed mother stared out with mild interest. No doubt she had heard of Kaia Craig, a thought that made Kaia extremely uncomfortable. She didn't stop and wait for the girl, hoping that the brief acknowledgment would be enough to sate her but also prevent a conversation. She couldn't have been much older than thirteen or so and her name was something like Becca or Bertha. No, must be Becca. No one called their kids Bertha any more unless they really hated them. A few other regulars muttered 'hellos' and 'good mornings' as Kaia pushed through the gates. She nodded and tried to keep her head down so as to avoid any other welcomes. As usual she felt the stares, always stares. The surf life saving season was just gearing up and she knew it would only get worse as more people returned to training. Kaia was prepared for it. Or so she told herself.

Flinders Park swimming pool wasn't much, but it was somewhat of a Gold Coast icon. It had been there since the fifties and – despite dozens of renovations – it still looked like it belonged in that period. The two Olympic-sized swimming pools certainly didn't, however, and even in the morning darkness their iridescent blue tiles gave off a science-fiction glow. Kaia walked soundlessly along the grey concrete towards an undercover area at the end of the pool reserved for training squads. The other pool was empty for now, but it would begin to fill with lap swimmers and elderly water aerobics enthusiasts closer to 8AM. A small group of fifteen or so people were gathered together talking and grumbling about being awake at this hour. She avoided all of them by taking the long way around the structure and placing her bag on a long, empty outdoor table.

Although it was nearly 5AM, no one looked keen to remove their beanies and scarves and get in the water. It was barely below 15C and the pool was heated. Yet for some reason everyone acted like a nuclear winter was coming right up until the moment a coach screamed at them to 'get in the blasted pool'. That coach was almost always BB – real name Brenton Booth. Kaia had always found it ironic that two important men in her life were better known by a duo of letters positioned together. BB was like most swim coaches: grumpy in nature, a chain smoker and a mad genius. He'd been on the world tour with her dad back in the day, before he retired to become a swimming coach. Since then he'd trained a dozen Olympic champions and countless surf life saving legends – from Trevor Hendy to Karla Gilbert. Kaia had been swimming with BB since she was ten, after her dad insisted she get a 'real coach'.

Most people feared BB and, true, he was fearsome man.

Barely over five foot five and wire-thin, he still managed to inspire dread in grown men and women alike. He was tough and his sessions were brutal when they needed to be. To train in his squad you had to work your way up through three other coaches – and even then, most people preferred to fly under the radar at BB's sessions. For those who understood him, they knew how to get the best out of his madness: show up often, on time, don't answer back and always give 110 per cent in the pool. It was a simple recipe and one that hadn't changed in all the years she had been training under him. Still, Kaia always marvelled at the rogue few who tried to butt heads with BB. They usually lasted no more than a few weeks.

She stripped down to her swimmers – a metallic green full-piece – and grabbed her bathing cap and goggles. Making her way to the usual lane (number three), she couldn't help but smile as she heard BB's raspy yell at the people standing around behind her. Placing a water bottle on the pool's edge, Kaia sat next to it and dipped her feet into the liquid below.

'Sheesh, he's not in a good mood this morning, is he?'

With a heavy thud, Jarna 'Cabby' Cabin plonked herself down on the tiled surface.

'It is a Monday,' Kaia muttered, twirling her hair into a knot at the back of her head.

'Yup, that makes all the difference,' Cabby said sarcastically.

She wasn't sure if she could call Cabby a friend, but since she began training with the squad over a year ago, Kaia had enjoyed regular banter and a familiarity with her that somehow never extended beyond the pool's premises. She could never put a finger on why that was. They competed for different surf clubs and swimming training was the only place they saw each other besides on the beach at surf carnivals, which made things difficult. Regardless, she dug what they had going on. When Kaia was at training she liked to train, not joke around and catch up on the latest gossip. Cabby and she had this in common. Plus, the girl could swim. She came from a competitive swimming background before making the cross over into surf racing, and it showed. She was easily the fastest person in the squad and Kaia strived to be a steady second.

'How was your weekend?' Cabby asked.

Kaia shrugged as she stretched the silicone of her bathing cap with her hands and pulled it over her head.

'You?' she asked, tucking the loose strands of hair underneath.

A year older than Kaia, Cabby had a sweep of dark brown hair that she kept in a pixie cut that somehow managed to remain stylish no matter what time of the morning it was. She had a typical swimmer body – six-pack and all – and everything about her screamed 'strong'.

'I got laid,' she said, mimicking Kaia's shrug.

'Good for you. Anyone we know?'

Cabby cast a casual glimpse behind them and nodded at a short girl in a purple two-piece. Imogen Tishop, a twenty-something from Cabby's surf club, West Port. She was a mediocre competitor, but a decent swimmer and genuinely one of the nicest people in the squad. Although from the brief conversations Kaia had with her, she was quite certain the wheel in her head was spinning but the hamster was long dead.

'She seems sweet,' Kaia said, impassive about Cabby's conquest and eager to start the warm-up.

'I knew you'd be no fun to tell,' she sighed.

Kaia shrugged again, unapologetic. 'Who else have you told?'

'No one. A gentlelady should never kiss and tell,' she said, putting on a terrible British accent.

'Except to me?'

'Except to you.'

'Bullshit.' Kaia smirked, thrusting herself into the water. She had grown up around surf club guys, not to mention she lived with two well-known ones in her father and brother. Kaia knew them and knew the culture: surf club guys *always* kissed and told. If not directly after the act, give it a day. The women were no different.

'The Frenchies got in yesterday,' Cabby said, throwing herself into the water after Kaia.

'Huh.'

She didn't need to glance at the figures written on the white board to know the warm-up would be four sets of 400 metres. It was the same every morning. She moved into position on the wall and prepared to push off.

'Apparently the South Africans land on Wednesday,' Cabby added, lowering her voice.

That got Kaia's attention. Her feet slipped on the tiled wall and she bobbed under the water as she tried to regain her footing.

'What? All of them?'

'Most. There's always a few new add-ons and a few who don't come back but yeah, from what I heard … Chris too.'

Kaia said nothing. She could tell Cabby was examining her face carefully. She could only imagine what she saw. It must have been something close to pity because she said: 'I'll lead.'

She was already halfway down the length of the fifty metre pool before Kaia even noticed Cabby had gone. She was paralysed, with her back pressed flat against the end of the lane. Each year a handful of elite ironmen and iron-women competitors from around the world travelled to the cluster of surf clubs on the Gold Coast to train. Put simply, the best athletes in the sport all came from the same stretch of beach and it made sense for the international competitors to try embed themselves within it. A mixture of French, British, New Zealand and even Swedish athletes would start arriving from now until the middle of the season in January. And the South African contingent would be here in a few days. Everything was about to get worse. Much worse.

CHAPTER TWO

'Kaia, you waiting to paint a sunset or are you gonna do a warm-up?'

'Huh?'

BB's gruff tone jerked her away from her dread daydream.

'Ah, right,' she mumbled quickly, ducking her head under and pushing off from the wall.

Kaia let the water rush over her before she popped to the surface and began placing body parts methodically in front of each other. Her hands barely gripped the water as she swam forward. She was off somewhere else completely. Her mind was with the returning South African competitors.

Six months earlier Kaia had killed someone. Unintentionally, of course. But the end result was still the same. It had been at the Australian Titles at Surfers Paradise during the Open Ironwoman final. Her recurring nightmare had most of the facts right. It was the last event of the season and she had been looking forward to defending her crown. Reflecting on it now, everyone said the carnival should have been cancelled or at least moved to a calmer location. It had been too rough. The surf was out of control, peaking at the ten-foot mark and sucking up something brutal on the sand bank. But the race had been one of the final of the carnival and officials had been desperate to finish.

The ski leg was first and only six competitors made it out around the buoys and back to shore to start the board leg. Kaia was neck-and-neck with a local girl, Silva Parks from North Tallebudgera surf club, when they paddled into the break. She got held back after being hit by side wash and Kaia saw a gap open up in front of her. Excited, she had powered for it. Her enthusiasm was short-lived, however, as she saw what had been building on the horizon. A bomb: the biggest wave of the day so far. It was easily twelve-foot and Kaia had felt a fearful lurch in her stomach as she realised she wasn't going to make it over the crest in time – she would be right in the drop zone. Kaia's entire family had been out on surfboards in bigger waves and sure, she couldn't duck dive on a paddle board like she could on a surfboard but she could still roll. She'd accelerated towards the bottom of the massive wave as it began to collapse on top of her like a small building. At the last minute she gripped her front handles and rolled off the board, flipping the craft with her. She clenched the front straps as tight as she could and tucked her feet under the handles of the back straps. Squinting her eyes shut, Kaia had waited for the impact.

It came with impressive force, dropping down on her with relentless anger and she'd done her best to keep the board clutched to her body. Kaia would never let go of a board. You couldn't finish a race without your craft, plain and simple. Yet she'd had no choice in the matter. Her feet were sucked out of their position first and she tightened her grip on the front handles. Her eyes burst open under the water in horror as she felt a release of pressure in both hands. The right handle had snapped off and Kaia was left holding a piece of rubber with no board attached to it. The final handle had only come loose at the front, but that was enough for her grip to slip free and the craft to be whisked out of her hands. She fought the churning wash to make it to the surface, hoping against hope that her board might be close enough for her to swim to.

It wasn't.

All she could see was white froth extending to the shoreline as the wave carved a path of destruction through the rest of the field. Silva had popped up beside her board some ten metres to Kaia's left, looking like she had just survived multiple drownings. Exhausted, she'd hauled herself halfway back onto her board before she paused.

'Kaia!' she shouted.

Kaia followed her gaze and saw another beast forming behind her, a ten-footer. Silva was already linking her hands through the straps to roll for a second time. Kaia kicked her legs furiously and threw her arms forward as she swam towards the mountain of water. A few seconds before impact she took a deep breath and dived down as deep as she could go. She heard an awesome thud as the wave exploded above and she watched the white foam roll over from a safe distance below it. Heading for the surface again, she'd muttered a breathless thank you to Silva as she swam past her towards the shore. Silva herself was struggling to get back on her board before the next onslaught.

Kaia body-surfed a broken six-foot wave as far in as she could, trying to milk the maximum amount of distance. Pulling off the wave, she'd looked around for the familiar lemon colour of her fibreglass board. It was then that she'd realised something was wrong. Seriously wrong. People were running into the surf and water safety were mounting I.R.Bs (Inflatable Rescue Boats) and pushing off into the waves. She could almost taste the general sense of panic in the air.

What had happened plagued Kaia for months and probably would the rest of her life. Bree Tyler had been the second youngest competitor in the field: a seventeen-year-old out from South Africa to train for the season. She and four other girls had still been on their surf skis from the first leg when the two waves had hit. Despite knowing they wouldn't make the race time limit, they had endured in a bid to at least complete some of the course. When Kaia's board had been ripped from her hands it had been picked up by the wave and propelled to the shore, directly into the path of Bree and the others. In a perfect storm of terrible timing, Bree had been paddling towards the wall of white wash coming at her when Kaia's board emerged from the foam. It hit her in the head with lethal force, knocking her unconscious and off her ski. The entire beach had seen in happen. When Bree didn't resurface, the thousands of people who had been watching the race – many of them capable lifesavers – had rushed into the water to save her before it was too late.

It was.

They'd continued to search into the night, but the powerful currents and relentless surf had kept her body hidden from rescuers. It wasn't until the next day that she washed up two kilometres north of the competition arena at the Southport Seaway. As if the horror of the accident wasn't enough, what followed was almost as bad – a circus in every sense of the word. Naturally there had been a film crew recording the race and they had captured the exact moment when the board collided with Bree's head. The footage was replayed over and over on every news bulletin for days after the incident as the media began covering just who was 'to blame' for the unlucky twist of fate. Officials, naturally, for keeping the event running when it should have been cancelled. Maybe even the local council for not stepping in when they should have. The bulk of the blame, however, fell on Kaia.

It didn't help that her father was who he was – *the* KC, famous surfing legend and media personality. It also didn't help that she had been positioned as the golden girl of the sport in the weeks leading up the event. Having just graduated high school a few months prior, the Australia Titles had been intended to mark her first foray into the sport as a full-time professional. Instead, they now had a death toll. Kaia never had much interest in school, her mind and passion usually focused on the ocean. She had done barely enough to graduate, whereas Bree Tyler on the other hand … she was less than a year younger, but she'd already had her sights set on a law degree while continuing to chase her dream of becoming an ironwoman. The contrast was stark.

Things escalated quickly from the footage of Bree's grief-stricken parents crying into the cameras to Kaia standing before a Royal Commission as one of the people called to testify about the nature of the accident. Bree's parents and her two older brothers had all been watching the race from the safety of the beach and were, naturally, devastated. They were desperate for someone to blame and Kaia Craig became that someone. Suddenly she was the 'irresponsible', 'reckless' *someone* who had 'no regard' for her fellow competitors. It couldn't have been further from the truth, but the Tyler family were struggling to come to terms. They found comfort in a common goal and the press found an endlessly sellable story.

A light brushing of fingertips on her toes alerted Kaia to the fact that she had let herself get too caught up in her memories. She had slowed down enough that the swimmer behind her was hot on her heels – literally – and she mentally kicked herself into gear, speeding up her kick so that a flurry of bubbles formed behind her. Kaia had a therapist now, it had been something advised by the lawyer who had represented her at the Royal Commission, but outside of those weekly sessions she found the pool her own kind of mediation. Sure, getting there was hell: dodging the stares and the whispers and the pointed looks. But once she was in the water, Kaia was safe. She was submerged and protected from all the mess that waited for her on land. Her mind was free to wander as she did lap after lap. Swimming training – besides being essential for her chosen profession – was good for her mental health, so long as she kept an eye on the clock and stayed on pace.

Kaia had become good at wearing a mask over the past few months. She'd never had reason to before, but now she'd been taught how to keep her face neutral for the cameras as she left the courthouse, bulbs flashing and reporters shouting horrendous questions at her. She had learned how to mask her hurt when someone would utter the word 'murderer' at training, loud enough that they knew she heard them. She had made herself impenetrable when she left board practice one day to find her tyres slashed. She had composed herself enough that every time her dad found another excuse for *another* trip – anything that would keep him away from home – he had no idea what her real feelings were. She felt as if she had let that mask slip somewhat with Cabby. The news that the South Africans' arrival was imminent had left her rattled for more than a few reasons. Would Bree's brothers be coming back as well? They were in their early twenties and embroiled in the clubbie culture of train hard, party hard, and had made the pilgrimage to race with Aussie surf clubs for the past two seasons. She suspected Bree's parents wouldn't return. After all, the Royal Commission was over. Kaia had been cleared of any responsibility, so too had the race officials and local council. Amendments to the safety regulations in light of extreme weather conditions had been advised and implemented almost immediately, but the general ruling had been that Bree Tyler's death was an accident: an unfortunate, preventable and public accident.

The Tylers took to the local papers, vocalising their outrage and their heartbreak. They didn't hesitate in continuing to point the finger squarely at Kaia: something she discovered by accident at home when her brother didn't manage to throw out the day's papers quick enough before she saw the headlines. Her mask had slipped then too. On her part, she had stayed silent. KC and her lawyer had both encouraged her to compose and release a statement, yet she just simply wanted the whole thing to go away. It hurt her image, the quietness, Storm said. But to Kaia there was no point. She had done enough. One way or the other, anything she said was going to hurt Bree's family and she had already hurt them beyond repair. In the long, silent hours she spent swimming up and down the pool, her chest slowly beginning to burn with exhaustion, these were the ugly thoughts that plagued her.

Their session was a long one that day, a full two hours, and BB punished them every minute they were under his control. They had only a half-hour break before hitting the gym for a strength session. Only the hardcore among the squad usually hung around for that, with the numbers thinning from thirty to about ten. Kaia always stayed and she was grateful to see that Cabby was staying too as the group began pairing off. She had expected to be on her own, with BB as her spotter, which was usually the way she preferred it. BB wasn't much of a talker, but Cabby? Cabby seemed to know everything that was going on.

'So,' she said, through grunts as she twisted from one side to the other and handed Kaia a medicine ball, 'Do you want the dirt or not?'

Sweat was forming at Kaia's temple as she gripped the

ball's leather, mimicking Cabby's movement before handing it back to her. She hoped her silence answered for her.

'Oh, come on,' Cabby pushed. 'When was the last time you even saw him?'

'The day it happened,' Kaia breathed.

'What?!' Her friend had dropped the medicine ball in shock, earning a scolding shout from BB who was strolling around the group.

'That's … that's cold. I mean, he jumped ships pretty quickly. I don't think there was a single day he wasn't at court with the Tylers.'

'Chris was friends with her brothers. He was kinda the main person responsible for getting so many South African recruits into Middle Beach.'

Cabby snorted. 'That doesn't mean shit and you know it. How long did you two go out for?'

'Two years.' Kaia sighed. 'And three months.'

'Uh-huh. And the last time you saw him was the day it happened. Never trust a man who dates teenage girls.'

This time it was Kaia who dropped the ball, quickly grabbing it and hiding a giggle before BB noticed.

'He was a teenager too, Cabby. We went on our first date when he had just turned eighteen.'

'How old were you?'

'Fifteen.'

'My point stands. I'd say never trust men, period, but I know you don't swing that way. Straightey-one-eighty.'

BB called time and the group let out a collective sigh of relief. Taking a moment to towel off and grab a sip of water, the girls moved to their next station at the rowing machines. Cabby waited until the rhythmic whirring sounds of the devices drowned out their voices so that only Kaia and she could hear each other.

'I'm gonna tell you what I know,' she started. 'That way you at least have the information, no surprises.'

'All right,' Kaia said, cautious.

'Chris's coming back, obviously, and he's not changing clubs.'

That surprised Kaia. Cabby registered her look and grinned.

'Come on, girl, you know better than that. You two as the *golden couple* might have broken up, but the boy attaches himself to winners. He's not leaving Middle Beach any time soon.'

'Australian champs six years in a row is a tough record to beat,' Kaia murmured, the bitterness clear in her own voice.

'The Tyler brothers are coming back too, but obviously they got transfer papers already sorted out. No one knows what club they're going to yet, which is weird cos the season isn't that far off from starting but—'

'Her parents?'

'Nah, they're staying behind in Cape Town. The boys are, what? Like, twenty-two and twenty-four? They don't need their mum and dad like …'

Her sentence trailed off.

'Like Bree did,' Kaia finished.

'Yeah.' Cabby looked apologetic as she shrugged, sweat droplets glistening on her dark skin as they continued to row.

Kaia fell silent for the rest of the session, the thought of crossing paths with her ex-boyfriend filling her with a whole new kind of anxiety. Thinking back to the last time Chris and she had spoken, the last time they'd touched, she could almost smell the salt that was in the air when he ducked down to give her a good luck kiss under the marshalling tent before the big race. Everything had changed after that. People had picked sides, with her brother and father sticking to hers. Chris's name should have been on that list too, but he'd never spoken to her again after the Australian Titles. Not a call. Not a text. Complete radio silence. Cabby wasn't the only one who had noticed his allegiance with the Tylers. He'd shown up to the courthouse every day in a trim suit – his dark brown hair smoothed back into an orderly ponytail. Kaia had seen him too, but only after Storm had spotted him and let out a string of curse words that caused a clerk to blush. Chris had embedded himself in her life when they first got serious, hanging out with her brother and even surfing with her dad. He was the first proper boyfriend she'd ever had, the first and only person she'd ever slept with, and he had fitted so seamlessly into her world that she never questioned what it would be like when he wasn't there … until the time came that he wasn't.

'TIME!'

Sliding off the rowing machines' seats, Cabby and Kaia headed for the bench press. As Kaia stretched out her limbs with a deep, satisfied groan, a question that had been playing in her own mind was vocalised by her friend.

'Do you think you'll see him?'

'I don't think I'll have a choice.'

Kaia knew that eventually, whether by accident or on purpose, they were going to cross paths at some point. And she was not looking forward to it. She'd spent the past few months trying to rebuild herself, rebuild her life, and a big part of that had been blocking out what had come before. It was one thing to tell herself that she could put Chris out of her mind when he was on a different continent. It was another thing entirely when he was not only back in the same city, but at the same surf club. Kaia tried to let the burn in her muscles distract her as she lifted up the weights balanced on each side of the bar. It was hard to distract yourself from the inevitable.

Driving down the coast's most expensive street of houses – nicknamed Millionaire's Row – Kaia felt only the slightest pang of relief at returning home. Usually she would try and get in a hearty meal and a nap before her afternoon training began, but it had been a long time since sleep had given her any rest. She lived on Hedges Avenue, a strip of mansions that were positioned on prime beachfront along the coastline. The avenue itself was one-way traffic only, but it was always heavily populated with joggers and walkers making the most of the scenic route. Kaia waited for two cyclists to pass her driveway before she pressed a button on the portable remote that opened the rolling gate to her family home.

A thick, concrete fence that was six feet high ran around the front of the property and blocked the most direct view of the front yard. The tops of frangipani trees hung over the fence, adding another dimension of privacy. When in season, flowers bloomed and fell onto the footpath below. The fence was rendered and painted a neutral beige colour that complimented the earthy tone of the paved driveway. Her father had a gardener maintain the lawn once a week so the grass was a vibrant green and sprang back up under her feet as she walked over it.

Kaia's hand was extended towards the long, silver handle that ran vertically up the length of the door when it swung back to reveal a dishevelled young woman. Only a few years older than Kaia, she was barefoot and gripping a pair of glittery gold stilettos in one hand. A matching purse was draped over her shoulder and long, black hair extensions hung in stringy clumps that fell to her waist.

'Oh,' the girl said, surprised.

She quickly licked her finger and wiped it under each eye

in a bid to remove the day-old mascara and eyeliner that had caked under her eyes. Dusting her hand off on her dress, she extended it to Kaia with a mega-watt smile.

'Hi there, I'm Ashanti!'

Kaia let a long pause hang between them before she replied.

'You a friend of my brother's?'

'Right! You must be Kaia, his little, like, sister?'

'Uh-huh,' she replied. As she looked down at the woman from her significant height, she didn't feel so 'little'. 'He in there?'

'Um, yeah, he was still … sleeping.'

Kaia nodded, slipping past the girl and into the foyer of her house. Dumping her bag in the laundry to wash her gear from that morning's session, she heard something that sounded like 'laters' before the front door was gently shut. Kaia internally counted down from ten before she heard a creak from her brother's bedroom followed by his footsteps padding softly across the tiled floor. His tousled white hair appeared in the doorway with a curious glance.

'She gone?' he whispered.

'Yeah, Storm. Ashanti is gone. Thank you again for fulfilling my morning ritual of returning from training to scare a new woman as she tries to sneak out of our house.'

'Come on,' he laughed. 'Ashanti's not new. She has been here *at least* twice before. You met her, she had short pink hair then? Spunky?'

'Oh my God, she's a return customer? Storm, you'd better get out now – this is as close to being engaged as you'll ever get.'

'That means I get a stag do, right?'

'Ugh,' Kaia gagged, pushing past him. 'You are the worst, you know that?'

He beamed, following behind her with glee. 'You too, KC Junior.'

'I hate it when you call me that,' she muttered, her gaze running over the contents of the fridge as she opened it up.

Storm pulled his shirtless frame onto a stool at the kitchen bench, then sat patiently as Kaia determined what she was going to cook. Grabbing some eggs, bacon, bread, herbs, butter and a handful of other ingredients, she began working on breakfast as her brother recounted his wild evening. The Craigs' house was like all of the others on Hedges Avenue – it cost as least three million and was on a plot of land worth five times that. It was two stories; the second floor was populated entirely by KC with his bedroom, bathroom, office and a second kitchen and living area. The bottom floor was where Storm and Kaia resided, each with their own large bedroom and en suite. Once you got through the front door and past their rooms and the laundry, the house went down a step and opened up into a massive living space. With all the prize money and sponsorship deals and merchandise contracts KC had accumulated over the years, when he had the finances to afford a place, he had wanted it to be his ultimate dream home. Everything was tiled, and come the sweltering Queensland summer the cooling effect was well appreciated.

With a state of the art kitchen, lounge that was frequently rearranged depending on who was over, flat-screen TV and sound system, French doors that gave the house the feeling of the indoors always being outdoors, and a barbeque area where they'd held some amazing parties, the only thing someone could say the mansion 'lacked' was a pool. Kaia's father hadn't seen the point when they had the ocean literally a few steps out their back gate. It was no secret why Storm still lived at home, despite most guys his age desperate to get out from under their parents' roof.

'And then Testy got picked up by the cops for skate-boarding home naked,' Storm finished. Kaia, only having half-listened to his account, paused by the frying pan.

'He got arrested?' she asked, spinning around.

'Nah, they just held him overnight. He sent me a text this morning saying he was out.'

'Isn't his real name Geoff or something? How did he get the nickname Testy?'

'Well, he has these really *huge*—'

'Ah,' she interrupted, holding up her hand. 'Actually I'm good, I don't want to know.'

He grinned, springing up from his chair. Pulling out a plate for each of them and cutlery, Storm began working on the refreshments.

'What do you feel like?' he asked. 'The usual?'

'Watermelon, apple, orange, ice and—'

'Extra ginger, yeah yeah. Have you got spinach over there?'

'Uh-huh,' she said, chucking it to him.

'How was training?' he called over the sound of the blender grinding ingredients to make fresh juice.

'Fine, it was long distance.'

'BB in one of those moods, I remember. What was the set?'

Storm nodded along as Kaia recited the full two-hour session, even flinching when she mentioned the staggered sprints. He'd trained with BB once, back when he was bouncing between different sports like a bee hunting pollen. He was one of the most naturally talented athletes Kaia had ever known: whether it was surfing or skateboarding, whatever he took up he mastered without shedding a bead of sweat. Maybe that was the problem: everything had come so easily to him. Storm could have been anything he wanted: a golfer or a tennis player even, he was that gifted as a sportsman. But since his early teens he had never been able to stick to the one thing. Her father had been hopeful that he'd take after him and end up on the world tour after Storm started winning comps on the grommet circuit. But her brother was never one for the order or rules of organised competition. What Storm did have – besides his looks – was a charismatic personality that was addictive to all he met. He was the opposite of his name and more a ray of warm sunshine.

'Brunch is served,' said Kaia, sliding two hefty plates of eggs benedict over the bench with a flourish.

'As is your fresh, cold press juice.'

'Teamwork,' she replied, a small smile playing on her lips. This was somewhat of a routine of theirs: a shared breakfast when she returned home from training and when Storm emerged from whatever he had got up to the night before. The siblings had always got along well, in fact, since they were old enough to chase after each other they'd behaved more like best friends than brother and sister. Yet sitting side-by-side, with their tanned skin, fair hair and long limbs, there was no way they could be mistaken for anything but blood relatives. A content silence hung between them, with the only noise a metallic clink of their knives and forks as they scraped against the plates.

'Dad's home,' Storm said, after several minutes had passed and he'd sated his appetite.

'What? When?' Kaia replied, pausing mid-bite. 'I thought he wasn't due till next week?'

'The low-pressure system they were chasing blew itself out.'

'Where were they trying?'

'It would have had the most impact on Jaws.'

'Sheesh. Near Mum.'

'I don't think they even made landfall,' added Storm.

'Dad would have had something to do with that.'

'If he was smart,' her brother scoffed. 'Anyway. He crashed upstairs while you were out and is sleeping off the jetlag.'

Jaws was the name of one of the world's most famous surf breaks off the coast of Maui, Hawaii. Maui also happened to be the island where their mother lived with husband number three. Or was it four? Kaia could never keep up. After her parents had split, KC wanted Leah to stay in Australia so she could be close to her children. She hadn't wanted any part of it. Once their marriage was done with, she intended to leave that entire life behind, which included Storm and Kaia. Her increasing lack of involvement was a source of much frustration and pain for her dad, despite the fact he'd done just fine raising both of them on his own. Their childhoods had been spent hanging out in the surf or going on tour with him, if they were lucky. While other kids went to the park, KC took Storm and Kaia to the waves where he taught them everything he knew about the big blue. His marriage had ended over a decade ago, but he'd never dated again – not even a girlfriend. When Kaia had quizzed him about it, he always replied that Storm and her were the only 'great loves' he needed.

'You done?' Storm asked, holding out his hand for Kaia's plate.

'Yeah,' she replied, handing it to him. Sipping the last of her juice, she watched Storm's back as he loaded up the dishwasher. She wondered if she should tell him about Chris and the South Africans coming back this week. She decided against it, thinking back to the time she'd had to physically plant herself between them during the Royal Commission. She'd appreciated Cabby giving her a warning.

'What was in that?' she said, stalling as she looked suspiciously at the green residue left in her brother's glass.

'The greatest hangover cure in history: celery, apple, spinach, lime, kale, cucumber and a pinch of pepper.'

'That sounds like crap.'

'And yet,' he mused, 'I feel *so* much better already. Plus, I gotta be sharp for tonight.'

'Tonight?'

'The Dirty Boogs, remember?'

Kaia blinked at him as she waited for her mind to catch up.

'I'm filling in for their drummer,' he elaborated. 'You said you'd come.'

'Oh! Totally, yeah, I just … forgot. They're playing in Cooly, right?'

'Yup,' he said, eyes narrowing as he watched her. 'What's up with you, sis?'

'Nothing, I—'

'You're doing that awkward twitch thing you do when you don't wanna talk about something.'

'I am not.'

'You are too.'

'Well, this is gonna get us nowhere.'

He sighed, crossing his arms and planting his feet where he stood at the sink. That was Storm's way of telling her that he wasn't going anywhere until she spat out what she needed to say. Kaia felt herself twitch under his gaze and cursed him for knowing her tell.

'Okay, fine,' she breathed. 'I didn't wanna mention it, but in case you run into him—'

'Run into who?'

'Cabby said the South Africans get in on Wednesday. Chris too.'

She watched as a muscle twitched in his jaw, the only indication of Storm's true feelings simmering under the surface. He was trying to keep himself in check, she realised, for her.

'How do you feel about that?' he said, after several moments had ticked by.

'I …. I dunno,' she answered, honestly. 'I won't know till I see him and there's no point worrying about that, as it mightn't be for ages. If at all.'

'If he tries to talk to you or makes you feel uncomfortable —'

'Storm, he hasn't spoken to me in *months*. That's not gonna change now.'

''Kay, but if he does or … anything. Just give me an excuse to punch him, Kaia, for fuck's sake. You know I'm living for that.'

'I know.' She laughed, letting out a burst of nervous energy. 'And that's sweet, but it would just make everything worse. Things feel like they're finally starting to get back to normal.'

There was a loaded silence and Kaia glanced up from where she had been fidgeting with her fingers. Storm was looking at her intensely.

'You're a terrible liar,' he said.

She shrugged, laying her hands down on the bench. 'What do you want me to say?'

'I want you to be mad, Kaia. I want you to be furious about the way people have treated you, even Dad! Just bailing at any opportunity so he doesn't have to be here to deal with what's going on. Instead you just …'

'What?'

'You just take it. You don't stand up for yourself, you don't fight, you just sit there quietly like you are right now.'

'Because it's exhausting, Storm,' Kaia whispered, looking up at the ceiling as tears welled in her eyes. 'It's exhausting and I'm *so* tired but I feel like I haven't slept in months. I can't fight every bad, horrible, toxic thing people say about me because I don't have the energy and I can't change their minds. I just … you just have to let it go.'

'You sound like your therapist.'

'You haven't met her so you wouldn't have the slightest idea what she sounds like.'

'Ha,' Storm snickered, looking more annoyed than amused. 'Look, I gotta go but I'm gonna speak to Cabby. Find out what else she knows.'

'The gig isn't till tonight,' Kaia protested, following her brother towards his room. 'You're gonna head in this early?'

'Yeah,' he said, noncommittal. 'The guys have been on tour for months and this is my first chance to hang out with them properly.'

'Okay,' Kaia murmured, feeling worried that Storm was up to something. As if sensing her concern, he spun to face her.

'I'll see you tonight, right? You come and have a good time and take your mind off all this bullshit.'

'Sure.' She nodded.

'Let your hair down, for once.'

She gave him a smile she hoped looked braver than she felt on the inside. He might have thought she was a bad liar, but he seemed convinced enough by the gesture.

'See that?' He grinned, pointing at her. 'That almost looks like the little sister I used to know.'

CHAPTER THREE

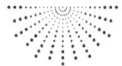

The band had already started by the time Kaia made it to the venue, but she hoped they were no more than a few songs deep at most. Ski training that afternoon had run late, then she had wasted another hour in her room agonising over what to wear and how mad Storm would be if she managed to get out of showing up. But her brother was always her biggest fan and he'd never missed an opportunity to be there for her. Tonight, it was her job to return the favour. The ends of her hair were still damp and they tickled the bare skin on her shoulders as she pushed her way into the crowd. The space was two levels, with the second storey barely more than a balcony that looked down on the stage and people below. Astro Surf as a club was designed for the kind of music The Dirty Boogs played: loud, raucous and disorderly. It thrived on the live scene but it couldn't fit more than a few hundred punters through its doors and tonight it was wall-to-wall. There was a cluster of people crowded around the bar and Kaia was grateful she didn't drink alcohol as she was able to weave right past them and towards the stage. She paused when she got to the edge of the mosh pit, not wanting to push any further into the sweaty, heaving mass that was made up of mostly skater boys and surf rats.

Despite standing a head or so taller than most of the other women in the room, Kaia felt a strange safeness in her anonymity there. Sure, there were a few people who recognised her but most of them weren't clubbies. They knew her as Storm's sister, not the girl who had killed someone. It was a nice feeling and Kaia wondered if that had been part of her brother's motivation in dragging her out. The Dirty Boogs were a blend of punk and surf rock and the band had blown up in the last six months thanks to two spots on Triple J's Hottest 100 chart. As they were old high school pals, her brother had occasionally filled in for their drummer in rehearsals and local legs of the tour. And Storm was in his element tonight, already shirtless and covered in perspiration as he thrashed away, wielding the sticks like weapons. His 'drumming' hobby had driven their mother mad when he was a kid, but Kaia was always somewhat in awe of her brother's musical ability. She herself couldn't do more than guess the difference between a keyboard and xylophone if it came down to it.

With a triumphant yell, the current song drew to a close and was met by a chorus of whoops and cheers from the crowd. Storm was beaming, his white teeth flashing even in the low light as he soaked up the audience's response. He was reaching for a sip of his beer – tucked just behind his drum kit – when he spotted Kaia from his position on the stage. Despite the fact that she had been late, that she was there by herself and that she'd been so anxious about going, it was all worth it in that moment. She saw her brother's smile grow even wider as he threw a wave in her direction. Kaia felt nerdy about it, but she didn't care as she returned his grin and gave him two thumbs up. The heads of a few girls around her turned to stare at the chick the drummer was giving his attentions to and assess whether she was a threat.

'Kaia bloody Craig, as I live and breathe!'

Kaia's body jerked forward as she was playfully whacked on the back. If she'd had a drink, it would have gone all over the people in front of her. She slowly turned around to meet the surprised but excited face of Cabby.

'What the hell are you doing out on a school night?' her friend shrieked.

Kaia jerked her head towards the stage. 'Being a supportive sister and all that. You?'

'Storm invited me but hell, when he said you were coming I didn't really believe it.'

'Yeah, me neither. But here I am.'

'And looking *good*, hun, white isn't even a colour and it's your colour.'

'Thanks.' Kaia laughed, feeling herself blush. 'You look incredible yourself.'

'Oh this?' Cabby mocked, doing an exaggerated swaying motion with her shoulders. 'I just spent an hour or so throwing it on.'

Cabby did look incredible, in tight jeans that hugged her curves so beautifully Kaia wished she was something other than just straight up and down. In a red top with the shoulders cut out, her friend was the kind of woman every man in this room would turn his head for. Though Cabby couldn't care less about them.

'You here with anyone?' Kaia shouted, her voice raised as the next song started. Cabby smiled and jerked her head in the direction of the bar where Imogen Tishop was bopping along with the music.

'You on a date?' Kaia asked, incredulous. 'Cabby, I didn't think that was your style.'

'Hit it and quit it usually, but we were chatting in the

changing rooms this afternoon and she's cute so … we're on a date.'

'I'm happy for you,' she said, nudging her pal. 'You gonna catch me up on everything that happens tomorrow morning at training?'

'Every single …'

Cabby's words fell away as she caught sight of something that made her face drop. Kaia frowned, following her gaze to a cluster of guys on the balcony that didn't seem that familiar until she spotted—

'Chris,' she whispered.

He must have seen her at the exact same time, as he was staring back with the slightest look of shock on his face. It was testament to how little Kaia liked going out that he was surprised to see her there. He nodded, just a tiny movement of his head in acknowledgment, and she gulped.

'Aw, shit,' Cabby breathed. 'I guess they got in earlier than expected.'

'It's okay,' Kaia said, trying to ignore the clench in her stomach. 'I'm okay.'

'You're a shocker, that's what you are. You look like you've seen a ghost.'

'I just … I think I'm gonna go. Is that lame?'

'No, no, Storm will get it. I'll mention it after the gig, don't worry about it.'

'I'd rather be home.'

'Don't explain yourself to me, flee his toxic arse. I'll update you in the morning.'

'Thanks, Cabby,' Kaia said, sweeping down to give her a kiss on the cheek.

'No probs, get outta here.'

Cabby slapped her on the behind as she turned to leave, like she was a race horse who needed the motivation. If Kaia hadn't been conscious of the fact that she was within Chris's line of sight she probably would have sprinted from the building. Storm would be fine, she reasoned, he always was and she never liked to hang around long once the band was swamped with groupies. She'd made an appearance and now she was making an exit. She had a small, tan leather handbag with her that didn't fit much more than her phone, some cash and her car keys. Kaia gripped the strap where it wrapped around her body, gently sliding her way between people as they squeezed into the hallway that was sole entry and exit to Astro Surf.

'That was quick,' the bouncer remarked as she dashed past him.

The second she was outside and inhaling the cool night air, she felt better. That was until she heard her name come from the lips of the very person she'd been trying to avoid. She froze, waiting a second to see if she'd imagined it. Nope, there it was.

'Kaia,' he said for a third time. 'Wait, please.'

There were a few people milling about outside smoking and they looked towards her with interest, as if they were about to see some exciting drama unfold. Kaia didn't turn around. Instead, she walked away from the club and down the main street, which was mostly empty at this time of night in Coolangatta. She knew he had followed her, she could hear his footsteps, and when she was satisfied that they were far enough from prying eyes she spun around to face him. He stumbled to an abrupt halt, steadying himself as she stared at him from just metres away. This was the closest they had been to each other in months, she realised.

'Kaia …'

'Chris, that's the fourth time you've said my name now. What do you want?'

'I … I want to talk, to you.'

'Now? Now you want to talk to me?'

'Yes, yeah, if you'll let me. I wanted to speak to you after the trial but …'

Kaia didn't jump in to finish his sentence. She didn't know what words were supposed to fill that space, so she let it linger there as her mind did that awful thing minds do and brought up everything she didn't want to be thinking about in that moment. She thought about the first time she and Chris had kissed – on the beach at party a friend of his had thrown. She thought about the way his lips had tasted and how she thought it was sweet that he had held her hand. She thought about losing her virginity to him, in her own bed, when her father had been out of town. She thought about all the times he had seen her naked, explored her body, and all the weakness in herself that she had left exposed to him. She thought about the first time he had told her he loved her – he had said it first – and she thought about how excited she was when she had first realised they were truly, officially, a couple. All of these poisonous thoughts ran through her head as they stood across from each other: her in a short, white summer dress that fell to mid-thigh, and him in a pair of cargo shorts with a shirt that had The Dirty Boogs' logo splashed across the front.

'I didn't think you'd be back this early,' Kaia said, breaking the silence between them.

'I, uh, yeah. Me and a few of the others flew in this morning. Everyone else arrives on Wednesday.'

Kaia nodded, shivering slightly in the breeze. She didn't know what else to say. This was super weird and super uncomfortable.

'Listen,' he said, taking a step closer. He was clearly as uneasy as she was, his hands running through his thick, brown hair, which was tied into a loose bun on top of his head. Chris was hot, *really* hot, and Kaia despised that about him in that moment. Like everyone in the sport, he was tanned and his body was ripped. But where Kaia was tall and lithe, Chris was short and stocky. Storm had always joked that he had 'short man syndrome' but that hadn't stopped the two of them hanging out together.

'I know I fucked up,' Chris pressed. 'After everything that happened, I know I should have been there for you. But I've known the Tylers since I was a kid, Kaia. They're friends with my dad and the whole situation, well, it just looked so bad.'

Kaia said nothing. She stood there in silence, her only response was to blink at him.

'I know I should have called or texted or *something*, but everyone was picking sides.'

Kaia shrugged, throwing up her hands in a noncommittal way. 'I don't know what you expect me to say to that, Chris.'

'It's a new year, a new season. I know we can't go back to the way things were, but I just want to know everything is okay between us.'

She felt her mouth drop open with shock at that comment, genuine shock. Her heartbeat seemed to be thudding through her temple as his words repeated in her head. Kaia moved her lips to say something, anything, but she couldn't formulate a sentence. Instead she took a step backwards, then another, before spinning on her heel and walking away from him. She didn't move quickly, in fact, she felt as if she was moving incredibly slowly as she continued her route back to the car. He called after her once, twice, but there wasn't a third time and he must have given up as she proceeded to ignore him. By the time she buckled her seatbelt and started the engine, Kaia finally was able to close her mouth which had been hanging open like a fly trap since she left Chris behind. She stalled the car twice on the way home, something she never did, as she took the back streets towards her house, driving in a daze.

Cabby skipped swimming training the next morning and so did Imogen Tishop. Kaia took that as a sign things had gone well on their date, but selfishly she wished her friend was there for companionship. When she'd arrived home the night before, she crept into the house, not wanting to alert her father to her presence. She could hear the television upstairs playing repeats of *Sons Of Anarchy*, his favourite show, so she knew he was up but she hadn't wanted to face him in that moment. She was still unnerved by the whole Chris situation and her emotions would have been painted all over her face. Thankfully the family dog, Quint, was her co-conspirator. She fed the German Shepherd a treat from the stash she kept in her bedroom to keep the eight-year-old quiet. Kaia had barely slept that night, tossing and turning, so that when her alarm went off it actually felt like a relief to have something to do. That feeling was short-lived, however, as BB was in another vicious mood and punished the squad with almost two hours of clocked fifty-metre sprints. By the time she pulled up in her driveway, the lack of sleep and abundance of exercise was catching up with her. Kaia felt exhausted as she slipped out of the car, her limbs like liquid.

'Kid Kai!'

'Hey, Dad,' she said, ducking down to accept a suffocating hug as her father met her on the driveway. Quint barked and jumped around them, trying to work out how he could take part in this human gesture.

'You just finish training? How's the ol' Ball Bag?'

'Ew.' Kaia flinched. 'I hate it when you call BB that. Why do all you surf rats have nicknames that centre around dicks or balls?'

'Tradition? I dunno.' He shrugged. 'Get your butt inside though, kiddo, I'm making tacos.'

'Tacos?'

'*Breakfast* tacos.'

As if on command, Kaia's stomach let out a rumble that reminded her just how starving she was. She followed her dad inside, dashing away for a rushed hot shower before returning in her most comfortable satin pyjamas as she towel-dried her hair. She rapped on Storm's door as she passed, knowing that he'd be pissed if he slept through one of their father's breakfasts. KC was happily humming to himself as he worked away in the kitchen, his hand tapping to the beat of a Hoodoo Gurus song playing from the speakers.

'Where did you learn this recipe?' Kaia asked, knowing that it must have been something newly acquired on his trip.

'Ah, we had this great Samoan fixer in Hawaii by the name of Uli, unbelievable cook. Wasn't even his job but he could whip up a croquembouche in the middle of a storm cell if he felt like it. Anyway, I managed to get him to teach me this and another dish that will be a surprise for dinner tonight.'

'Aw yeah, Dad's on dinner duty!' Storm whooped, emerging from his room with wild hair and his arm half inside a shirt that he was throwing over his head.

KC grinned at him as he pulled up a stool next to Kaia at the bench. 'Morning, mate, nice to have you with us.'

There was a distant call of 'see ya' followed by the front door closing and Kaia cast her brother a sideways glance.

'What was *her* name?'

'Bek, but with a "k". She made a real point of making sure I knew it was with a "k" and not a "c".'

'She probably didn't want you to confuse her with her friend Bec with a "c", who you shagged last week.'

Storm snorted. 'I did not shag anyone called Bec – "c" or "k" – last week. Also, can we not discuss who I'm rooting while Dad makes us breakfast?'

'Firstly,' KC started, spinning around, 'You've been working your way through the alphabet since you turned sixteen so Kaia and I are both used to it by now. Secondly, I don't mind what you do in this house as long as you kids are safe. I was cool with Kaia having Chris stay over and …'

Her dad looked uncomfortable for a moment, glancing briefly at her before back to Storm who was shaking his head ever so gently.

'Anyway,' he continued. 'Point is, I made breakfast tacos.'

'That was the point?' Kaia remarked, her sass almost immediately evaporating as KC slid a hefty plate in front of her.

'Good God,' Storm breathed, looking down at the feast.

'Wait,' their dad cautioned, grabbing his phone and poising it over their plates. 'Let me just get a quick pic to send Uli … there, dig in.'

The meal tasted as good as it looked, with Kaia groaning in pleasure at the first bite – a mix of tomato salsa, egg, bacon, avocado and the tiniest hint of spice in the aftermath. The three of them were dead quiet, the only sound being generated from Quint who shuffled between each family member depending on who would toss him a leftover.

'So,' Kaia said, voice somewhat muffled through a mouth-ful. 'The trip was a bust?'

'Yeah, we were spewing,' KC replied. 'The low blew itself out before it even got to us.'

'You got nothing?' Storm asked.

'There was a messy little six-foot swell, which was good to shoot some aerial manoeuvres on with the GoPro. Nothing great, though. Good people, shit conditions. How was the gig last night?'

'Awesome,' Kaia and Storm said in unison.

'It was sick,' Storm continued. 'Greg, their regular drum-mer, has been on and off most of the tour so they've been

49

switching people in and out. They want me to play again tonight in a secret show they're doing.'

'That's great, Storm!' Kaia beamed. 'Do you reckon they'll ask you to join full-time?'

'I dunno,' he said, pausing with a mouthful midway to his lips. 'There's a lot of complicated contract shit they'd have to work out before that happened. I don't mind filling in casually. How was training?'

'Eh, hectic. My shoulders are killing me.'

'You did gym afterwards again?' her brother asked.

'Yeah.'

'You gotta ease up on that, right, Dad?'

'Storm's got a point, you need to be careful not to burn yourself out during the off season.'

Kaia tossed Quint a scrap of bacon, which he gulped almost instantaneously.

'Listen,' Storm started, collecting their plates as they all finished up. 'What else have you got on today?'

'Board training this arvo, then that's it.'

'Okay, well, how about I run you through some stretches beforehand? Just a light Pilates workout on the deck. I know your problem areas.'

'Yeah?' she said, getting to her feet. 'That would be great. I think I'm going to crash now and have a nap, but in a few hours?'

'It's on like pong.'

Kaia left the two men of her family chatting casually in the kitchen, sighing with relief as she curled up with the thick doona that lay across her bed. For whatever reason, she never had her horrific nightmares during the day, only at night. Her mattress squeaked as Quint jumped up, following his tail in a circle for a moment before he settled down beside her.

'Please let me sleep,' she whispered. 'Please just let

me sleep.'

'Like, if it wasn't for her face she would totally look like a man.'

'I know, right? I can't believe Chris went out with her for two years! What did he even see in her?'

'Um, her money – duh. Her dad's super rich and famous.'

'Please, he's Gold-Coast-famous at best. You know, I heard her brother—'

'Oh, he's really hot though.'

'Whatever. Her brother manages their dad's social media for, like, a job.'

'That actually sounds great though, I would nail that.'

Kaia had been listening to this shit for the last five minutes, hoping – for the love of God – that the two gossips would move their boards into the gear lockup quicker so she could leave. She had been putting hers back into storage at the rear of the shed after training when they had trailed in after her with their crafts. Not realising she was there, they launched into a full-on dissection of her life while simultaneously blocking the exit so Kaia couldn't get out without having to walk past them. It was close to her worst nightmare, standing there in the shadows as she heard all of the most horrible things people imagined about her and her family vocalised. Her eyes were stinging and she told herself it was because of the choppy, windy conditions that afternoon, which had seen salt water blowing into her eyes for the past hour and 20 minutes. It was nothing to do with what they were saying, nothing at all. Finally the girls started to move away, their voices growing faint as they headed towards the change rooms. Carefully, quietly, Kaia tiptoed out of the darkness. Her bag was waiting on the concrete just a few metres away and she skipped the idea of a shower, wanting the sanctuary of her car instead.

Throwing a towel down on the seat so her wet sports bikini didn't soak through, she jumped into her ride and turned the radio up as loud as she could stand it. It didn't matter what was playing, she wasn't listening to it anyway. She just needed the noise as she pulled out of the club car park and started the drive home. She only lived 10 minutes away from Middle Beach, but she was halfway home when she realised that was not where she wanted to go. Kaia found driving therapeutic, it soothed her, yet it wasn't working today. She needed to clear her head. She needed to go somewhere she wouldn't be seen. Driving away from the beach and towards a more suburban section of the Gold Coast, Kaia planned to go to a place she thought would be quiet as the day progressed into early evening.

Lake Pelutz was a sprawling, man-made freshwater lake that was the basis for the name of the suburb she began driving through: The Lakes. It was one of the few bodies of water on the Gold Coast that didn't connect to anything else. That is to say, although the south east coast of Australia was home to some of the best surfing breaks in the world, the beaches were just the beginning. The entire city was once a swamp but now was wedged between a labyrinth of canal and river systems stemming from the ocean and winding through into the mountains. Looking at the Gold Coast on an aerial map, there was just as much water as land mass. On the rare occasions Kaia had come to Lake Pelutz, she had liked it because there was a long footpath that ran along its perimeter. Perfect for a five-kilometre circuit. The Lakes were also inhabited by rich retirees or older, child-free couples. This was ideal because she knew no one in that demographic. She could go for a run without bumping into a familiar face. Amen.

Discreetly throwing some jogging clothes on over her wet ones, she did a few light stretches before cranking the volume on her iPod shuffle so The Cars were blaring into her ears. She had grown up listening to her father's music and had never got over a love of seventies and eighties rock. Maintaining a steady pace, she slowly started to feel better as her body fell into a familiar pattern and she watched the fading light reflect on the water. It was dark before Kaia knew it and she relished the anonymity as she moved through the cool night air. When *Dangerous Type* came on through her headphones – her favourite song – she increased the volume until it couldn't go any higher.

It wasn't surprising that Kaia didn't pick up the sound of two extra sets of footfalls. She did sense something, however, and turned to see a pair of dark figures jogging in unison behind her. They were far enough back that she couldn't see their faces, but from their shape she could tell they were men. Both were quite short, or at least smaller than her, which wasn't exactly a great measure of shortness. Turning around, she ignored them and told herself to relax. It was a beautiful evening and there was no need to be alarmed. These were just two other people wanting to go for a run, like her.

When Kaia looked behind her again, they were closer. The Gold Coast was a relatively safe place, but like any growing city there was crime: murder, robbery, rape, even the occasional abduction. The Lakes was one of the safest suburbs she could possibly be in, so she tried to keep herself calm, collected and quell that rising anxiety. She had already been on the homeward stretch when they appeared and she spotted the incline of the hill that led to the car park some 500 metres in the distance. Increasing her pace slightly, Kaia hit pause on her music so she could hear if they tried to move closer again. She did so a moment too late.

The Cars faded from her ears just as the thundering footsteps of a man sprinting towards her took over. She spun around in time to be tackled to the ground, the impact knocking the wind out of her and with it any ability to try and call for help. Dazed, Kaia kicked as the man attempted to straddle her and was joined by his accomplice. They had both put on balaclavas. Panic spread through her as she realised these guys were seriously out to hurt her. Kaia increased her thrashing and tried to roll the main one off her, but he was too stocky and too strong. A jarring blow to the side of her head – delivered by the second man – stopped any kind of resistance as sparkly specks danced in front of her eyes. Her body stilled as she reeled from the hit.

'HOLD HER!' one of them shouted at the other.

'Fucking *help me* then!'

Their voices were muffled through the material of their masks, but there was one thing that was unmistakable to Kaia even in her dazed state: their South African accents. While they were arguing, she slowly moved her leg into position before slamming it upwards and kneeing the man on top of her in the back. He was taken by surprise and lurched forward with the impact. His grip on her hands loosened slightly and she was able to push him off and towards the other guy. She scrambled upwards and sprinted away from the two attackers as they stumbled over each other to catch her.

'HELP!' Kaia screamed.

Her voice was no more than a rasp. She tried to clear her throat to shout again when her feet went out from under her. One of the men had made a dive and grabbed her ankle. She fell forward and felt her teeth pierce her bottom lip as she thudded onto the path. He dragged her backwards, Kaia yelling out at the burning sensation as the concrete grazed along the side of her face. She had a second to wonder how they had managed to catch up to her so quickly before determining that they were fast on their feet, faster than she was. As one tried to secure her free leg, she kicked him square in the face once, twice, three times, until he released her other leg as well. His accomplice caught up just in time and dived on top of her. He linked his hands around Kaia's throat and squeezed.

'*Guh*,' was all she managed to get out as he tightened his grip.

Kaia struggled to breathe, couldn't, and felt her legs and arms flailing uselessly beside her. With her last morsel of strength she tried to scratch the man's face. Her hands could barely make an impact on him through the balaclava, so she went for the only part that was exposed to her: his eyes. They had been staring down, full of menace and hate, when she pushed her fingers into them.

He screamed and she pushed harder, feeling the soft texture squish under the pressure. As soon as he released her and clutched at his face, she was up again, wasting no time in stumbling away from them. She knew they were quicker than she was and they both had a working set of windpipes. Kaia was barely succeeding at staying on her feet as she lurched forward, trying to suck in as much air as she could. If she couldn't outrun them, she was fairly certain she could outswim them. Teetering off the path and without a second thought, Kaia dived into the lake. Being underwater and away from more air was the last thing she wanted, so she pushed her way to the surface and began thrashing towards the centre. She hadn't thought any further ahead than getting in the water and swimming for her life, but she kicked off her sneakers as she swam and they started to weigh her down. Kaia's head was lowered as she charged forward, willing her legs to kick hard and her arms to move faster. Her thighs were powered with desperation as the water churned and she tried to get her six-beat kick going. If she could make it to the other side of the lake before the South Africans – where the houses were directly on the waterfront – then she could run inside one of them for help. Kaia had barely set herself that goal when she felt fingertips brushing her toes. Not stopping for a second, she glanced backwards with a breath and saw that both men had jumped into the water after her. One was further behind and struggling – the one with the sore eyes, she assumed – while the other was right on her feet.

She panicked and in a bid to inhale another gulp of air swallowed a mouthful of water. Choking, she had a moment to feel horrified at her decrease in speed as she stuck her head up to take a breath. A scream suddenly rang out in the night air and, unlike Kaia's, it was extremely loud. It was also masculine. She stopped swimming and looked back in the direction of where it had come from. One of the South Africans, the one furthest away, had stopped swimming. He was treading water and looking around frantically, swivelling his head this way at that. A large splash broke the surface to his left. He tried to let out another scream but it was cut short as he was pulled under the water. Only a few bubbles hinted that anyone had been there a few seconds earlier.

All the fear Kaia felt was immediately discarded as she became distracted by a more immediate problem. The second South African ploughed into her, swimming headfirst directly into her body, and his head shot up to investigate the sudden stop in movement. His balaclava had slipped off his face, but Kaia was unable to get a good look before he grabbed her shoulders and jerked her towards him. His fingers dug deep into her skin and she let out a yelp of pain. He was reaching for her face when a movement pulled him under the surface. He was still holding onto Kaia with a vice-like grip and she was dragged downwards with him. The pair were being pulled at tremendous speed and water was whipping past their faces in cool streams as they went deeper and deeper. Kaia could hear the baritone sound of his attempt at screaming underwater as he was tossed to the side. Naturally, she was pulled in that direction as well.

Her ears popped as she was tugged deeper once again. Everything was dark. The only source of light was dim, coming from the night sky above. Kaia looked down at the man who had once been her attacker. She could just make out the pinkish tinge of his skin and the whites of his eyes exposed in full horror. Following the direction of his stare, she let out a scream of her own as a hand slowly wrapped its fingers around the wrist of the man. There was a sudden gesture and she heard a snap ring out in the silence of their underwater world. Instantly the man released his grip on her and a stream of bubbles extended from his mouth as he tried to yell. A dark and vaguely silver object abruptly covered her view of the man as it pushed him downwards with rapid speed. It wasn't until he was no longer visible to her that Kaia recognised the heavy burn building in her chest as her lungs protested for air. She had been slowly floating back up, but with a glance skywards she felt a whole new kind of fear.

The surface was far, too far.

She wasn't going to make it in time. Kaia started kicking her legs feverishly and tried to pull through the water with her arms. As the lava started spreading through her chest, she tried to increase her pace, desperate. *I can't die like this*, she thought, *I can't drown*. The faint glow of the starry sky above was beginning to fade as Kaia's vision blurred with the lack of oxygen. Her lungs were on fire, with every limb protesting equally as loud. She urged her hands to keep tugging, for her legs to keep kicking. Kaia's last tangible thought was of Bree Tyler. It was fitting, she mused, that she should die the way Bree had: underwater and alone.

CHAPTER FOUR

K aia came to, coughing and wheezing. Her throat burned from all the trauma she had put it through. The water passing into her windpipe felt like acid as she wretched up what must have been the entirety of Lake Pelutz. Panting, she leaned over onto her elbows and took deep breaths in and out, savouring every precious taste of air. Finally she opened her eyes and found water just inches from the tip of her nose. She jerked upright then and took in her surrounds.

She was sitting in the shallows and had been propped up against the knee-high concrete wall that separated the path from the water of the lake. In some places the edge dropped right off into deep water, but she had been placed in one of the shallower parts. As she peered over the ledge, she could see green grass and a children's playground, followed by a dimly lit path leading to one of the main streets. Her head was pounding and she squinted her eyes shut as she reverted back to her half-reclining position.

How had she got to the surface? More importantly, how had she made it from the middle of the lake all the way back to shore? She tried to recall what had happened. The attack, trying to swim to safety and then being pulled underwater by ... something. No, *someone*.

Her eyes flew open as she remembered the calculated movement of a single hand snapping her attacker's wrist. Kaia tried to slow her breathing as she looked around, searching for any sign of the mystery person. There was no one. The surface of the lake was black, smooth and still, like an expansive pool of oil. Everything was quiet in The Lakes: there was no hint of what had happened earlier. A movement to Kaia's left caught her eye. She sat up as she tried to get a better look at what had drawn her attention. She winced as she became aware of various hurts, but she never took her eyes off the spot where she thought she had seen something. A sudden splash erupted from the surface of the lake and that was all Kaia needed to spring out of the water and leap the edge in a single bound. Her shoes were gone and she sprinted towards the main street in bare feet, her soles slapping on the asphalt. She kept running straight out onto the road and waved frantically at the first car she saw. It screeched to a halt mere inches away from her.

'Good gracious,' came the voice of the female driver. 'Are you all right?'

The woman had come to a stop in the middle of the road and other cars began to pile up behind her. Kaia sank down to her knees with the relief of knowing she was safe.

'Please,' she croaked, 'I need to call the police.'

'And then he just disappeared?'

'Yes.'

'Just ... gone?'

'I told you, I couldn't see exactly because I was further

away, but yes. There was a splash and then it looked like something pulled him under the water.'

'Something?'

'Yes.'

'And you didn't see a fin or anything like that?'

'Officer, it wasn't a shark.'

'How can you be so sure?'

Kaia sighed. 'It's a freshwater lake.'

There was a long pause before he replied. 'Bull sharks can survive in freshwater.'

'And how do you get them into a lake?'

That question obviously stumped the young constable, given the quizzical expression his face.

'Well, got to cross off all the possibilities,' he said, in an official tone. 'I helped fish that old chap out of Burleigh Lake a few years ago when the bull sharks had at him. Ugly business.'

Kaia didn't reply. Instead she tried to look exhausted so the officer would leave her alone. She was wearing a white hospital gown and sitting on the edge of one of the beds in the emergency ward at Gold Coast Hospital. Having already been interviewed by three different police officers, which meant telling the same story over and over again, she was getting pretty frustrated. The woman who had picked her up ignored her repeated requests that they stay at the scene until the police arrived. She took Kaia straight to the hospital and had her daughter in the back seat call the police to tell them where they would be. As soon as the cops arrived, the questioning began. Recounting the event was simple enough in theory, but it was the excruciating detail they wanted Kaia to go into that was proving tough. She was still in shock. Not at being attacked mind you, but by what followed.

What had she seen under the water? What had attacked *her* attackers? Were they killed? Eaten? And that hand, a human hand ... Those were the questions spiralling through her mind as she did her best to answer their queries. The curtain to her bed was suddenly ripped back as the commanding officer returned. He looked from Kaia to the constable and back again with an air of agitation.

'Rosenberg, what are you doing?'

'Sir?'

'I said what are you doing?'

'Uh, questioning the victim. Sir.'

'No, Rosenberg, you are not. This girl has already been questioned three times: by the reporting officer, myself and once by Constable Jones over there. Do you think we really need a fourth line of questioning? More importantly, do you think that perhaps, maybe, she would like to rest?'

'I didn't think about that, sir.'

'No, you clearly didn't. Now get the heck out of here and help Jones file her report.'

'Yes, sir.'

Dismissed and belittled, the constable left with his tail between his legs. Kaia couldn't say she was sorry to see him go. A few curious stares from the nursing staff at the counter was all it took for the man – who had introduced himself as Senior Sergeant Warun Ferris – to give them an annoyed look before pulling the curtain shut again.

'Most of them recognise you from the papers,' he said, giving Kaia an apologetic shrug.

'Oh,' she murmured. That was not a good thing. Her eyes skimmed the dark features of this cop, who was clearly the one in charge. There was a small, enamel pin that depicted the Aboriginal flag and was clipped to the pocket of his blue uniform. It glinted under the harsh fluorescent lights as he moved closer towards her.

'Your father is on his way, brother too. They should be

here any minute. We also have a female officer coming who's going to take some photos of your injuries.'

She nodded.

'Is there anything else I can get you while you wait?'

'Thank you, no, I'm—'

'WHERE IS SHE?!'

Kaia registered the panic in her dad's voice instantly as he entered the emergency ward. Within seconds the curtain to her bed was whipped back again as his tanned, usually happy, face stared at her with concern.

'Kai,' he said, his voice cracking as he gave her appearance a once over.

'Dad, it's oka—'

She didn't get a chance to finish as her dad came in for a bone-crushing hug. Despite the still-tender nature of her body, Kaia closed her eyes and ignored the pain as she leaned into his shoulder. She loved being hugged by her father. He was a frequent giver of the one-armed half-hug, but a full-on two-arm assault was rare. His thin, shoulder-length blond hair was almost the same shade of whitish blond as Storm's and hers. It tickled her cheek as she inhaled his familiar scent. Salt. KC always smelled of salt from the ocean, which both comforted Kaia and slightly stung her nostrils. Keeping one hand on her shoulder in a comforting gesture, he turned to Sergeant Ferris.

'What happened?'

'Well, Mr Craig—'

'Call me KC,' he said, reaching out a hand for the officer to shake.

'Sure. Okay, KC,' he said slowly, as if trying the letters out on his tongue. 'While Kaia was going for a jog around Lake Pelutz, two men attacked her from behind and physically assaulted her. We're not sure what their intentions were—'

Her father's grip tightened on her shoulder as he realised what Sergeant Ferris meant.

'—but thanks to some quick thinking from your daughter, she dived into the lake in a bid to swim to safety on the other side. What happened after that ... we're not sure.'

KC turned to Kaia expectantly, obviously hoping she would fill in the blanks. She couldn't do more than shrug and tell him what she had told the police.

'There was a big splash and I saw one of them get pulled under the water. The other one tried to pull me under too and then ... that's it. That's all I remember. Next thing I was on the shore at the opposite side of the lake and I ran for help.'

Sergeant Ferris nodded with understanding. 'It's common in traumatic incidents like this for the victim to block out parts of what happened as a coping mechanism, especially after such a violent attack. We see it all the time, in even the most simple Post Traumatic Stress Disorder cases.'

Anger and sympathy filled her dad's eyes as she watched him cast a glance in her direction.

'Did you find these punks?' he said, turning back to the cop.

'Not yet. We've found evidence of where the assault occurred, there's blood we think must be Kaia's, and a discarded balaclava, which we may be able to get DNA from. We've been unable to find the attackers but it's clear there were two of them, going off your daughter's injuries and what we found at the scene. We have officers searching the area and speaking to residents who might have seen or heard anything.'

'What about the lake?'

'We're waiting on police divers coming up from an incident in Byron Bay. They should be here tomorrow morning to do a sweep of the lake.'

Kaia gulped. She didn't know what was down there or what had attacked the men, but the thought of people diving back into Lake Pelutz looking for it was a terrifying concept.

'It's a freshwater lake, right? So it couldn't have been a shark.'

'That's what your daughter said.'

'Lake Pelutz isn't linked up to any of the canals so nothing could have got through the catchment,' KC mused. 'You didn't see any fins, Kaia?'

'Dad, I honestly didn't see anything except for a splash and the guy going under the water.'

'There would be eels in there but—'

'WHERE THE BLOODY HELL IS SHE?!'

The emergency ward was dealing with a lot of crazed Craigs that night. Her brother's entrance was just as dramatic as her father's and KC ducked away for a second to calm the impending Storm. There were a few muttered words, spoken low enough that Kaia couldn't hear them properly, before Storm joined Sergeant Ferris at her bedside.

'Sis,' he said, plunging in for a hug as soon as he saw her. Storm didn't even take a second look at her, just dove right on in there. Kaia welcomed his hug. He had just come from playing at Astro Surf again and reeked of bourbon and cigarette smoke.

'Ow,' Kaia choked out as he gripped her tightly.

'Ah, sorry!'

'It's okay, I'm still a little bit sore.'

He leapt back and held his hands out in a gesture that looked as if he was ready to protect her from anything: whether that be a gust of wind or a grizzly bear.

'Technically, that would be *very* sore,' came a heavily accented female voice from behind the curtain.

The doctor who had been treating Kaia earlier emerged from the other side with a stern look that contradicted her external appearance. With stylishly cropped black hair, Doctor Andersen was a plump woman with a figure of almost spherical proportions. She was also Russian, or at least Kaia thought so given the strong accent that required her to concentrate extra hard when the doctor was talking.

'You've had quite the night, Mizz Craig. Family?' she asked, looking at the men assembled at the bedside. Kaia nodded by way of response.

'I'm sorry to say, gentlemen, but Mizz Craig will be staying ze evening.'

'What?' Kaia protested. 'I feel fine, seriously.'

'That may be ze case, but you are not – as you put it – fine. You have a concussion from several knocks to the head, bruising on your face and severe bruising around your throat where you were strangled. You have five stitches in your lip and numerous other cuts and bruises. Your windpipe is damaged, which should be of concern to the police officer here who haz been continually making you talk for ze past hour and a half despite my demand that you rest.'

'Yes, well, we needed to interview her as soon as possible while the information is s—'

'Not my concern, officer. My concern here iz the patient who has been through a great deal tonight and needs to stay for observation. We both know who has jurisdiction here, so let's avoid ze embarrassment and have you bid farewell for tonight, no?'

Kaia watched with interest as the two struggled silently for power. She could almost see Sergeant Ferris chewing the inside of his cheek in frustration as he said goodbye and promised to return in the morning to see how Kaia was feeling.

'We have private health, we can get you moved to a better hospital if you want?'

'Dad, I'm fine. This hospital is fine. I'm only going to be here for one night,' Kaia sighed as they wheeled her to a room. She would have liked to protest the use of a wheelchair as well, but the adrenaline was wearing off and she was beginning to feel the effects of that concussion.

'All right, they've got you in a private room,' said a breathless Storm who had just returned from talking with the ward nurses.

'Oh for Pete's sake,' Kaia muttered.

Her father wanted to help her into bed, but given his lack of height and Storm's abundance of it her brother was the better candidate to negotiate the feat. They both settled in chairs next to her as if they intended to camp there.

'You're not staying.'

'Yes, I bloody am,' said KC.

'Darn straight,' replied Storm.

Kaia glanced between the two identical, stubborn expressions and the determined sets of their jaws. There was no arguing.

'Fine. This will be very boring for you both. I'll be going to sleep soon and—'

'No sleep, remember?'

Blast it. Her dad was right. Dr Andersen had forbidden her from going to sleep until she could come in and check on her at 1AM to see how she was coping with the concussion.

'So you two are setting out to keep me awake until then?'

'Yup,' said Storm, stretching his enormously long arms above his head.

'Why don't you go and get some beers or something then, make it interesting?'

Storm and KC looked at each other with thoughtful expressions, both very keen on the idea but neither wanting to be the one to admit they intended to sneak booze in to a hospital.

'I'm up,' said her father, rising from his chair.

'There's a bottle shop across the road on the corner of Scarborough Street,' Storm added.

KC nodded. 'You want anything, kid? Chocolate?'

Chocolate sounded good. Namely, chocolate chip cookies sprang to mind. Then she thought of her red, sore throat and winced in anticipation of the pain.

'Yoghurt?' Kaia offered. 'It will be easiest when I can eat again.'

'You got it.'

As she watched her dad leave, she felt something warm press into her palm. It was a hand, Storm's hand. She linked her fingers through his and returned his smile.

'You okay?' he whispered.

She nodded.

'For real?'

Kaia thought about that question longer. No, she was pretty shaken up. Although not for the reasons people thought. The attack had been terrifying, but it was what had happened in the lake that was still raising goose bumps along her arm. Storm noticed and placed his other hand on her forearm.

'Don't worry, you know Dad and I won't let anyone hurt you again,' he said.

She heard the truth in his voice, in his words, and Kaia gave him a grateful look. It was a lovely sentiment. However, if she had learned anything in the last year it was that no matter how much your loved ones tried, no one could stop life from hurting you – physically or otherwise. She had been dealing with emotional injuries for what felt like forever: Kaia almost welcomed seeing physical ones that she could combat.

'Do you have any idea who it was?' he asked her.

'No,' she replied. 'There were two men. That's all I know. They were wearing balaclavas.'

Kaia was lying. More importantly, she was lying to her brother, which was something she *never* did. She was fairly certain she knew exactly who the two attackers were. They had been stocky, athletic men with South African accents. It also wasn't a crime of opportunity: those men acted like they had a personal vendetta against her. Kaia couldn't think of any two people with a better reason to want her dead – or seriously beaten up – than Bree Tyler's older brothers. Both fit the physique of the men who had attacked her and both had most likely returned to the country the same day as Chris.

Kaia had avoided telling the police these details for two reasons: first, because she hoped she was wrong. Second, she didn't know if they were alive or not. If they weren't, well, she thought that family had been through enough without having to know what last act the two Tyler sons committed. The second reason was linked to the first. If they were still alive, she didn't want them connected to what had happened. If it came to it, she wouldn't press charges. So much pain had been inflicted on the Tylers directly and indirectly because of her, Kaia didn't want any more. Frankly, she was aching for the whole saga to be over. If they were linked to this, then who knew when it would end? Would there be a trial? That meant more time in a courthouse and more TV cameras and more fingers being pointed.

So Kaia would keep quiet and pray the Tyler brothers had emerged shaken but otherwise fine from Lake Pelutz. She would hope they decided against pursuing her further. Maybe it was even one of them who dragged her to shore? It was a dark fairy tale, but it was all she had. As Kaia fought to keep her eyes open, one image kept replaying in her mind: a strong, grey hand as it wrapped around the man's wrist. Her thoughts were interrupted by a gentle knock on the door before Storm called for whoever it was to come in. Cabby's anxious face appeared from the other side, her mouth dropping open as soon as she saw Kaia sitting there in the bed.

'Holy shit, hun, I came as soon as I heard,' she said, closing the door behind her and rushing forward.

'Cabby,' Kaia breathed, surprised at how much relief she felt at seeing her friend. They'd always been acquaintances, buddies at most, but there was something to be said for those who came through when you needed them. Cabby hadn't shunned her after the Bree Tyler thing and here she was now, late at night and rolling up to the hospital in a pair of ripped denim jeans and a baggy Bikini Kill T-shirt. Kaia felt a wave of appreciation wash over her as Cabby pulled up the spare chair next to the bedside and acknowledged Storm with a slap on the shoulder.

'Wait,' he said. 'How did you hear? The police said they didn't release any info about who the victim was yet.'

'They also said it wouldn't stay quiet for long,' Kaia countered.

'Uh,' Cabby said, running a hand through her short hair. 'I kinda used to have a thing with one of the nurses here. She knows we're friends and sent me a message when they brought you in.'

'Nice,' Storm said, nodding with appreciation.

Cabby gave him bashful grin. 'I'd appreciate if neither of you mentioned it, she's not supposed to share info about patients, obviously. She could lose her job.'

Storm made a motion that indicated he was zipping up his lips and throwing away the key while Kaia muttered 'of course'. There was a loaded silence as Cabby settled in, her eyes moving over Kaia's face and the hospital gown she was wearing. As if sensing some invisible signifier, Storm got to his feet.

'I'm gonna go try grab a cup of coffee or something,' he said. 'Anybody want?'

'No thanks,' Cabby said, while Kaia shook her head as she watched him leave.

'Not the subtlest of creatures, is he?' her friend noted.

'You're immune to his charms.' Kaia smiled. 'Straight women? Storm is their Kryptonite.'

'I can't imagine. Anyway, how are you? Genuinely? Are you okay?'

For what felt like the one thousandth time that evening, Kaia recounted her story. She left out the part about who she suspected her attackers were, just like she had with the police, but for some reason when it got to the section in her tale where she saw that eerie grey hand reaching out, she kept going. She wasn't sure why, maybe it was too many secrets bottled up on top of each other, but Cabby became the first person Kaia actually told about what she *thought* she saw. There was a prolonged pause once she finished talking, her friend seemingly taking a moment to process all the information.

'Did … did you tell the cops this?' Cabby asked.

'Are you kidding? No way, they'd think I'm crazy.'

'Good. What about your dad and your bro?'

'No,' Kaia scoffed. 'I'm not even sure *I saw* what I saw. Apparently your brain does all kind of things when you experience trauma and can create—'

'Kaia.'

'I … yeah?'

'Do you remember that time last season when the surf was dead flat and instead of doing board training in the surf, they dropped us off at the start of Tallebudgera Creek? Told us to paddle back?'

'Of course. We were going against the tide the whole way and it took us an hour to make it to the creek mouth.'

'Right. It was dusk, there were twenty of us, all exhausted, and there was this flock of seagulls floating on the water about fifty metres away when there was that huge splash and a *fucking* shark sprung out and ate one of the birds.'

'Oh my God,' Kaia said, half laughing. 'I totally remember. Jesse was at the front of the group and screamed so loud he fell off his board.'

Cabby was properly chuckling now as she recounted the story. 'We all freaked out. I swear we never paddled so fast in our lives as we did back to the shore that arvo.'

Kaia remembered the afternoon clearly. They'd all seen sharks before, dolphins too: it was inevitable considering the amount of time they spent in the ocean. It wasn't a huge deal, they were in *their* playground after all, and for the most part people got out of the water quickly enough and there were no major incidences. Plus, everyone knew that the highly publicised 'protection' methods of the shark nets and drumlines did jack all except catch unfortunate sea turtles. Being in the water as often as clubbies were, you were going to see a shark eventually – it wasn't anything to go postal about. But seeing a shark leap out of the water and eat a seagull just metres away from you – while you were still in the creek – it made sense everyone in the group had freaked out. When they'd got a passer-by to call their coach to come and pick them up, even they had been blown away by the account.

'That story got mileage for months,' Kaia recalled. 'Jesse tried to say he stayed soooo calm the whole time.'

'And that it was *my* scream everyone heard. I mean, please.'

'I know.' She smiled.

'We had been paddling through that shark's territory for almost an hour, none of us any wiser about the fact it was

71

there. Hell, it could have been following us! Just waiting for the right moment to take an inquisitive nibble on the smallest person.'

'What's your point?'

'None of us really know what's beneath us, Kaia. They're discovering new sea creatures and species all the time.'

'Yeah, but, Cabby, this looked human. If it even existed it all, which is a big if.'

'I know.' She shrugged. 'All I'm saying is don't discount yourself as "crazy" so quickly. Maybe you did see what you saw. Maybe it was your trauma. Or maybe something saved you, whatever it was, and you finally caught the break you deserve.'

'Cab—' Kaia cut herself short as the door to her room opened again, revealing Storm and her father, who was rather sheepishly carrying a plastic bag.

'We interrupting anything?' KC asked. 'We come bearing snacks.'

'No no, come on in, Mr Craig,' Cabby said, shooting Kaia a look that distinctly said 'later'.

'Ah, mate, no one has called me Mr Craig since I got divorced. Call me KC.'

'Sure,' Cabby said, smiling as she shook his hand. 'Mr KC.'

He laughed, assembling seats with Storm around Kaia's bedside until it felt like she was holding court.

'You're Cabby, right? Or Cammy?'

'Cabby,' she said.

'That was you, wasn't it, last year at Aussies – swam one of the best open surf races I've ever seen.'

'That was her.' Kaia grinned, knowing that Cabby would be bashful about it.

'That was incredible. You were twenty metres ahead by the time you reached the first buoy.'

'Yeah, I got jagged on the way in though. Managed only third place overall.'

'Third.' KC nodded. 'That's nothing to sniff at. Where are you from originally?'

'DAD,' Storm and Kaia hissed in unison.

'What? I didn't mean, it's not cos you're—'

'It's okay,' Cabby said, with patience. 'I get it, you don't see that many black women doing surf sports.'

'Alotta Hawaiians and Brazilians,' KC pressed, as Kaia cringed and buried her head in her hands. 'I swear that was half our world circuit back in the eighties.'

'Dad,' Storm said, looking horrified. 'Can you stop talking now? Cabby was born here, on the Gold Coast.'

'Oh, cool. I thought you might have come over from one of the international clubs but you've got that Aussie accent.'

'Nah,' she replied. 'Born at Pindara Hospital, raised here. My parents moved up from Melbourne; Ghana before that.'

'Cool, cool. Do you drink, Cabby? Or do you stay dry like Kaia?'

'That we definitely do not agree on.' She grinned. 'I'm wet as fish.'

'Excellent!' He beamed, bending over to get beers for Storm, Cabby and himself.

Kaia mouthed the words 'I'm so sorry' at her friend. Cabby made the smallest shrug gesture with her shoulders, giving Kaia the impression this was not the first time she had been asked that question. Storm waved and pointed at the Southern Cross tattoo exposed on KC's shoulder as he bent down. Cabby had to do her best to stifle a giggle as Kaia's father handed her a V.B. The past 24 hours had been horrible for Kaia. Hell, it felt like the last half of the year had been. Yet crossing paths with Chris and what she'd overheard at the surf club as people gossiped about her all seemed to pale into insignificance compared to what she had lived through that night. She was battered, she was bruised, and as Storm handed her a napkin to dab at her lip, she realised she was bleeding. And still, there she was: sitting there surrounded by her small family that loved her unconditionally and a friend who had come through in a way she hadn't entirely expected. For the first time in what felt like forever, Kaia let herself entertain the smallest morsel of hope that things *could* be better.

It was an optimism that barely lasted the night, as when she left hospital the next day the press were waiting for her. Someone had tipped off the media: a dozen or so journalists with cameras and microphones were shoving them into Kaia's face as she was rolled out the doors. Dr Andersen had insisted she stay off her feet until she made it to the car. Kaia internally cursed the woman as she thought about how this would look on the 6PM news. *Poor Kaia Craig, how things have flipped: once the perpetrator and now the victim.* To make matters worse, her throat had come up a disgusting shade of black and blue that she knew was going to catch the camera's eye. The left side of her face was red, swollen, and covered in cuts from where she had been dragged along the concrete. It wasn't a good look.

'Kaia, Kaia, do you know who attacked you?'

'Is it true you were stabbed?'

'Kaia, how did you fight off the attackers? Who were the perpetrators?'

'Have the police been able to corroborate your story?'

'Do you have any message for other women who have survived violent assaults?'

'Kaia, how do you feel about being a hero?'

'Do you think they will strike again?'

'KC, how does it feel to have something like this happen to your daughter?'

'How will this affect your upcoming season, Kaia?'

The questions came in a relentless barrage. Thankfully Sergeant Ferris had been standing nearby when they went to exit and he had some officers clear a path to Storm's car. Even when they were safely inside, flashes continued to erupt from the cameras as they snapped pictures of Kaia and her family.

'Fucking hell,' muttered Storm, who spun around in the driver's seat to reverse.

'Take it easy now,' said their father, who had purposefully sat in the back seat with Kaia. 'If you accidentally run one of the pricks over, we'll never hear the bloody end of it.'

'Be worth it though.'

'Storm.'

'Yeah, yeah, I'm taking it slow and easy.'

Storm turned up the radio – playing one of his favourite bands, Liars – to try and drown out the noise of reporters thumping at the side of the car and continuing to shout questions.

'Who did I save?' Kaia asked quietly.

'What's that, sweetie?' her dad responded.

'One of them asked how it feels to be a hero. Who did I save, then?'

Kaia's brother and father fell silent as they realised why the question had bugged her.

'You saved yourself, kid,' said KC, slipping a hand around her shoulder. 'You saved yourself.'

She thought back to the question Sergeant Ferris had asked that morning: 'Can you think of anyone who would want to hurt you?'

Kaia had exchanged a look with Storm and KC before she answered.

'You must not have been following the news over the last six months.'

He looked stumped for a moment, then realisation

washed over his face. 'You think this might have something to do with the girl who drowned? The South African kid, what was her name?'

'Bree Tyler,' Kaia supplied.

'You think it could have something to do with that?'

She raised the palms of her hands up in the air to indicate that she didn't know.

'I was under the impression that was an accident.'

'I'm glad you think so,' said Storm. 'But there are plenty of others out there who don't. You should have seen the kind of mail we got.'

Sergeant Ferris tilted his head. 'I'm more surprised people still use mail.' 'Someone even spray-painted a death threat on our fence,' her brother continued. 'I'd start with anyone who might still have a grudge against Kaia. A bunch of them flew in over the weekend.'

She was surprised her brother had known this. Even most of the clubbies thought the rest of the South African team didn't arrive until Wednesday, but Storm had known there were already a handful back in the country. He cast her a quick, guilty look and she wondered if he had seen Chris at the gig. He had obviously wanted to keep it from her in case she was upset. Maybe she wasn't doing as good a job of holding it together as she thought. Her dad hadn't missed the look that passed between them and without skipping a beat he suggested their first suspect.

'You should look into Chris Ritter.'

'Dad!'

Storm seemed mildly amused.

'What? He's someone that has ties to both you and the South African girl.'

'Dad, come on. We both know that's not why you offered up his name.'

'Who's Chris Ritter?' interjected Sergeant Ferris, notepad out.

'No one,' Kaia hissed.

'His name is Christopher Ritter,' her brother started. 'He's Kaia's ex-boyfriend. He's a beach competitor at her club, Middle Beach. They should have his contact details and know where he's staying.'

'Storm!'

He gave her an unapologetic shrug. 'I'm with Dad on this one.'

'He a big guy?' Sergeant Ferris asked, not looking up from his note taking. 'Strong?'

Storm and KC shared a glance, before her brother answered. 'Sure, I guess. Every clubbie is fit and in good shape: it comes with the territory.'

'Why?' Kaia frowned.

'The markings around your throat are thumb and finger-nail impressions made from an angle directly above you,' he said.

Kaia self-consciously felt her fingers creep towards the black and purple bruising that she now wore like a choker.

'It's hard to manually strangle a person, you have to exert maximum force, so we're looking for someone or someones with considerable upper arm strength.'

And so the first person the police would be going to about the incident was her ex, which should no doubt make things even more uncomfortable next time they bumped into each other. At least Kaia was going to be a little more difficult to run into for a while. In fact, she was on strict orders to rest up and not leave the house for the next two weeks. She was even banned from going in the surf until her stitches could come out, which she was hoping would be the end of the week. Kaia knew that last restriction was going to kill her.

CHAPTER FIVE

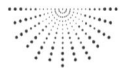

K aia was going mad and, in the process, driving her brother and father mad along with her. She had been stuck inside the house for six days, 13 hours and 24 minutes. To be fair, being stuck inside a beachfront mansion was most peoples' idea of heaven. The first few days had been spent trying to avoid any of the coverage about the attack, which included staying off the internet and not turning on the TV. After what had happened last time, Kaia didn't want to see a single story about herself or what the press 'claimed' went on. She also didn't want to see any pictures splashed across the papers. The damage was blatantly obvious in her reflection: she didn't need to view it from the other side of the lens as well.

At first a few reporters had staked out positions at the front of the house. When she had avoided stepping out the door or leaving the property, the interest had died off. The rest of her family was now free to come and go as they pleased. Storm, KC and Kaia watched Netflix. Then they watched DVDs and, oh yeah, rounded that up by watching more Netflix. She hated being inactive and after six days of being allowed to do nothing more than get out of bed, walk to the couch, then walk back to bed, she was getting antsy.

'What do you want to do, then?' asked Storm, after she complained about being stuck inside for the zillionth time.

Kaia gave him a death stare.

'I know you want to go out, but you've gotta stay in for at least a few more days. That scary doc said you're doing really well. It will probably only be another day or so.'

'Errrrggghh!'

She stormed off in the direction of her room.

'Do you want to watch *Cleverman* later? *Insecure*? *Teen Wolf*?' he called after her.

Damn it. He'd gone for her favourite shows, knowing she couldn't resist.

'FINE!'

Slamming her bedroom door, she flopped face-down on her bed like a petulant teenager. Okay, she *was* a teenager, but Kaia firmly believed she was rarely petulant. She could hear Quint whining at her door and it hurt her heart, but not enough for her to drag herself up off the bed. Kaia's phone pinged and she ignored the message tone. She didn't care who it was. Cabby had called a few times and speaking to her on the phone had kept Kaia busy and entertained. She'd come around for dinner earlier in the week and that had helped too. KC had a small gathering organised for Sunday night and Storm was helping him with it. She knew what they were both doing. Although Kaia wouldn't exactly call herself a people person, being trapped inside the house was making her loco. So if she couldn't go out into the world, her brother and father were going to try and bring the world to her. And she loved them for it.

Her father was supposed to go on a mentoring trip with the Silver Swell Quest grommets in two weeks, but he'd pulled out indefinitely. He'd simply said it was because he needed to be 'home more' and Kaia knew that meant he was hanging around to watch out for her. When everything had gone down after the Australian Titles, KC was great initially. He'd made sure she got the best legal representation possible and went above and beyond to speak out to the press in support of her. However, she couldn't pretend she hadn't noticed the increased frequency of his trips. Since the incident, he had been home less and less, sometimes for only four days before he was jetting off again.

Kaia sighed, rolling onto her back and looking up at the ceiling. What she was really desperate to do was return to Lake Pelutz. Not the most likely place a victim of a recent physical assault would want to return to, but she was possessed. Or obsessed. Perhaps both. She'd thought a lot about what Cabby said and thought about what she'd seen. In the hours that she'd had alone to run over what had happened again and again, she had become convinced that she hadn't been 'spared'. She had been *saved*. There was something in the deep, dark depths of that lake and that something had saved her life. Maybe she truly had lost it under the pressure of two horrendous events back-to-back. Maybe she was experiencing PTSD symptoms like the doctors and cops had suggested. Either way, Kaia needed to know what was in that lake.

Later that night, when she was certain everyone was fast asleep, Kaia did probably one of the stupidest things she had ever done. She snuck out of the house and rode her bike to The Lakes. Taking her car would have made too much noise: between the lights and the engine there was no way she wouldn't have woken either Storm or KC And how would she explain it? Since she didn't know the fate of her attackers or if there was anyone else out there ready to step up and finish the job, she wasn't making the wisest choice. Yet Kaia was consumed with the idea of *something* living in that lake.

The bike ride to Lake Pelutz was only 20 minutes, which was slower than it took to drive there but quicker than it would have been if she jogged or walked. As she peddled through the dark, the night air rushing past her face, she felt like she was peddling towards some kind of certainty. The figure that had swept in front of her eyes and pushed the second attacker down into the depths of the lake kept popping into her mind, along with the grey hand prying another away to give her freedom. She'd gone over it so many times she had started to see intricate scale patterns on the skin that she was fairly sure hadn't actually been there.

When Kaia cruised down the final path to the lake edge, the entire scene was deathly still. It was almost identical to the night she had been attacked. She positioned her bike facing her quickest exit on the grass next to her so she would be ready to go at a moment's notice. She also slipped a butcher's knife out of her backpack and held it loosely in one hand. With the other she grabbed a torch, then headed towards the edge of the path that dropped off into the deepest section of the lake. This part wasn't lined with houses, merely a few portions of shadowy bush that looked menacing in the 2AM darkness.

'What the hell am I doing?' Kaia whispered to herself.

Once she found a spot that looked perfect, she crouched down and peered into the black water. Right. *What now?* She placed the butcher's knife on the grass next to her as she balanced herself with one hand and used the other to hold the torch up high. Skimming the light over the lake's surface, she started close to shore and moved it out as far as the beam would reach.

Nothing. Not a ripple.

Kaia was certain there was something there. Although she had doubted herself before, she didn't now. She sensed it. It almost felt as if someone was watching her. Or perhaps she was just paranoid after her last experience at the lake. Kaia wasn't certain how many times she repeated this process, at least a dozen, skimming the surface with her flashlight. An hour passed and morning crept ever closer, but she was determined to stay longer. Absent-mindedly she had begun stacking some of the loose stones that lined the edge of the lake to pass time. There was one wobbly column constructed when guilt finally got the better of her and she thought about how angry Storm and her father would be if they found out what she was doing, despite their best efforts to keep her safe and inside the house.

Kaia's last resort was some salmon she had cooked for a salad at lunch that day. If there was a – she struggled to even think the word – *creature* down there, she hoped they liked fish. What else could they survive on? Cooked salmon would be a rare treat, she reasoned, as she unwrapped the foil and placed the fish on the grassy edge. Kaia did one more sweep across the water with the light before giving up. With a heavy sigh, she got on her bike and rode home. It was nearly 5AM when she made it back to her bed with barely a sound. No one in the house was any wiser as she lay down on her pillow, Quint snoring softly beside her, with a feeling of utter disappointment.

Kaia couldn't say what it was that drove her back those next four nights. Maybe it was a relentless desire to prove to herself that she wasn't mentally ill. Maybe it was boredom. Whatever it was, when she returned after 1.30AM the following night and settled in at the same spot, she got a surprise. The salmon was gone, as she had expected. Anything edible sitting in a park with a hundred other birds and dogs eager to snack on it would have disappeared. In its place, however, were three small stone columns. The one she had built from the night before was at the centre, with six rocks stacked on top of each other the way she had left it. But next to it were two smaller towers with four rocks positioned in descending order. She squinted, bending down close to the piles as if to investigate any sign of life.

Any person could have built these, she reasoned. This particular area of Lake Pelutz was the most deserted, but that's not to say a child couldn't have stumbled upon her rock column and added two more as part of a fun game. Heck, even a bored adult walking their dog along the bank could have made them. Kaia stayed at the lake for another two hours, her hopes ignited by a silly stack of stones. Nothing happened. No one showed. The surface of the water remained as still as the stoic pile of rocks in front of her. The last thing she did before she left was leave another piece of salmon wrapped in foil.

The following night was much the same: salmon gone, another stack of rocks in its place. The two new towers were smaller, only three rocks this time. Kaia waited as long as she could and tried to occupy her mind by flicking through the latest surf reports on her phone. She couldn't stop herself from checking the surface of Lake Pelutz every few minutes. She repeated the cycle of the previous evenings: leaving fish before riding home, deflated. The fourth and fifth nights were the same and she was growing agitated. Had she genuinely gone nuts? Was everything all in her head? Was there some local kid chuckling away to themselves every day as they added to the stone pile? There were eight columns now and Kaia still had no idea who was adding to them. Frustrated, she peddled home in a huff.

Cabby came over that next day, along with some of KC and Storm's friends, for the barbecue they had promised. Kaia's stitches had been removed a few hours earlier and her lips were feeling strangely liberated. She kept running her fingers over the skin as she tried to grow accustomed to the sensation. It was twilight and the small party of about ten were sitting in cane chairs on the balcony outside as her father cooked sausages, kebabs, mushrooms, onions and patties on the barbecue. KC was the only person allowed to touch the elaborate cooking monstrosity, which was his pride and joy. He chuckled at something Storm said to him and Kaia noticed he was wearing a novelty apron.

'Oh no,' she muttered.

'What?' asked Cabby, following Kaia's gaze to the apron that depicted a cartoonish version of a woman's body on the front. The stylised figure was wearing an Australian flag bikini.

'He has a rotating collection of "hilarious" aprons,' Kaia explained. 'He even has the male version of that one he's wearing now, with the cartoon dude having a hairy chest and fluoro budgie smugglers.'

'At least it's not a chef's hat,' she suggested.

'You know, I'd almost prefer that. It would be more earnest.'

Cabby watched KC thoughtfully as she took a swig of her beer. 'I like it.'

'You would,' Kaia laughed.

Storm handed them paper plates loaded up with meat and seared vegetables all fresh off the hot plate. He offered Kaia a beer, testing the waters, but she shook her head and gestured to the diet ginger beer in her hand.

'Diet?' he asked, scrunching his nose. 'Since when do you drink "diet"?'

'Since normal ginger beer is too strong it burns my throat,' she replied.

He nodded with understanding before leaving the women to their own devices. They ate in comfortable silence for a few minutes.

'How are things going with Imogen?' Kaia asked.

Cabby grinned, batting her eyelashes with faux innocence.

'That good, huh?'

'I don't want to alarm you, but a few more dates and I think I might actually be seeing someone.'

'Cabby!' Kaia exclaimed, 'That's so great! I'm really happy for you. I thought it—'

'I know, I know. I kind of thought that too, that it would just be casual and then probably get awkward. But I really like her.'

'She's a sweetheart,' Kaia added.

'Right? At first she seemed a bit dim, but once you get to know her—'

'Are you going to meet the parents and everything?'

'Whoa, slow down. We're not quite there yet.'

'But she's out, right?'

'Yeah, she came out to her folks when she was, like, thirteen. Brave kid.'

'You came out to your parents when you were sixteen, I still think that's pretty damn brave.'

'It's okay.' Cabby smiled at the compliment. 'Although my parents are African, so I think I get bonus points for that.'

'Totally.'

Cabby had finished her plate of food long before Kaia finished hers. With her lip still slightly tender and her injuries fading, she was taking her time. She felt her friend watching her as she ate and she glanced up.

'What? What is it?' she asked cautiously, certain that she had sauce or something smeared on her chin.

'How are you?' Cabby asked. 'You seem a little less stir crazy than the last time we hung out.'

'I'm … I'm okay. I never thought I'd miss people whispering about me and giving me weird looks, but I'm actually keen to get back to training.'

'I wouldn't be if I were you. BB has been slamming us.'

Cabby cast a look over her shoulder to where their swim coach was standing with KC. The pair were engaged in an animated discussion and just from looking at them Kaia could tell it was about the 'good ol' days' on the surfing tour.

'Anyway,' Cabby said. 'He'll probably take it easy on you when you're back, not that you would have lost that much form in a few weeks.'

'Storm took me for a few long jogs along the beach when Dad was out and I've been cycling, so hopefully that will have helped.'

'Cycling?' Cabby said, grasping Kaia's words. 'Cycling where?'

'Um, nowhere just … on Dad's exercise bike. Upstairs.'

'Kaia,' her friend whispered, voice dropping low. 'You are the shittiest liar I have ever seen.'

'Why do people keep saying that?'

'What the hell have you been up to?'

Kaia felt her pulse quicken as Cabby's gaze seemed to pierce right through her. Before she could stop herself, she was pouring out the details of what she had been doing those past few nights.

'I kept thinking about what you said, and what I saw, and how we don't really know what's beneath us and … and I wanted answers.'

'You have got to be fucking kidding me,' Cabby hissed. 'Do you know how dangerous what you're doing is?'

'I know, especially if the guys who attacked me are still out there—'

'That's just the tip, Kaia. What if there really is *something* down there? What makes you think it's friendly, just because you've been playing stone checkers or whatever? Because it didn't eat you once, that doesn't mean it won't the second time.'

Kaia blinked at the passion in her friend's words. 'You don't seem to think I'm entirely crazy though, right? You think there could actually be something in Lake Pelutz?'

Cabby sighed, leaning back for a moment and looking frustrated. 'Look, I don't know. None of us know. Police divers were in there last week and they found nothing.'

'So why are you so convinced I'm gonna get eaten?'

She made a clicking sound with her tongue, as if she was annoyed. 'When I was a kid, my auntie used to tell me stories about Mama Wata.'

'Mama what?'

'*Wata.* It's this old myth my people used to tell each other to teach kids not to go in the water on their own or to trust strangers. Basically, you'd see this beautiful woman near the shore of the ocean or a river. And she's so babin, right, that you can't help but be drawn to her. But when you finally get there, she drags you to the bottom and drowns you.'

'Jesus.'

'No, Mama Wata.' Cabby smirked. 'Now, some would say the drowning was accidental, it was just her way of playing with you and it always got out of hand. Other stories would concentrate on her luring you there.'

'Like mermaids leading sailors to their deaths on jagged rocks.'

'Exactly.' Cabby nodded. 'I mean, these stories aren't unique: every culture has 'em. But whether it's mermaids,

Mama Wata, sirens, sea serpents, Nessie or whatever, the end result is always the same, Kaia.'

'What's that?'

'*Death.* They always lead unsuspecting idiots – you – to their death.'

Kaia didn't realise she had been holding her breath and as Cabby finished, she let out a shaky gust of air. Her friend looked worried and she leaned forward, grabbing her hand.

'Look, girl, I don't want to scare you but you should be scared,' she whispered. 'There's enough human things to be afraid of by going back there, then there's things we mightn't understand.'

'But, Cabby, I *need* to know.'

'Why? Why is this so important to you?'

'Because why me? I didn't deserve to be spared, I killed someone.'

'Kaia, you know that was an—'

'Accident, sure, but Bree Tyler is still dead because of me. If there is something down there, if something choose to save me, I want to know why. I wouldn't have chosen that.'

'Kai …'

Cabby looked saddened by her friend's words, clenching her hand a little bit tighter.

'Okay. Fine. If you're determined to go back, you have to promise me one thing?'

'Anything.'

'You take me with you. It's safer if there's two of us on the shore anyway.'

Kaia thought about it for a moment. She couldn't explain why, but this felt like something she had to do alone. It was cathartic for her in some weird way. And yet, Cabby was *really* worried about her. And she hadn't immediately done what so many others would have and called her a nut job.

No, Cabby believed that Kaia *believed* what she had seen. And that counted for something.

'Okay,' Kaia said, cautiously. 'What are you doing later tonight?'

'Shit,' Cabby breathed. 'What have I got myself into?'

———

The new plan didn't vary much from the old: Kaia left her house on her bike, riding a few blocks away until Cabby was waiting there in her car. Cabby lived in a house with several other surf competitors and didn't have Kaia's issue when it came to sneaking out of the house under her father's nose. Kaia threw her bike in the back and together they drove to Lake Pelutz at 3AM in the morning. Cabby was smart, switching off her lights as soon as they drove into the car park so as not to alert any locals to their presence. While Kaia still had her butcher's knife, Cabby came armed with a baseball bat *and* a can of pepper spray.

'If the cops find us, I'm throwing the pepper spray in the lake,' she said quietly, following Kaia as she led her to the usual spot that she frequented.

'How come?' she whispered back.

'Technically it's illegal, which is some bullshit when you think of all the things guys get away with. Just let us have our pepper spray, you know? It makes me feel safe.'

Kaia pressed a hand over her mouth to prevent a giggle. 'How did you even get it?'

'My mum.' Cabby beamed. 'She gave one to each of my sisters and me, saying that there was plenty more where that came from if we needed it.'

'What a champ.'

'Damn straight. This the spot?'

'Yeah,' said Kaia, frowning as she realised there wasn't a

new stone pile. It was the first time in days there hadn't been an addition. What was there instead was the aluminium foil the salmon had been wrapped up in. It had been torn in two pieces and scrunched into round balls. Arching over the top of the two spheres was half a circle made out of stones in various sizes. Tilting her head to the side, Kaia looked at the strange positioning of objects. And then it hit her. It was upside down. Shuffling around until her back was facing the lake, suddenly she was looking at a smiley face.

'What is it?' Cabby asked, bat poised over her head as if she was ready to attack at any moment. She didn't bother to look at what had been left there for them to find, instead her eyes were trained on the water.

'It's, uh, an upside down smiley face,' Kaia said.

'Upside down?'

'Well, yeah it's … wait, no. It's not upside down.'

Kaia let out a quick burst of laughter as she realised what this meant.

'This is exactly how you would have made a smiley face if you were *in* the water,' she whispered, spinning around to look at the smooth expanse of Lake Pelutz. No movement, no ripples, no nothing. Cabby and Kaia waited for a full hour and a half before they gave up, the excitement of the smiley face having worn off by then. Before they left, Kaia decided she wanted to leave something different behind. But she'd only brought salmon again and had nothing else to offer. Looking down at the torch in her hand, she smiled at the waterproof sticker plastered on its side. She switched it off and left the torch and fish next to the smiley face, while Cabby had silently watched her as she rearranged the pebbles to spell out 'hi'.

The following evening there was no foil and no pebbles. The torch and salmon were gone, but Cabby reasoned anyone could have taken it. Kaia's throat had finally healed up enough that she was able to eat harder foods and the two girls sat at the edge of the lake, munching on chocolate chip cookies. With Cabby still on her normal training schedule, the second late night adventure had drained her. It was less than 20 minutes before she was curled up on the grass and dozing next to Kaia, a gentle snore the only sound. For her part, Kaia managed to stay awake – and if she hadn't, she may have missed it all together. It was close to 2AM when she first saw it. She had been aimlessly gazing out over the surface of the water when – about 150 metres from the edge – a faint glow appeared. She choked on her cookie and dropped it in surprise. It landed in the water with a soft 'plop' as the light continued to move closer. Her feet had been dangling haphazardly in the water and she yanked them out. Kaia was frozen in place as the small light inched closer and closer. It was barely a few inches under the water and she watched the surface of the lake, anticipating that something would break the surface. It didn't. Instead the light kept encroaching until, less than five metres from her, she panicked. Waking Cabby in a rush, she dragged her friend to her feet and they both backed away from the edge in a tangle of limbs. The light blinked out almost instantly, leaving Kaia staring at the once again serene surface of Lake Pelutz.

'What is it, what did you see?' Cabby asked, her speech somewhat slurred from having just woken up.

'I-I don't know. I thought I saw a light, maybe.'

'A light? In the sky? Aliens now too?'

'No,' Kaia said, unable to smile at Cabby's quip. 'In the water. I think it was my torch. You didn't see it? It was coming closer and closer.'

Cabby looked from her friend to the lake and back again. 'I didn't see squat. You sure you didn't doze off as well?'

'It was … yeah, yeah, maybe I did.'

'Come on,' Cabby said, gently grabbing her by the elbow. 'I'll drive you home.'

Kaia wasn't sure why she had lied. She *had* seen the light. She *had* been wide awake. Yet as soon as she had woken her friend, the light had disappeared. She ran the scenario over in her mind on the drive home, streetlights flashing by as Cabby hummed along to whatever was playing on the radio. She began to feel furious with herself. What had she done? The answer she wanted had been waiting at the end of her flashlight and she had reacted like a scared little kid. When Cabby dropped her off, Kaia peddled the final streets home in a daze. She didn't go back to sleep that night. That whole following day she was more agitated than usual. The brief swim she was allowed in the surf with Storm and KC brought little comfort as she counted down the hours until she could sneak back to the lakeside. Kaia knew what she had to do to discover what was down there and this time, she'd be going alone. The only question: was she brave enough to do it?

CHAPTER SIX

The night air was cool on Kaia's skin as she took off her clothes. It wasn't quite far enough from winter for her not to feel this, so she gritted her teeth as she laid her hoodie down on the soft grass and wiggled out of her tights. She let her toes curl over the edge of the path that dropped off into Lake Pelutz. The water was still, as usual, but tonight it seemed even more so. It was a clear evening and the starry sky was reflected perfectly in the surface of the lake. If anyone was watching it would have looked like Kaia was diving into the universe as she took a deep breath and leapt off the path. She relished the sensation of the water running over her swimsuit and through her hair as she propelled forward and down into the depths.

Stay calm, she told herself, rising to the surface, *keep calm*. If she was going to get eaten by some mysterious sea creature, well, then that was what was going to happen. But no, Kaia had faith that she had been saved *not* spared. Whatever was down here had saved her life once, so she prayed it wasn't in the mood to eat her. The nights of sneaking out had showed Kaia that the thing didn't like it when she came with someone else. Those nights were the quietest, the most inactive. If there was something there, it wanted her alone. And it also wasn't willing to come to her: she would have to go to it. So there she was, swimming out into the middle of a lake at 1.30AM in the morning, doing her best to put all thoughts of Mama Wata out of her head. Yup, Kaia felt like she was definitely on the cuckoo's nest side of crazy.

With her eyes shut and her head trying to keep a thousand different terrifying scenarios at bay, Kaia purposefully swam on until she guessed she was in the middle of the lake. She stopped slowly and lifted up her head, treading water. She had swum almost exactly to the centre of Lake Pelutz. Now she just had to wait. The tension was building in her body and she found herself calculating the distance to the shore on every side. As her heartbeat raced, she didn't feel the same confidence she had some minutes early. Rather, she was beginning to feel like this wasn't a good idea. In a bid to calm herself, she took a deep breath and plunged under the water using her hands to push herself downwards. Somehow almost everything seemed better underwater. On instinct, she opened her eyes and saw nothing but black water surrounding her. Preparing to kick her way to the surface, Kaia spun around and saw ... a face.

A stream of bubbles escaped her mouth as she screamed. She slapped a hand over her lips to stop them. There, under the surface of Lake Pelutz, was the face of a man staring back at her. Not much older than she was, he was looking intently at Kaia with what could only be described as avid curiosity. She didn't trust herself to remove her hands from her lips, she feared the second she did more screams would emerge. So she left them where they were and used her flailing legs to keep herself under the water. Unnatural blue eyes stared at Kaia through a mop of black hair that blended perfectly into the colour of the water. The pale, grey shade of his skin was offset by a heavy beard that started under his nose and seemed to consume the bottom half of his face. The facial hair hid most of his neck, but it couldn't hide the lean, muscular torso that extended beneath it. Kaia followed the path of eight perfectly formed abdominals and pronounced hip bones to see something that made her choke on the water she had been trying to block out. As she coughed, she inhaled more fluid, and in a fit of heaving gestures kicked to the surface.

Kaia burst through the water retching and spluttering as she tried to digest what she had just seen. A fish tail. The man had a fish tail. Where the bottom half of a normal guy would be – legs, butt, penis, feet, toes – his body turned into a single limb covered in grey scales. It looked long, but she hadn't got a good glance at it before she spluttered her way to the surface. Kaia was still coughing when a black head silently popped up beside her. She stared at him, eyes wide, while taking loud, deep gulps of air.

'Don't be frightened,' he said in a voice so soft and quiet it brought on a whole new wave of choking.

'What … *are*… you?' she asked through strangled breaths.

'Amos,' he said, thrusting a hand through the water at her.

Freezing on the spot, Kaia stared at the sudden grin that had emerged within the black wilderness of his beard. A row of perfectly white, slightly serrated teeth lined what would otherwise be a friendly smile.

'Amos,' she repeated. She slid her fingers to her carotid artery, feeling her thumping pulse and just double checking that she wasn't actually dead. Nope, still very much alive. Moving her hand slowly through the water, Kaia shook his outstretched limb in a gesture that was made awkward by her need to keep treading water. His skin was oily, much the way a fish's felt, and she jerked her own hand back too quickly. He noticed, with a flash of something crossing his face. They floated there for a time, neither talking, just star-ing. Finally, she felt the need to break the silence.

'I'm Kaia,' she whispered.

'I know,' he said, still grinning. 'I heard the police talking about you when they came searching.'

She must have given him an astonished look because he felt the urge to explain.

'I watched through the reeds over there.'

He gestured to a far-off end of the lake where the shal-lows were covered with long, green plants that looked like grass and rustled in the wind.

'What about when the divers came?' she asked, uncertain why she was asking *this* question and not the most obvious one of 'how are you a bloody merman?!' His smile dropped slightly, but his eyes remained animated as he explained.

'I followed them for a bit, but they didn't stay around very long.'

He looked disappointed at that. Given the fact she was having a conversation – an actual conversation – with a merman, Kaia initially hadn't noticed the burning in her legs from the exertion of treading water for so long. She was starting to feel it now, however, as the shock wore off.

'I-I need to sit,' she said feebly.

He looked from her face and down to her legs, as if remembering they were there for the first time.

'Over here,' he said, pointing at a spot to the left of the reeds.

Kaia kicked forward and extended her arms, pulling herself in the direction he had suggested. Her progress was stunted somewhat by her desire to keep her head above water so she could watch Amos's every move. Amos … he had a name. The sea creature from deep below had a name and it was *Amos*. His shoulders remained above the surface as he moved forward slightly in front of Kaia. He didn't need to use his arms, for obvious reasons: he was propelled by the strength and power of his massive tail. Kaia fought an urge to dive under the water and watch. For some reason she thought that might be intrusive.

Instead she wondered how this could be the same creature she had been so afraid of. He surged onwards, before looking back at her with an expectant smile and darting across her path. He zigzagged like this all the way to the shore and it was truly becoming harder and harder to believe that this *fish guy* could want to eat her. Or maybe that was the point, to seem harmless when in reality he was anything but? Amos hung back as Kaia stretched her feet down and made contact with the sand. Stepping forward like an astronaut trying to walk along the surface of the moon, she stopped when it was shallow enough for her to sit down with the water coming up just below her armpits. Her legs were bent out in front of her and Kaia rested her elbows on her knees as she leaned forward to watch the merman. He stayed where the water was deeper, his tail floating limp while he inched forward lightly, using his hands. It was still dark, but thanks to a slight glow from a far-off streetlight and Kaia's eyes having adjusted to the night, she could still get a fairly good view of him. Until the halfway point, Amos was just a normal man. A fine specimen of a man, Kaia noted, given the definition in his back and the arm muscles that she could see. Her gaze caught on something at the side of his body that was moving ... gills. He had actual gills.

'Oh my God,' she said, her hand instinctively reaching out towards the skin surrounding them. Most of him was still under the surface and Kaia watched in fascination as the gills expanded and contracted as Amos's body converted the oxygen in the water like a fish. Her fingers were about to touch the side of his stomach when she paused, suddenly realising what she was doing.

'Uh, sorry,' she mumbled, feeling embarrassed as she slicked her blonde hair back off her face with water. Amos looked from his gills to Kaia's now clenched hand with interest.

'It's okay,' he said, grabbing her wrist. 'They're just gills.'

He pressed her palm against them and she let out a small sound of shock as she felt the movement under her finger-tips. He held her there for a few seconds, before releasing her hand. She drew it back to her body instantly, like her limb was attached with elastic.

'It can't be covered all the time,' Amos said. 'Otherwise I can't breathe.'

Kaia was still staring at him in disbelief. Where the buttocks on a human would begin, his skin took on a different texture as it evolved into scales. They seemed to be a dark grey colour, but as the water glided over them and they reflected against the surface she thought of them as closer to blue. The tail extended some four feet before split-ting into two opposing directions, much like a dolphin's tail. Her gaze returned to his skin, the pallor of which looked similar to a normal human – but as if it had been left in the water too long so it was a faint grey. Kaia reached out again, examining his expression to make sure it was okay.

'Can I ...?'

He nodded. She touched his exposed shoulder blade as it sat out of the water. His skin felt strangely just like her own, except there was a certain ... She wouldn't exactly describe it as slipperiness, but as she ran her hand over his shoulder and down his arm there was a texture to his dry skin that made it feel as if it was still submerged in the water. She followed the trail of her fingertips with her eyes and let out a gasp of surprise when she saw intricate silver patterns forming. They were identical to the shape of his scales and appeared raised off his skin like goosebumps. Kaia's nose was inches from his skin as she examined the effect her touch had on the strange surface.

'I'm not crazy,' she muttered, feeling a newfound appreciation for her brain. Despite everything she had been through, the horror and the doubt that followed, she had remembered this. Her mind had filed away the details: from the colour of his skin to the patterns that decorated it.

'Why would you think you're crazy?' he asked.

She blinked, looking at his expression closely to see if he was as genuinely confused by her comment as he sounded.

'Because I'm sitting here talking to a merman: a living, breathing merman with gills and the whole package.'

'I'm an aquatic humanoid, actually.'

There was an air of recital as he said those words, something that made Kaia think he'd said them many times before.

'Who told you that?' she asked.

'Told me what?'

'That you're a … how did you say it?'

'Aquatic humanoid.'

'That's it.'

He shrugged, nonchalant, but there was a sadness underling his words. 'My father said merman or mermaid was what they used to call us in myths.'

'You have parents?' she questioned, suddenly looking around as if an entire family of *aquatic humanoids* would pop up at a moment's notice. 'Where's your father?'

'I don't know,' Amos whispered, something like hurt and confusion crossing his features. He flipped over from his stomach until he was on his back, body propped up on his elbows.

'We used to live over there,' he said, pointing to the opposite side of the lake and a long house that was sitting in darkness. 'He used to take me swimming in here on special occasions. I thought we were going somewhere better the last time I saw him. He said we were preparing for a trip but ...'

His brow crinkled as he recalled the memory.

'He was destroying everything: all his work, the computers, everything. And then he let me go. He pressed a button and next thing all the water was sucked out and I ended up at the bottom of the lake.'

'You were in a tank?'

Kaia tried to imagine a tank big enough to fit him and thought it would have to be closer to a pool. Even then, a *big* pool.

'Yes.' He nodded. 'Sometimes I'd stay in the tank, sometimes I'd stay in a pool that was long and narrow – '

'A lap pool?' Kaia offered.

'That's it. Father added a … a drain, I think is the word your people use? He had transferred me to the pool that night which is something he only ever did when I was getting to swim in the lake. He hit the button and *whoosh*, here I was. I kept waiting for him to come. I knew it was dangerous to be seen, so I only looked at night. But the house was full of people for a time and then nothing. No one ever came back. That was a while ago and I think surely he must be dead. He would never leave me otherwise.'

A long pause hung in the air between them as Kaia pondered the weirdness of her current situation. Amos seemed to be thinking about his father, his family, but truthfully she had no idea what kind of thoughts would occupy a merman's mind.

'What month is it?' he asked suddenly, breaking the silence.

'It's August. August 20.'

'August,' he repeated, mulling it over. 'I have been here for five months.'

'You've been here by yourself in Lake Pelutz for five months?'

'Yes.' He nodded.

'What have you been eating?' The question was out of her mouth before she had a chance to stop herself. Kaia swallowed an unwelcome thought about stray swimmers.

'There are plenty of fish in the lake. Or at least there were to begin with. I have to eat them raw, which I like because Father never let me do that. But there are less fish now. Sometimes I steal food that people leave behind close to the shore if the birds haven't eaten it. Or if I look really carefully for them, I can find some fish deep at the bottom. The salmon you keep leaving is good.'

Kaia grinned. 'So that was you! You did the smiley face?'

'Yes, I'm glad you saw it. Do you have any more?'

'Uh, no, I didn't bring any food with me.'

He looked disappointed and Kaia thought about how hard it must be relying on other people's scraps.

'I ate the fish too quickly in the beginning because I thought Father would come back,' Amos said. 'By the time I realised he wouldn't, I had to learn other ways.'

'I can come back tomorrow with food,' Kaia said, cautiously. 'I can bring as much of it as you need.'

'Really?'

'Of course! You're stuck here and you're hungry, it's the least I can do. You saved my life.'

They both paused at that. It was the topic they had been dancing around, but now there was no avoiding it.

'You're not afraid of me then?' He asked the question so meekly, Kaia was surprised at the trepidation behind it.

'As long as you give me nothing to be afraid of,' she said, watching his face for any clue as to what he was thinking. When he said nothing, she pushed on. 'I was afraid that night. And then afterwards, I guess, but my friend Cabby would call me reckless. Fear got replaced with me obsessing over what I saw and whether or not I had lost it.'

'Lost it?'

'Gone crazy,' she explained.

'Cabby, she was the woman you came here with?'

'Uh-huh. She's a good pal, she looks out for me.'

Kaia had a weird moment of clarity then and a deep, internal shiver passed through her. He noticed, leaning back slightly.

'You should go,' he said. 'Your body doesn't run like mine, you humans get cold if you stay in water too long.'

She nodded, feeling the full extent of just how freezing she was for the first time. Her teeth started to chatter as she got to her feet, carefully climbing up the ledge that led back to the path that wrapped around Lake Pelutz. Looking back at Amos as he slipped into deeper water, there was one more thing she had to know.

'You pulled me to the surface, didn't you?' Kaia asked, the words coming out as almost a stutter as she stood there, shivering. 'And dragged me to shore?'

He nodded. 'I thought I was too late at first. You were floating there like you were frozen. Once I got you to shore I could see you were still breathing, so I just waited until you woke.'

'Why?' she asked softly.

'You didn't deserve to die.' He stated it as if it was a fact of the universe.

'How do know? Maybe I did.'

Amos considered her carefully as she said this. 'No, you don't. I can tell. A bad person wouldn't fight that hard to survive. A bad person wouldn't have come back every night afterwards.'

Kaia smiled, not quite agreeing with his theory, and feeling as if 'goodbye' didn't necessarily fit this scenario.

'I'll see you tomorrow,' she said.

She had already turned and started walking away when she heard his reply slide over the surface of the water towards her.

'It was nice to meet you, Kaia.'

CHAPTER SEVEN

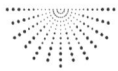

'We're doing our utmost to locate them.'

'Kaia?'

'Hmm?'

'Did you hear what Sergeant Ferris said?'

'No, sorry. I was just … thinking.' She stifled a yawn and gave her dad an apologetic glance. Turning to face Senior Sergeant Ferris, who was sitting on the couch opposite her and KC, she mumbled an apology.

'It's okay, Kaia,' he said, giving her an understanding smile. 'I know you've been through an ordeal. You've got a lot to cope with and you must be exhausted.'

She nodded, as if agreeing wholeheartedly with him. After all, she couldn't exactly explain the reason she was so exhausted was because she had been up late the night before having a deep and meaningful with an aquatic humanoid. Just thinking the words 'aquatic humanoid' made her need to sit down. Kaia had said the words out loud in her bedroom when she was by herself and the effect was overwhelming.

On the plus side, she wasn't mental.

'You suspect the Tyler brothers?' Storm asked from his

position leaning against the kitchen bench with his arms crossed. Kaia sat up a little straighter and tried to look more interested in what the police officer was saying.

Sergeant Ferris sighed. 'I don't want to draw conclusions, but the fact they're missing looks suspicious. That's the line of questioning we're pursuing at the moment.'

'And you've ruled out Chris Ritter?' asked KC.

Kaia groaned as her father put a hand on her shoulder in a supportive gesture.

'Seriously?' she asked, looking up at him.

'I have every right to ask, honey.'

'We did speak to him,' Sergeant Ferris said cautiously. 'But he had a solid alibi. He did mention that you two had a conversation in person the night before the attack?'

'What?' her dad said, swivelling in his seat to face her. 'When?'

'You didn't tell me anything about this,' Storm added.

'We just crossed paths at The Dirty Boogs gig,' she said, trying to downplay the situation.

'He said things got quite heated?' Sergeant Ferris countered.

Fucking Chris, she thought, rolling her eyes. 'We saw each other from across the room so I left, not wanting to have to speak to him. He followed me out onto the street and wanted to talk. I didn't.'

'What did he want to talk about?' the officer asked, taking notes.

'Didn't he tell you this?'

'Just following up, cross-checking the information.'

'Sure,' she said. 'Well, he wanted to apologise for … I guess, siding with the Tylers after the accident. And breaking up.'

'And how did you respond to that?'

'I told him I didn't want to speak to him, that what was

done was done and I was just trying to move on with my life. And then I walked to my car.'

'And he left you alone?'

'Yeah.'

Sergeant Ferris nodded, his pen making a final few scribbles on his notepad before he got to his feet, signalling the end of the interview. If you could call it that: essentially he had had wanted to update the Craigs on how far along they were in the investigation. Put simply, not far. When he had started working his way through the list of potential suspects, Bree Tyler's two brothers had quickly moved to the top when he discovered they were a) back in the country and b) unable to be located. Their disappearance was being treated as intentional, he told Kaia, given that their wallets and mobiles were gone, as well as some clothing. Their car had been located several blocks away from Lake Pelutz, but it had remained untouched. None of their credit or Eftpos cards had been used since the night of the attack. Among their friends and known associates, no one seemed to know where the Tyler brothers were.

Kaia did. Or at least, she thought she did.

However, her lips were indefinitely sealed. Everyone shook hands with the officers and Sergeant Ferris led the way to the door. Quint was trotting beside her and she patted his head as she followed the police officer outside, pretending to be the polite host while her father and brother stayed inside. When the gate rolled back, she casually trailed after him as he made his way to the car.

'Sergeant Ferris,' she started. 'Can I ask you something quickly?'

He paused, surprised. 'Sure thing, Kaia.'

'Have there been any other attacks in the area over the past few months? Around Lake Pelutz?'

In the broad daylight, Kaia became properly aware of his

age for the first time. Sergeant Ferris was much more mature than the other officers she'd met at the hospital. He was on the other side of fifty, and his forehead was wrinkling in concentration as he thought about her question for a few seconds. He was still a fit guy, kind of like her dad, but retirement didn't seem that far off for the officer.

'Actually,' he said, his silver eyebrows raising with the realisation. 'There was one months back, I think. I didn't work the case.'

'Really?' she said, trying to keep her tone casual. 'Was it a similar kind of thing?'

Sergeant Ferris looked at her, concern etched into his expression. 'It was a murder.'

Kaia heard the breath escape from her mouth. 'I … I didn't hear anything about it.'

'I suspect you wouldn't have, it was just before the Australian Titles.'

'Oh,' she said, with understanding. Kaia would have missed any sort of coverage because she had been embroiled in her own drama. 'Did they ever catch the killer?'

'Killers,' he corrected. 'There were two. And no, it remains an open investigation. A colleague of mine is still working the case but the media theory was that it was a home invasion gone wrong or a case of mistaken identity. The place was trashed.'

'Who was the victim? How could you confuse someone you intended to kill?'

'The MO has never really been clear,' said Sergeant Ferris. 'The deceased was a professor at Hodgkins University, no known enemies or reasons why anyone would want him killed.'

'But there were two attackers? Just like there were two men who came after me?'

Sergeant Ferris had been reaching for the car door when

he paused, looking back at her. 'These were very different crimes, Kaia. And in my experience as a cop, usually the simplest explanation is the right one.'

'Right,' she murmured. 'The Tyler brothers had the most reason to hurt me and if they're missing, then it's probably the Tyler brothers.'

'Spot on,' he said, before pausing again. 'But let me check in with my colleague anyway. See if there's anything in it.'

'Thank you,' Kaia replied, smiling as she took a step away from the car and he started the engine. She was about to walk inside when he wound down the window and leaned out slightly.

'You know,' he said, a smirk pulling up one side of his face. 'If you ever think about swapping the surf for a *real* job, let me know.'

'Police?' she asked, with a grimace.

'Just a thought,' Sergeant Ferris said, turning on his indicator to pull onto the road. 'We always need more women on the force.'

Kaia let out a small laugh at that, watching as the officer drove off and Quint barked his farewells.

———

Kaia was nervous about going back to Lake Pelutz that night. A part of her wondered if she had dreamed the whole thing, meeting Amos and discovering what really was *below* the surface. But then she thought about how she had believed she was crazy, that it had all been in her head. She had doubted herself then. It was time now not only to believe in the extraordinary, but to believe in herself. As she slowly dismounted her bike, jogging alongside it before placing it in the bushes, Kaia's nerves were increased tenfold. Across the opposite side of the lake, at the house where Amos had said he and his father once lived, there was something going on. The property was illuminated and she could see half a dozen silhouettes moving around inside. Torchlights irradiated the back of the property as two other people looked for … something. Even though it was pitch-black and she couldn't have been further away from them across the water, Kaia stayed crouched down and low to the ground as she scurried to the start of where the reeds were thickest. She kept her eyes trained on the house, fearful of whether those torchlights would keep expanding further around the lake.

'Police.'

Kaia jumped, falling back off her heels and onto her butt in an ungraceful fashion. It was Amos, obviously, his face peering out at her and barely visible from within the reeds.

'Amos,' she breathed. 'You scared me to death.'

'Sorry,' he said, moving closer to the edge of the path and resting his chin on the concrete there. 'You looked worried.'

'I am,' she whispered, trying to pull herself together. 'It's midnight, what are they doing at your old house at this time of night?'

'They've been there since dusk. They're going over it "one last time" I heard a man say.'

'Amos, how close did you get? You should be careful, if any of them saw you—'

'I can hide myself when I want to. They saw nothing.'

She gulped. 'Right. Of course you can.'

'My father was very clear about what would happen if people like that found me. It wasn't good. What's that?'

Looking down at the package in her hands, Kaia handed it to him. 'It's for you. Food. Probably more than you want, to be honest, but I hated the idea of you having to wait for peoples' scraps.'

He had had been rapidly undoing the aluminium foil she

had wrapped six different types of fish in when he paused, staring at her intently.

'Well, go on,' she said, waving away the feeling of slight discomfort. 'Dig in. I didn't bring any drinks or anything because I guess that—'

'I don't,' Amos blurted, cutting her off as he swallowed an entire piece of salmon whole. 'But thank you.'

'You're welcome.'

Kaia brought her knees together, hugging herself as she remained sitting on the edge of the lake while Amos ate in the darkness. Her gaze flicked back to the police as they continued to go through the house, looking for God knows what.

'I think that's my fault,' she said, nodding at the scene.

'The police?' he asked, pausing mid-mouthful.

'Yeah. There's an officer who has been staying in touch with me and I started asking him some questions today, trying to find out what happened to your father.'

'You did?'

She turned to face him, feeling guilty about having to tell anyone this kind of news. 'It's not good, Amos. You were right: he's dead.'

He nodded, eyes dropping downwards. She knew it was what he had suspected, but that wouldn't make hearing the information any less painful.

'They said he was shot by two men, but they never came up with any real suspects.'

'Did he suffer?'

'What?'

'Pain. Did he suffer pain when they killed him?'

'In the news articles I could find online,' Kaia said, 'the killers apparently shot him once in the leg and then again in the head.'

110

He was silent at that, placing a piece of fish that had been destined for his mouth back down into the foil.

'The police told the media they thought it was an accident, an execution that was meant for someone else. He had some kind of home lab set up that they destroyed as well.'

'Thank you,' he said, quietly.

'What for?' Kaia frowned.

'For finding out. For telling me.'

She nodded, not sure if she really deserved a thank you for that. He didn't look up at her, instead focusing his gaze intently on the fish. Something glistened around his neck and for the first time Kaia noticed he wore a necklace. Well, it wasn't a necklace as such: it looked like an old, long, silver chain that was designed more for practicality than aesthetic appeal. It seemed to dangle to midway down his torso, but she couldn't see if anything hung at the end of it because the rest of his body was covered by the reeds. Glancing at the expression on his face, the grief that was evident there, and she knew he needed to be alone. Even though she'd been there for little more than twenty minutes, Kaia got to her feet.

'I'll see you tomorrow, Amos.'

He nodded, but didn't vocalise a goodbye. With the slightest bristling sound, he disappeared and Kaia took her leave. On the ride home, she figured it was probably a good thing they kept their visit short that night. There was too much activity at the lake. All it would take was for someone to find her there and suddenly Kaia would be forced to respond to questions she didn't have the answers to.

———

It was well after midday when Kaia finally woke up. Even

Storm had been active for hours when she emerged from her bedroom, bleary-eyed. He shouted a quick 'afternoon sis' as he dashed out of the house, surfboard under his arm. Kaia followed his movement as he leaped off the back steps and sprinted across the sand. She could see why: clean sets of five-foot waves were breaking off-shore thanks to a steady southerly wind. She was only surprised Storm hadn't been out there earlier. A quick check of the family surfboard rack in the garage confirmed what she had suspected: KC was out there too. He'd probably been in the water since sunrise. This suited her intentions perfectly, as Kaia had work to do. She was officially taking herself off house arrest and heading to the library. It was not somewhere she frequented, ever, and she had to look up the address of the nearest branch. It was only a fifteen-minute car trip and she whipped up a quick bowl of muesli, fruit and yoghurt that she could eat while she drove. She had a spoon dangling out of her mouth as she stepped out of the house only to find Cabby at her front door.

'Hey!' Her friend grinned.

'Hey,' Kaia replied, awkwardly swallowing a mouthful. 'What are you doing here?'

'I was bored, it's a Saturday. Thought I'd come and annoy ya.'

'I'm honoured.'

'Actually, I'm surprised you're not out in the surf like, I dunno, everyone else we've ever met ever.'

Kaia laughed. 'No, I slept in and fancy staying dry for one day. I'm actually off to the library.'

'The – I'm sorry, what? You? At the library?'

'I read!'

'I'm having a very hard time imagining it. What could you, Kaia Craig, possibly be going to the library for on a glorious Saturday?'

'Uh,' she started, fidgeting where she stood. 'I was going to go look up … er, mermaid stories.'

'Girl.'

'Just a few.'

'You still on that?'

'Well, no. I mean, I've stopped going to Lake Pelutz,' Kaia lied.

'Good.'

'But I'm still curious.'

'It's cos I got talking about Mama Wata, isn't it?'

'A little bit, yeah. Then I started reading about other stories and—'

'Fine,' Cabby said, crossing her arms. 'Let's go to the library and look up mermaid stories.'

'Really?' Kaia said, surprised. 'You'll come with me? Judgement-free?'

'Oh no, my judgement is coming too, but *after* we do this we're going somewhere to get pizza and have a drink.'

'I don't drink.'

'It's not all about you, blondie.'

With a smile, she followed Cabby to her car and they piled in. Kaia started to give her directions to the local branch, but her friend already knew where it was. It was situated next to a day care centre and the excited cries of children playing rang out as the girls navigated their way through the car park. The outside walls of the building had been painted as part of a community art project and it was difficult to spot the entry among the colourful patterns and amateur designs. Inside, it didn't feel like the kind of library Kaia was expecting. This was the Gold Coast, after all, not New York, so she quickly dispelled any notions of spiral staircases and towering columns of ancient volumes. Instead it was well-lit with beautiful natural light filtering in through several skylights. There wasn't anyone hunched over dusty books, reading by the dull illumination of a lamp. Rather, readers were propped up on colourful pillows or wedged into spaces at various window seats that lined the circular structure. It was like a big sphere of learning, Kaia thought, passing a bench of computers that were occupied by people busily tapping away on the keyboards.

Kaia wasn't precisely sure what she was looking for – or even how to search for it – so she began absentmindedly browsing the aisles while Cabby strolled off towards the LBGTQI romance section. Passing the fantasy area, children's books, and finally true crime, she began inching her way towards the encyclopedias. There were so many thick volumes with tiny gold writing, she almost turned around and went home. Her fingers trailed over the names of the various titles until she got the distinct impression someone was watching her. She jumped as she passed an empty spot on the shelf, only to see Cabby's face staring back at her from the other side of the aisle.

'Boo.'

'Cab, you freaked me out,' Kaia whispered over the top of her friend's high-pitched laughter. 'Why would you do that?'

'Why not?' she said, joining Kaia on the other side. 'Anyway, you are so in the wrong spot. Follow me.'

Cabby grabbed a book by its spine as she passed, then gestured for Kaia to come with her. She took a sharp right turn until they were standing in a very narrow aisle. Her eyes followed the subject headings until she came to a stop under one that said 'MYTHS/FOLKLORE'. Kaia's head was in line with another reading 'UFOS/PARANORMAL', and she wondered, not for the first time, what she had got herself into. Cabby was stretching to try and reach a dark blue book – *Medieval Mermaids* – and Kaia made use of her height, grabbing it for her.

'Thanks,' she said. 'I'm a hobbit.'

'I'm a giant, so let's call it even.'

'Can you grab those two? Oh! And that big one, yeah, that should about do us.'

Two hours later, Kaia was somehow sitting at a workstation with Cabby, their heads both buried in books about historical accounts of mermaids and mermen. Cabby was scrolling rapidly on a tablet, consumed by the information and consulting back to the book she had open in front of her. Kaia was hypnotised by the illustrations of a man named Gustave Dore. He had drawn horrific images of gigantic sea monsters snarling and hissing at ancient heroes or snapping at the feet of naked damsels in distress. The black and white drawings were so detailed she kept getting lost in the bleakness of his work. There was a deep unease spreading through her stomach and Kaia tried to direct her attention back to the text.

'Huh. This is interesting,' she started. 'It says here in 1493 that Columbus reported seeing mermaids near the Caribbean. He said they "rose high out of the sea, but were not as beautiful as they are represented".'

'Yeah, I keep coming across a lot of old accounts from pirates and sailors right up until the late 1800s then it kind of just … stops.'

'They were supposed to be an omen of bad luck, tricking men into giving up their gold and drowning them in the depths.'

Cabby smiled. 'There's a widely accepted theory they were just dolphins, that the men had gone nuts from spending too much time at sea. Or they were horny and everything looked bangable to them at that point.'

'That sounds—' Kaia's sentence danced away in her mind as it hit her. These men most likely weren't crazy. What if they had seen actual mermaids and mermen, just like she had seen Amos? What she had taken for a superfluous myth, like the Loch Ness monster or Yowie, was now suddenly much more relevant. These could be some of the first historical accounts of humans coming in contact with Amos's people. Because if she was sure of anything, it was that there had to be more than one. He had to have come from somewhere: she just hadn't built up the courage to ask him yet. The aspect that creeped her out the most though, was that universally merpeople were considered not a good thing. Whether that's because their beauty cloaked evilness or they were malicious tricksters, there didn't seem to be a positive story among the accounts – excluding a fairy tale by Hans Christian Andersen.

'The most recent sightings I can find are these two,' said Cabby, passing over her iPad.

'What's that?' Kaia asked, staring at a grainy picture of a dark blue object. She zoomed back until the whole scale of the image was clearer. It was still a mystery to her.

'That's supposed to be a mermaid off the coast of this town in Israel in 2009. Someone tried to take a photo of it. Apparently dozens of people spotted it doing aerial tricks, that kind of thing.'

'Sounds ridiculous,' she murmured, thinking of how shy and secretive Amos was. It made sense to assume most of his kind were like that, if they were out there.

'I know, but a one million dollar reward was offered up to anyone who could bring in proof of its existence.'

'By who?'

'What?' Cabby asked, glancing up from the screen.

'Who offered up the reward? I mean, a million dollars is a lot of money, but even more so when you think about how crazy this story sounds. Who would risk a million dollars on that?'

'Either someone who was really sure or really desperate,' she mused. 'Anyway, in 2012 in Zimbabwe, work was stopped on these two reservoirs because the workers claimed they were being pestered by mermaids and mermen.'

'Any proof?'

She shook her head. 'As usual, no. But the national water minister did put out a press release about it.'

'As you do,' Kaia snorted.

There was a crackle over the intercom before an announcement that the library was shutting in 15 minutes. With a triumphant roll of her shoulders, Cabby slammed shut the book that was resting in her lap.

'Welp, come on. I promised I'd help and you promised me pizza.'

'That's true.' Kaia smiled, getting to her feet. 'Where were you thinking?'

'Ninja Turtles,' Cabby said, strolling back to the section where they had first retrieved the books.

'Storm loves that place.'

'Of course he does, he's a twenty-one-year-old man-child. A Teenage Mutant Ninja Turtles themed pizza bar is exactly the kind of joint built for people like him.'

Kaia laughed, acknowledging that Cabby wasn't wrong. In fact, if she remembered correctly Storm either knew the owners or had made friends with them. It was less than a ten-minute drive to Burleigh Heads and Ninja Turtles, which had been a butcher's shop when Kaia was growing up. The butcher had closed down a few years ago and this place had opened up instead, surprising a lot of locals who didn't think 'themed' anything could work on the Gold Coast. But the café and food culture in the city was changing, evolving, getting hipper. Ninja Turtles was the result of that, with a cluster of tables and deceptively comfortable old couches out the front of the restaurant. Inside was basically just a bar designed for hanging out, with a few novelty pinball machines and arcade games – featuring the totally radical turtles, of course. It was early on Saturday afternoon so the place wasn't yet packed, only a few stragglers left over from the lunch crowd and otherwise too early for the evening rush. Ordering at the counter, Kaia got the impression she had been right about Storm knowing some of the staff. The guy behind the counter gave her a nod as if he recognised her and she smiled politely, her gaze darting back down to the menu.

'Over here,' Cabby said, waving Kaia over to a choice spot she'd wrangled under a display of skateboard decks that had been painted with different version of the characters.

'What did you get?' Kaia asked, flopping down into a huge armchair.

'The veggo supreme. You?'

'Four cheeses.'

'Oh that's good, with the thin crust. Mmmm. I'll be stealing a slice.'

'Heh, course you will.'

'In my defence, I'm riding the crimson wave right now and have the will to eat three times what I would usually.'

'No judgement here,' Kaia replied, holding up her hands. 'My PMS just consists of painful cramps and a weird craving for pickles – always pickles for some reason.'

'I sense you mean *actual* pickles rather than—'

'God, no,' she laughed. 'Real pickles: the kind you get from a grocer.'

The two girls laughed for a moment, settling in to the conversation.

'So,' Cabby said, taking a slow slip from the glass of red wine she'd ordered and watching Kaia.

'So?'

'So is your curiosity sufficiently sated after the library?'

Kaia let out a breath. 'I mean, maybe? I don't know, it's just an itch I felt I had to scratch.'

'You've swapped late night adventures for books though, which is an improvement.'

'Yeah, sure. Thank you for coming with me by the way and not …'

'Burning you at the stake?'

'Whoa,' Kaia scoffed, raising her eyebrows.

'Metaphorically. And you're welcome. I don't think what you saw, or what you think you saw, is impossible. It's maybe more likely that it was something else, but there's no harm in trying to get answers.'

'Answers?' she said. 'I don't know if those—'

'Peace of mind, then. My ma is a big believer in that shit as a psychiatrist. She reckons healing yourself is a journey and you going to that lake, looking up books, whatever else you need to do, those are steps on that journey.'

Kaia considered her friend for a moment, leaning back in her chair. 'You're pretty damn wise, you know?'

Cabby grinned. 'It's the wine.'

'Ha,' Kaia laughed. 'Of course! I should have known adult drinks maketh the adult.'

'Plus, I've got a whole twelve months on you. When you're nineteen, you can sort this all out for yourself.'

'Nah.' She smiled, taking a sip of her apple juice. 'I'd rather still rely on you to help me.'

'Fair enough.'

Physically, Cabby and she couldn't have been less alike. When Kaia stood to her full height, she towered over her friend by several inches. In a pair of denim cut off shorts and blue thongs, she was a stick. When she was growing up, the boys had called her 'beanpole' and shouted about her chest being 'so flat it made the walls jealous'. Boys were assholes. Cabby, on the flip side, was short, curvy and muscular: she looked like an athlete. Her skin was closer to black than brown and when she smiled, it seemed to light up everything in the nearby vicinity. Kaia envied her ability to hand out smiles like that so liberally and naturally. It had been quite a while since hers felt anything but forced. Their pizzas were delivered to the table and they remained in silence for a while, tearing into the first few slices. One thing they definitely had in common was a ferocious appetite.

'Listen,' Cabby said, wiping her hands on a serviette as she swallowed a bite. 'If the books don't do it, if there's still more stuff you wanna know or—'

'Steps to take on the healing journey?'

Cabby laughed, clicking her fingers at Kaia. 'Yes! Exactly! I know a marine biologist you could talk to.'

'You do.' Kaia blinked. 'Who?'

'I'm at uni too, you know. I got other shit going on besides this sport.'

'I know, I just … I don't think I've ever even met a marine biologist, which I suppose is weird, living on the Gold Coast.'

'Okay so full disclosure, I kind of know him. I've met him once, but if you wanted to go talk to him I could set it up.'

'Is he local?'

'Yeah, it's actually one of Imogen's older brothers. He works at Sea World.'

'Really?' Kaia murmured, thinking about it while she bit into another slice of pizza. 'Thing is, the only person I've spoken to about this is you. And I'm super fortunate you haven't told anyone that I've lost the plot; how would I broach this with a stranger? How would I talk around *that* subject?'

Cabby nodded, taking another sip of her wine.

'I couldn't just show up at Sea World and start asking questions. It would be strange as hell.'

'You're right,' Cabby agreed. 'Go on a date, maybe?'

'*What?*'

'I think her brother's straight, or at least I got that vibe.

He's definitely single. You could go on a date with him and start asking questions about his work.'

'I'm terrible on dates,' Kaia admitted. 'It took forever for Chris to get me to go out with him on our first date – and I liked him.'

'Okay, well, just a thought.'

'Let's park it,' she said, before picking up her last piece of pizza and finishing it in a matter of seconds. Although she'd been reluctant to go out – to do anything social – Kaia actually enjoyed her time there with Cabby. They stayed right up until about 8PM when the Saturday night business really began to roll in. When Cabby dropped her home that evening, Kaia had already resolved to head back to Lake Pelutz. Amos had enough food to last him for a few days without a visit if it came to that, but now she had questions – hundreds of them – and she was burning to ask them.

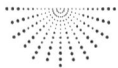

CHAPTER EIGHT

The second Kaia dipped her toe cautiously into the water, she felt like a weight had been lifted off her shoulders. She had been anxious to get to Lake Pelutz and worried about whether there would still be police activity at Amos's old house across the water. But thankfully, everything was quiet and she was able to slip down to their usual meeting spot without any drama. Amos was waiting for her, slowly appearing from the depths with a smile on his face. They had left things in an uncomfortable spot the night before, but it seemed to have all been forgotten. He genuinely looked excited to see her.

'Kaia,' he said, beaming.

'Hi,' she replied, steeling herself before jumping straight off the ledge and into the water with him. She'd worn one of her full-length wetsuits in preparation for being in the water for a while and immediately felt better for it.

'How are you?' he asked, inching closer to her.

'Warmer, thankfully. And you? Anything exciting happen? Cops? Sea monsters?'

'No, it was quiet. Well, it was busy – a lot of families come here on weekends. A lot of people swim from one side of the lake and back again. There's usually a lot to look at.'

'How old are you?' Kaia blurted.

'I'm nineteen, almost twenty,' Amos answered, seemingly not minding how direct she was. 'I turn twenty on December 2, or at least so my father thinks. Thought. That's the date he found me so that's the date we've always celebrated.'

'Where? How did he find you?'

He grew silent as he thought back. 'I don't remember much about that day. I was a kid, not much older than five or six and I was swimming with someone.'

'So there are others like you?'

'Others like me? Of that I'm sure. I think I was with my mother, maybe. Then I got caught in a net and I was terrified, screaming for help.'

She could see it was a painful memory and he lightly shook his head to draw himself out of it.

'My father was a scientist, you see. He had been doing a catch and release study on his boat when he found me.'

'Why didn't he just let you go? Put you back in the ocean?'

'I was hurt at the time, from trying to get my way out of the net, so he treated me and then … I don't know. I always wondered if maybe his curiosity got the better of him. There was too much to learn from me.'

'Or perhaps he got attached.'

'Perhaps.'

'Did he teach you how to talk? How to act so … human?' Kaia wondered if that question was offensive, but it was too late to take it back.

'Yes. Father taught me very well. He was a smart man. He taught me and looked after me and tried to find more of my kind. He spent most of my life trying to track down my people and where they might be from. He studied me and I tried to teach him things, but everything I know about this—'

he gestured to himself '—I know naturally. I've never had to think about it. It comes as easily as walking does to humans.'

'When I looked into your father's death they said he worked at Hodgkins University.'

Amos nodded. 'He used to teach classes there a few times a week, but once I got bigger … well, he was one of the few professors who was able to work from home mostly. He was old and research was what Professor Viktor Waldman preferred.'

It was the first time he had used his name properly instead of 'father', Kaia noted. She was almost sorry for asking him so many prying questions, but not sorry enough to stop. Her toes were barely touching the bottom of the lake as she bobbed there, listening to him talk.

'Do you know the time?' he asked suddenly.

'Yeah,' Kaia answered, checking her digital wristwatch, which she usually used to monitor her heart rate and time herself with sprints. 'It's 9.57PM. I came earlier than usual because I don't have to sneak around on a Saturday night.'

His eyes lit up as he looked over at her watch, but he was distracted for only a second.

'Can I show you something?'

'Uh, sure,' she said, nervously.

'We don't have much time and we need to be over at the other side of the lake.'

'Much time for what?'

'The fireworks,' he whispered, his eyes widening with excitement. 'They have them every Saturday night at 10PM. I used to be able to hear them from my tank but never see them. Now that I'm in the lake I can watch it all from just over there.'

Kaia gaze followed to where he pointed. It seemed like a long distance to cross before 10PM.

'I don't know if I can swim that fast,' she said.

'I know. I'll take you.'

She paused. 'What do you mean "take me"?'

He made a gesture with his hand that looked similar to the motion of waves.

'Okay,' she said, not sure whether she would regret this.

'Come out to where it's deeper.'

Kaia did as she was told, her toes skimming the sand for a little bit longer before she pushed off and paddled forward.

'I've always wanted to try this,' he said, with a devilish grin.

'Try?' She was doing her best not to let her wariness show.

'Wrap your arms around my chest, like this.'

He grabbed Kaia's hands and pulled them around himself from behind until they were wedged under his armpits and gripping the front of his body.

'Now hold your breath and hang on.'

'Hold my—'

She had barely taken a gulp of air when they shot forward at alarming speed. Water surged on either side as the tremendous power of Amos's tail propelled them onwards, Kaia pressed flat against his back. She felt sure that she would slip off at any moment. As they neared the other side of the lake he ducked under the surface. Kaia's hair was pulled back off her scalp as they tore through the water like a bullet. She saw the familiar glow of the yellow sand at the shore ahead of them and they shot up at the last moment, slowing to no more than a calm paddle. Blinking water out of her eyes, she let out an exhilarated laugh as she realised how quickly they had covered the distance. Unlinking her arms, she slid off his back and stood up to touch the grainy bottom just as a loud bang signalled the start of the fireworks. Spinning around, she watched the sky fill with coloured stars that exploded in a burst of noise and smoke.

They could just see them, with the display taking place a few suburbs away, but as she watched Amos's face react to what he was watching she could tell it didn't matter. This was clearly something he looked forward to every week.

'That was amazing,' she said, when the last firework had fizzled out. He grinned at her, looking somewhat like a drowned caveman.

'Is it ever hard to swim, with all that …'

She gestured to his long beard and he looked down at it, his grey hands running through the thick texture.

'I used to cut it and shave. Father taught me. It was easier, but I haven't been able to find anything to use since I've been in here.'

'I can help you with that.'

'You can?'

'Sure, I can bring a razor and clippers. My dad or brother will have some, I'd be surprised if they even noticed they're gone.'

'Your family,' he said, looking a little startled. 'What are they like?'

'My brother Storm is a few years older. He's tall and lanky, just like me.'

'You are very long,' Amos murmured, solemnly. Kaia couldn't help but stifle a giggle.

'My dad, his name is Ken: Ken Craig. Everyone calls him KC.'

'And your mother?'

'My mother, yeah, well … she doesn't live with us. She and my dad broke up a long time ago and she moved back to Hawaii.'

'She left you?'

'Uh-huh. Some mothers do that, I guess. Probably not yours.'

When she looked up, she noticed that he was staring at her intently.

'W-what is it?' she asked, uncertain.

He leaned forward, slowly, until their faces were almost touching. Kaia was frozen in place as Amos moved closer and closer towards her. *My God*, she thought, *he's about to kiss me*. But at the last moment he stopped and brought his hand slowly to a spot under her lip. His fingers traced a mark there, a still-fresh scar from when she'd bitten through her lip during the attack. It had taken seven stitches to close the wound up, but the doctor had told her she would have a permanent scar there thanks to the awkward placement. Kaia wasn't concerned about having a visible reminder of the incident, but she knew Storm was finding it hard to get used to the small line that started at her lip and ran down to the crease in her chin.

'That's from when they attacked you,' Amos whispered.

She nodded, still frozen. His hands slid down to her neck and she knew he was looking at the bruising there, which had faded considerably but was still visible enough.

'That too,' she said, looking up at the sky as his cool fingers ran along the marks, almost willing them to disappear. When his arm returned to his side, she turned to look at his face: *really* look. She wanted to see if she could read the truth there while she asked him her next question.

'What happened to the men who attacked me?'

'Do you really want to know?' he asked, sensing her hesitation. She didn't want Amos to shut down on her, but she had to learn their fates. Kaia took a deep breath and closed her eyes, before opening them again in a stare that answered the question for her.

'I drowned them,' he said simply.

Hearing it out loud like that gave it the finality that made her realise that – indirectly or otherwise – she was responsible for the deaths of all the Tyler children.

'They're dead?' Kaia whispered, knowing that deep down she had accepted this. She had simply been hoping to avoid the truth.

'Yes.'

'You didn't, er, eat them?'

'What?' He spat water out of his mouth with shock.

'Well, I've been researching merpeople and there's a lot of accounts where they devour their victims and I noticed you had serrated teeth so I didn't want to assume—'

'Kaia.'

'—and there's only so much you can eat being trapped here, I guess, so—'

'KAIA.'

Her mouth stopped moving as she peeked at him from under her eyelashes.

'I do not eat people. I don't think any of us eat people.'

'Are … are you sure?'

'Positive,' he said, almost laughing but clearly trying to keep a straight face.

'Oh. Okay. That's good to know. So where are, um, their bodies?'

She followed the movement of Amos's arm as he raised it and pointed to an area of the lake far to his right. It was a break-off spot – a smaller circle sitting outside of the larger circle that made up Lake Pelutz but still connected to it.

'It's too deep for families to swim there and the path stops a few hundred metres before it.'

'There's no foot traffic,' she said, knowing that when she had come here previously with her family or friends it was an area most people avoided. Not for any specific reason, mind you, but it was also the spot where birds seemed to congregate in the lake, so it was a bit grotty. Kaia was looking at the calm space with newfound horror. Within seconds it had taken on a more sinister feel.

'They're weighted down with rocks,' he said. 'I moved them there once the divers left.'

'Thank you,' she said, her voice sounding forced and foreign. 'I never said thank you for saving my life. Thank you.'

'Do you know who they were? Why they wanted to hurt you?' he asked, his expression darkening.

'They …' Kaia struggled to explain the situation. Amos liked her, he thought she was a good person. She wanted to maintain that illusion for just a little bit longer. 'Let's just say they had their reasons. I'll save the rest of that story for another night.'

He nodded. 'You need to get back to the other side.'

'Yes, my bike and everything is over there.'

He sat up a little straighter, as if his brain was suddenly overcome with an idea. 'Could I watch you swim?'

'What?'

'Swim. Could I watch you do it?'

'Uh, sure. Why?'

'It's fascinating to watch, the way you humans move—'

He trailed off as he mimicked the way he thought people looked underwater, jerking his head and throwing his arms awkwardly.

'Sure,' she said, tying her hair back in a bun as Amos splashed away excitedly and disappeared beneath the water. Bouncing up and down on her toes for a second, she plunged in and emerged on the surface a few seconds later. She took a quick gulp of air before throwing her head back under and swimming five solid strokes. Turning her head to the side, she took another breath before paddling in the direction of the opposite shore. She wasn't going at top speed, but she wasn't cruising either. She was somewhere comfortably in the middle and it felt great to be properly swimming for the first time in ages.

Amos wasn't anywhere to be found and Kaia scanned the blackness for his features. Goggles would have given her better sight, but she had thought it seemed a waste to use them when it was fresh water and her eyes wouldn't sting if exposed. Suddenly a flash of silver shot past her line of vision. It had come and gone so quickly she almost questioned whether she had seen it at all before Amos's face popped up beneath her, wearing a huge grin as he swam past. Kaia saw a jet of bubbles escape her mouth as she laughed underwater. He disappeared before returning again, this time swimming directly beneath her from head to toe. He was watching her movements with genuine curiosity, the smile having disappeared from his expression. She began to find it hard to focus on the simple task of kicking while placing one hand in front of the other. He swam into her eyeline again, pointing to the left and indicating that she was off-course. She adjusted slightly and spared a thought for what she was doing: swimming across Lake Pelutz, in the middle of the night, guided by a merman.

By Sunday, the great surf from the day before had not only hung around but it had got *better:* it was up to seven-foot breaking off Burleigh Point. Storm and KC had managed to recruit Kaia out into the waves with them. Carefully negotiating their way over the rocks off the headland so they wouldn't have to paddle all the way out from the beach, Kaia felt a joy building in her bones. The waves were meaty, clean, and coming in consistent sets. It had been a while since all three of the Craigs had been out there, like this, together. And it felt really bloody good.

'Come on, old man,' she called to her dad, who was behind Storm and her. He was taking a little more time to negotiate jumping from rock to rock.

'Yeah yeah yeah,' he barked back, subtly increasing his speed.

'Don't tease him,' Storm murmured. 'You don't want him slipping and cutting his arse open on a barnacle.'

'Didn't that happen to you once?' she countered.

'Shut up.'

Kaia laughed, closing her eyes for a moment as spray and foam from a wave crashing against the rocks splashed onto her face. She was poised on the edge of the last rock that wasn't partially submerged by the swell. She watched as the water drew back and the wave receded, surfboard positioned on her hip as she focused on getting her timing exactly right. Storm was one rock over, beside her, and they were both waiting on a wave big enough to cover the rocks in front of them. They'd leap off from where they were standing and utilise the momentum, paddling out as quickly out as they could before duck diving under the next few waves. If they timed it wrong, they'd land on the rocks below that would no longer be submerged under the water.

'You ready?' Storm called. 'This looks like it.'

She agreed, watching the last wave of the set building to a crest before them. 'Ready when you are.'

The wave broke, foam splashing up in a white flurry as it rolled towards them. The moment it was about to hit the rocks – the split second – Kaia and Storm jumped, throwing their boards out in front of them and landing in the cool salt water. There was an excited shout behind them and Kaia glanced back to see her father's head appear on the other side of the wave, splashing down with them. She grinned, feeling energised, and used her arms to power forward as quickly as she could. Storm should have been faster than her, but she was fitter and soon she was gaining on her brother. They were nearly at the back break – that calm area of water behind where the sets collapsed – when two more waves began to form. Kaia positioned her knee in front of her, pushing her board deep down under the water as the wave broke. She popped up on the other side, a smile spreading across her face. When she opened her eyes, there was nothing but clear water in front of her and she paddled forward to find a spot in the line-up.

'Don't you look pleased as punch,' Storm said, as Kaia sat up and balanced herself on her board.

'I kicked your butt, didn't I?'

'It's just nice to see you smiling like this,' her dad said, catching up to them and waving at someone he recognised further down the line. I haven't seen you this happy in forever.'

'How can I not be?' she replied, splashing the water around her. 'Look at this day!'

'We live on the Gold Coast, sis, every day looks like this. Blue skies, sunshine, chicks in bikinis.'

'I think Kai's the only chick out here,' her father said, looking around.

'No way,' Kaia snorted. 'There's a little grommet on a purple board. So there, ya sexist.'

'Hold that thought,' KC replied, swivelling on his board as he spotted something behind her. She followed his gaze to where an impressive wave was forming, the group of surfers moving around them to get in position. But KC was already ahead of them, the muscles in his back rippling and his short legs kicking up a froth as he pulled onto the wave. Storm and Kaia straightened up to see what little they could from the back of the wave, their dad's silhouette visible zooming along the course of the barrel. There was a small crowd of people clustered on the headland to watch and they were letting out cheers and whoops as KC did what he was famous for.

'Welp, this is me,' Storm said, seeing his own prime choice and paddling desperately for the next wave.

Kaia spent a little bit more time waiting to choose hers, a crisp six-footer, and as she descended the drop and got to her feet, she felt invincible. Gaining speed, she crouched down as she whipped along the line, cutting up and down the crest of the wave before it closed out on her. When it finally broke behind her, she jumped off her board and into the white wash. Popping up through the surf, she used her leg rope to drag her board back towards her and paddle out into the break. She spent some three hours out there with her family, probably longer than she should have, given her sunscreen would have well and truly worn off. But her dad was right: she hadn't looked this happy in a long time because she hadn't *felt* this happy in a long time. She wondered if it had anything to do with what she'd discovered at the bottom of Lake Pelutz, but she didn't want to think too deeply on it.

Calling out a farewell to her brother and telling him she'd meet them at the car whenever they were done, Kaia caught a snappy four-foot wave to the shore. Undoing the velcro on her leg rope, she wrapped it around her board then started to make her way up the sand. It was an unseasonably warm day for late August – hot, even – and she had worn her favourite surfing bikini: a black, floral number that had thick straps crossing over on her back like a sports bra. Glancing down at her stomach, she touched the slight red rash that was forming at her hip where her skin had rubbed against the wax on her surfboard over the past few hours. She located her vehicle in the car park and carefully propped her board alongside it as she glanced over her shoulder. She couldn't see anyone looking. Discreetly she crouched down near her back tyre and fiddled until she found the small, plastic box she'd had added to the underside of the car. It was the place she left her keys whenever she went surfing or did any other activity that meant she couldn't take them with her out into the water. As her fingers recognised the casing, she pressed down on the magnetic clasp and felt the weight of her keys drop into her open palm.

'You know, I always said one day your car was going to get nicked that way.'

Kaia froze, her spine stiffening as she recognised the voice. Slowly, she spun around and got to her feet.

'Hello, Chris,' she said, suddenly very aware of her lack of clothing. It shouldn't have mattered: she was a professional in a sport where as little clothing as possible was required, for both men and women. Yet standing there in just her bikini – and him, shirtless and barefoot in only a pair of striped board shorts – Kaia felt exposed.

'We're having a barbeque over in the park with some mates,' he said, jerking his head behind him to where a cluster of about twenty clubbies were hanging around, eskies and fold-out chairs assembled. A few of them were trying to do a good job of sneakily watching whatever was unfolding between Chris and Kaia, but they ducked their heads as soon as she glanced over.

'I saw your car over here and thought I'd come and say hi,' he continued.

'Chris,' she murmured, looking at her feet. 'That probably wasn't a good idea. I know the cops came and spoke to you.'

'You can't think I had anything to do with happe—'

'I don't know,' she snapped. 'But you're *so* close with the Tyler family, you used to flat with the brothers and now they're … missing.'

'I told the police everything I knew,' he said. 'That's what I wanted to come over and say. I thought about calling you, but I wasn't sure you'd answer and I would've understood that. You just need to know that if I thought for a second they would have ever tried to hurt you—'

'You would have done what, fucker?'

Kaia and Chris's heads both swivelled in the direction of the new voice, which belonged to Storm, who was sprinting towards them. Kaia recognised the fire in his eyes and she was able to jump into his path as Chris backed away.

'Storm,' she cautioned, placing her hands up against his chest as he tossed his surfboard to the ground.

'WHAT WOULD YOU HAVE DONE, YOU PRICK?!'

Her brother was screaming at him, pointing his finger squarely at Chris as he tried to get past Kaia.

'You would have done exactly what you did before,' he yelled. 'Fucking nothing. Where were you when she needed you then? Nowhere.'

'Storm, listen, mate. I was just trying to—'

'This family doesn't want you anywhere near it, okay?'

'Okay, okay,' Chris pleaded, taking further steps back. His friends nearby had started to wander over and the commotion had drawn the attention of onlookers.

'Hey! Hey! What's going on here?' her father called, running to catch up.

'Dad, grab him!' Kaia hissed, pushing Storm backwards towards KC. He stumbled, giving her father the opportunity to clutch him from behind and properly hold him back. He was muttering urgently into his son's ear, trying to calm him down and speak some sense into him. Kaia seized the opportunity, turning her back on her family for a second to face Chris.

'Get out of here,' she told him, shoving gently at his arms. 'You know Dad's not gonna be able to hold Storm back much longer. Leave, Chris.'

'I just wanted to see how you were,' he murmured.

'I was doing okay, right up until about five minutes ago.'

He winced, looking almost apologetic before spinning on his heels and walking as quickly as he could back to his people. Kaia watched Chris leave, making sure he had enough bodies around him before she grabbed her surfboard. Tossing it onto the roof of the car, she angrily grabbed her brother's and her father's as well, stacking them on top of each other.

'Get him in the car,' she said, tossing KC the keys. He did as she said, half-hugging and half-shoving Storm into the back seat before locking the doors. Kaia had almost finished securing the boards to the roof racks and she tightened the straps holding them down with more force than was necessary.

'You okay, Kai-girl?' her dad asked, gently squeezing her shoulder.

'No, Dad,' she huffed. 'We just created a huge scene, everybody saw and is going to be talking about it. I'm not okay.'

'Hun, Storm was just—'

'Being Storm, I know. This is the shit we've had to deal with when you weren't around and we're not perfect at it. I'm not mad at him, I'm just mad at *all of it*.'

She saw the hurt cross her father's face at the pointed remark and she regretted it almost in the same instant. But she was also furious and hyper-aware of the dozens of pairs of eyes that were on them. Snatching the keys out of KC's hand, she stormed round to the other side of the car and jumped behind the wheel. Her father told her she probably shouldn't drive, he offered to instead, but she was determined as she gently revved the engine before throwing the car into reverse. She was desperate to be behind the wheel and, for once, feel just a little bit in control of her life.

CHAPTER NINE

A thunderstorm had broken the afternoon heat and since then, the Gold Coast had been blanketed in a consistent rain shower. The surface of Lake Pelutz, which was usually so still it looked like glass, dimpled as the rain made contact with the water. It was past midnight, with all of the surrounding houses at The Lakes plunged into darkness as their residents snored safely inside. No one heard as Kaia sprinted down the grassy slope towards the lake edge and dived off the path into the water with the smallest splash. She stayed under the surface until she was a few metres from the shore and threw herself into a confident stroke of freestyle.

Kaia had been blessed by the weather, which had seen many retire earlier than expected and had brought an untimely end to a few of the picnics people had been having around Lake Pelutz. She felt her appearance at the lake was somewhat cloaked by the storm rather than just the unusual hour. As she swam to the centre, the physical exertion felt like a sigh of relief. She felt perfectly safe here, protected, even comforted by the knowledge that she wasn't alone. Sure enough, it was less than a minute after she'd dived in that a sliver flash crossed her path. It was just a glimpse at the side of her vision at first, before another – this time slower. Amos's face finally popped into view, smiling at her. She smiled back and slowed down enough that they would be able to have a proper conversation. Using her legs to keep herself afloat, Kaia took a gulp of air as she began to tread water. The black seaweed of Amos's hair appeared next, only half submerged as he kept everything below his nose underneath the water.

'I've got a surprise for you,' she said, gesturing back towards the shore. 'Besides fish.'

'Besides fish?'

'Well, I brought chocolate too, but this is something you'll be really excited about.'

'I already am,' he said, raising himself higher out of the water and offering her his back.

Kaia had been taken by surprise the first time they did this, but she was more prepared now as she wrapped her arms around his and they propelled forward at speed. Amos slowed down when they got to the shore and Kaia stumbled to find her footing as her body adjusted to the sudden decrease in momentum. Wading through the water until she was at the edge, she reached towards a small bag she had left there. She perched it on her knees and gave Amos a smile as she unzipped it and started laying out the contents on the path.

'Assorted fishes,' she said, naming the treats. 'Chocolate: white, dark and milk, because I didn't know what your preference was.'

'Milk,' he chirped.

'Okay, good. And finally, this!'

She held an electric razor up in the air triumphantly. Amos's smile faded as he looked at the object with wonderment, like it was some bizarre foreign treasure.

'To shave,' she said, wiggling it in his direction.

'You didn't have a razor?'

'This *is* a razor. The sharpest. There are lots of them, spinning over each other again and again electronically. It's also waterproof and battery-powered. I stole it from my dad's cupboard, but he has about a thousand so this is yours. Just don't take it very deep, I don't think it would survive more than a five-metre depth.'

He was still looking at it sceptically.

'You've never used an electronic razor?'

He shook his head.

'Only old-school barbershop stuff?'

He nodded again.

'It's okay, I can teach you. I had to shave my dad's face for a month last year after he broke his right hand. But first, I'm going to use these scissors to clip away some of the larger parts of your beard.'

She thought explaining everything to him carefully and clearly would help any wariness he might be feeling. When she was done getting rid of some of the length, she placed the scissors on the lake edge and dusted her hands together. Kaia motioned for Amos to move out into the deeper water. She walked until the surface was dancing around her shoulders and turned the razor on. She handed him a small torch and got him to hold it in the right spot so she could see properly. His expression grew even more alarmed when the buzzing started, but she gave him a reassuring smile. He grew still as she moved forward, cupping his left cheek and tilting his head. Kaia started shaving. Amos kept looking down at the tuffs of beard falling off into the water around them as she quickly did the first half of his face.

'One sec,' Kaia said, wading back to grab the mirror she had also brought with her. She held it up for him to see the effect so far and he blinked at his reflection there.

'Wow,' he exclaimed, running his hand along the smooth surface of his face.

'Told you.' She chuckled, shaking her head as she moved in to finish the rest. 'How much do you want off your head?'

He considered for a moment. 'I like it when it's all gone. It feels strange when it's long and the water runs through it.'

'I love that feeling.'

Amos reached out and lifted a strand of Kaia's own hair as the tips of it floated in the water. It only extended to her shoulder blades – that was as long as she could handle it thanks to being in the water all the time – but it was smooth and naturally straight. It always had a certain fluffy volume to it that looked like freshly dried hair, which it often was, given it was usually emerging from the 'being wet' state.

'This is your natural colour.'

'Mmm-hmm.'

'It's beautiful,' he said, genuine awe in his voice.

Kaia paused at the front of his head, where she had just started shaving. Here was a man who was literally from fairy tales and whose scaled tail was one of the most hypnotically enchanting things she had ever seen. Yet he thought her hair was beautiful?

'It's like sunlight,' he continued.

'I am in the sun a lot.'

'And you swim.'

She tilted her head, a question in the gesture.

'You're very fast,' he explained. 'Especially for a human. You can see it in your muscles.'

So there, in the middle of the night, while she shaved the head of an aquatic humanoid, Kaia began telling a perfect stranger all about her life. She told Amos more about her brother and father, she told him all about Cabby and how their friendship had grown, she told him about what she did for a living and how she had wanted to be a professional iron-woman for a long time. And she told him about Bree Tyler. While she'd hinted at it before, it all seemed to come gushing out of her that night as she explained what had happened, her part in the horror and everything that had come afterwards. She had long since finished with his hair and beard, but she stayed standing there in the water as she talked.

'I think those men were her brothers,' she added, finally.

'Really? The men who attacked you?'

'I'm certain of it. They're both the same build and I picked up South African accents. I never did get a good look at their faces, but the police said they had arrived in the country a few days earlier and they have been missing ever since. They also had the strongest reasons for wanting to hurt me. Not that there aren't others out there who would feel justified in doing it.'

'Who?' Amos practically barked. 'What are their names?'

She jumped slightly at the fervour in his voice. His features were tight with anger and for the first time since the attack, Kaia almost felt afraid of him.

'I, uh, I don't know. I just said it. There are a lot of people who still think what happened was my fault.'

'It wasn't. You held on as tightly as you could, the wave was too big!'

'Preaching to the choir.'

He looked frustrated by this, the injustice of it all. It was in that instant Kaia realised what a sheltered life Amos had lived – literally in a glass house his entire existence.

'Amos,' she asked. 'How did you learn to speak so well? Do your people—?'

'No, Father taught me. He taught me English, French and Chinese.'

'Really? You're multilingual?'

141

'*Père disait que le language était la porte d'entrée du monde et qu'il voulait que j'apprenne autant que possible.*'

She laughed, impressed. 'What did you just say?'

'I said "Father said language is the gateway to the world and he wanted me to learn as many as possible". We were learning Arabic together when he …'

'Died?'

Amos nodded.

'What do you remember about that night? Was he acting strange or was it just a normal day?'

'He came home from the university in a panic. I'd never seen him like that. He was terrified.'

'Sergeant Ferris said the men who shot him trashed your house as well.'

Amos shook his head quickly. 'No, that was Father. He was doing that before they came. He poured acid on the computers and burned all of our things, all of my pictures.'

'Why would he do that?'

'All his research was in there, everything he worked for.'

'Maybe that's what they were after, his research? Maybe it wasn't a case of mistaken identity at all.'

'Professor Viktor Waldman was a doctor of marine biology, Kaia. He only studied fish and aquatic life.'

'I get it, he wasn't exactly the keeper of state secrets.' She nodded, but was still unable to shake the idea once it had taken hold. 'What was the last thing he was working on before he was killed?'

His mouth popped open in understanding and Kaia saw a whole new pain wash over his face. He swam away from her and then back again, like the human equivalent of pacing. Amos fingered the chain that hung around his neck and Kaia was finally able to catch a glimpse of what hung at the end of it: three keys.

'Amos, what do they open?' she asked, pointing to his chest.

'I don't know,' he said, absentmindedly. 'Father gave them to me that night.'

'You never knew what the keys were for?'

'This one—' he held up a more modern-looking key '—was used to unlock the cupboard where he kept all of his dangerous chemicals. Acid, mercury, everything harmful was in there and you couldn't get to it without this. The other two ... I have no idea what they open. I've never seen him use them for anything in my life. But he used to wear this around his neck, always. I never saw him take it off.'

Kaia swam closer, picking up the two mystery keys in her hand. 'These ones look older, almost like antique keys.'

'Maybe.' Amos shrugged. 'Father had a tendency to make things look like what they weren't. We used to play games where he would camouflage toys in the pool and I had to try and find them. He said they were brain exercises and he would laugh and laugh as I tried to make things work one way, when he had changed how they looked so they actually worked another.'

'Like riddles.'

'Yes. He said they helped my problem-solving skills develop. When he gave me this chain, it was the first thing he did when he got home that night – the last night. I didn't realise how scared he was until he put it over my head and I could see the fear in his—'

Amos's voice broke as he recalled his final moments with his father. He looked down at the surface of the water, which was still rippling thanks to the rain. Kaia felt like she was finally able to see his face and properly judge the emotions that were dancing there. No longer hidden behind a *Cast Away* beard, the dark, almost black colour of his eyebrows only highlighted the largeness of his eyes. His irises were an unusual colour, she couldn't decide whether they were dark blue or grey, and they were directed downwards as he tried to control his feelings. He had a long, soft nose that seemed almost Italian in origin. His lips were insignificant in nature, small and thin, and she wondered what the greyish tone of his skin would look like in direct sunlight. Kaia felt like she was encroaching on his grief, but she didn't want him to feel like she was abandoning him. She reached out, her hand intertwining with his own. Amos looked up at her, as if surprised.

'I think I should go,' she whispered. 'Maybe you need to be alone.'

'No,' he said, the words coming out in a rush. 'Please don't leave just yet. I feel like I spend too much time by myself and I just want you … to stay. For a little while.'

'Okay.' She nodded, moving towards him. Awkwardly she sat down where she was, butt resting on the sand as she remained half in and half out of the water. Amos seemed to fold his tail beneath him, wrapping and bending it in a manner that meant he could sit alongside her. They stayed like that for a very long time. All the while, her hand remained locked in his.

When Kaia got home that evening, she sent Cabby a text that she was surprised to see a reply to almost instantly.

'What are you doing up at this hour?' Cabby's message read.

'Can't sleep,' Kaia replied. 'You?'

'Actively not sleeping' was followed by a winking face emoji. Kaia laughed, wrapping a towel around herself from the warm shower she'd just had.

'Do you reckon you can set me up on a date with Imogen's brother, the marine biologist?'

Cabby inundated Kaia's phone with a slew of emojis followed by a question: *'For sleuthing or seducing?'*

She replied to her friend with the first option written in capital letters, making sure her intentions were clear. Cabby said that she would organise it in the morning and Kaia lay down on her pillow with a relieved sigh. Quint was snoring ungracefully next to her and she thought about booting him off. She ran a hand through his fur, feeling comforted by the presence of someone else – even if that 'someone else' was a lazy German Shepherd. Closing her eyes, Kaia thought about sitting with Amos in the lake that night. Her presence had comforted him and she began to more fully comprehend just how lonely he must have been in the months since his father was killed. She wondered what he must do, in the long hours between her visits when the only thing he had was one big, empty lake and a lot of time.

———

When Kaia eventually pulled herself out of bed the next day, she gulped as she scrolled through a stream of messages Cabby had sent her. Not only had she managed to set her up on a blind date with Imogen's brother, she had organised it for *that night* at The Den in Broadbeach. Her friend worked fast and she couldn't begrudge her proactive approach to her dating life. It had been years – actual *years* – since she had gone on a date and a lot had changed since then. Kaia wasn't going out with the cute South African guy from her surf club and she wasn't fifteen any more. Rolling out of bed, she drew back her blinds and took a moment for her eyes to adjust to the light. Quint had long since abandoned her bed and snuck out of her room, obviously in the direction of whatever food was available. Stretching her long body with a yawn, Kaia opened up the doors to her wardrobe and stared at what lay before her. Okay, so this was a proper date with a proper adult. At The Den. People would recognise her there and they would recognise the scenario. She needed to look nice, but not *too* nice: she was there to get into this guy's brains after all, not his pants. She was distracted from her clothes crisis by a knock on her door and looked up to see Storm there. He was holding a tray full of food, but not just any food – it was a mish-mash of some of Kaia's favourites, including French toast and Kiwi fruit.

'Hey sis.' He smiled, meekly. 'Can I come in?'

'Sure,' she said, watching with amusement as he laid the feast down at her desk.

'I made you brunch.'

'I can see that.' She crossed her arms and leaned against the wall. 'That's a big gesture, Storm.'

'Yeah, well, you know. I kinda wanted to say sorry, I guess. For yesterday. I'm not sorry that I wanted to hit him and I'm not sorry I tried to.'

'Okay,' she said, her lips twitching.

'Dad spoke to me after, about how a scene could make things worse for you and how what I did could make things harder. So that's what I'm saying sorry for. I'm always going to want to protect my little sister and I got caught up in how that would make me feel, not what would happen in your life.'

'Storm.' She smiled. 'I think that might be the most emotionally mature sentence you've ever said.'

He laughed, nervously running his hands through his hair. 'I'm not gonna lie, I wrote a draft on my phone and practiced it.'

'What? Seriously, that's pretty damn adorable.' She punched him lightly in the arm as she made her way towards the food. The first bite of the French toast was so good she thought she might cry.

'Dad said you were really mad and once I calmed down, I understood why.'

'Hey,' she started, forking some Kiwi fruit into her mouth. 'Any apology that comes with brunch is going to be immediately accepted, just so you know.'

'Ha,' Storm chuckled, throwing himself down onto her rumpled bed. 'I'll remember that for the future.'

'You've even got maple syrup, bless you.'

'I'm good.' He smiled, tucking his hands behind his head. 'Anyway, what are you up to today? What are your plans, schemes, motivations?'

'I'm going on a date,' she said, grinning at the choking sound she heard coming from his direction.

'A DATE?!' he shouted, jerking up on the bed. 'With who?'

'It's a blind date.'

'You? Going on a blind date? No fucking way.'

'Cabby set it up—'

'God help me.'

'—with Imogen Tishop's brother.'

'Wait, which one? *Trevor*?'

'Travis,' she corrected. 'Travis Tishop. You want to help me pick something to wear or get outta here?'

'More like I'm coming with you.'

'Uh-uh. Not happening, Storm. You're not my personal bodyguard.'

'That's exactly what I am. For tonight, anyway.'

'Storm, no way in hell!'

'Where are you going?'

'The Den.'

'Perfect.'

'Storm!'

'Look,' he said, his expression softening. 'I'll be at the bar. He doesn't even know what I look like. It will be an invisible safety net. If you need me, I'll be there.'

Kaia stared at Storm, a forkful of toast hovering near her mouth. He had a stubborn look in his eyes that she knew all too well was unlikely to budge.

'I'm not getting out of this, am I?'

'Nope.' He grinned.

'Fine,' she huffed. 'Be ready to go at eight. And, Storm?'

'Yeah?'

'Be invisible.'

'I'm a ghost,' he whispered, making his best attempt at a poltergeist sound as he slipped from her room with a flourish.

The Den was everything you would expect of a place with such a name. It was a small, cosy venue with warm lighting. Travis had chosen the location, not Kaia, and as she negotiated her way through the many tables to his position she did her best to look like she wanted to be there. She absentmindedly made sure her lemon halter-neck top was tucked into the high waistline of the three-quarter-length denim skirt she was wearing. Simple gold hoops adorned her ears and she had brushed her blonde hair smooth. Heck, for the first time in a long time mascara was even highlighting her eyelashes. Kaia needed to make it look like she was on a real date, like any other normal girl her age. She needed to make it look like she wasn't trying to pump information from someone to learn more about her merman friend.

'Hi there, Kaia, lovely to meet you in person,' Travis said. Kaia smiled as she recognised the man from the photos Cabby had sent through.

'You too,' she replied. He was short, no more than five foot four, and Kaia did her best to bend to his height as he stood on his tiptoes to kiss her cheek.

'So, do I call you Doctor or Pr—'

'Travis is fine,' he laughed, as they both took a seat on the tall stools that were positioned at their table. 'I'm still a little embarrassed Cabby sold me on having a PhD.'

She nodded, noting that he was an attractive man despite an unruly head of hair and a somewhat dishevelled appearance. Considering he was wearing a pair of thick-framed glasses of the style favoured by hipsters, she guessed he was in his late twenties.

'Do you want something to drink?' he asked as a waitress lingered.

She glanced quickly at the menu. 'Could I have a ginger beer, please?'

'And an apple cider for me,' he added.

An awkward silence fell between them as they struggled to find an opening topic.

'I've seen you on TV,' he said at last.

'Oh?'

'Competing in the Energen X Ironman Series.'

'Oh,' Kaia said, with understanding. 'I always forget they televise that. I mean, I don't *forget* – the cameras are right there – it's just that there's usually a lot of other stuff going on.'

'I bet. Imogen tapes it and likes to watch them back for racing tips.'

'Ha, yeah. I used to do the same thing.'

'I've been to a few, the one they held at Kirra last year. I don't think I'm built to be around that many people though. Crowds, yeesh.'

Storm, she noticed, was doing what he'd promised: sitting at the bar, sipping a beer and only occasionally throwing a look her way. The waitress returned with their drinks and she took a sip, enjoying the bubbles as they worked their way down her throat.

'Your job must be great,' she said, trying to direct the conversation where she wanted it to go.

'I love it. I know how lucky I am to get up every day and do something that I enjoy.'

'How did you first get into it?'

'I actually did work experience at Sea World when I was in high school and then that was it for me. I studied marine biology at Hodgkins uni and began ticking all the boxes I needed to get in there.'

'Do you get to work with sharks?'

'Yeah, I've done a fair bit of research with them.'

'They freak me out.' Kaia shuddered.

'I thought you would be able to handle that fear better than most, being in the water all the time.'

'Sure, I guess. It's the black eyes that do it. And the teeth.'

'Those things are like steak knives.' He nodded. 'A Great White can shed over 35,000 teeth in its lifetime and all of them are just as deadly, just as razor-sharp. They're perfectly designed for tearing flesh.'

'But just because shark teeth are serrated, that doesn't mean they're all designed for killing – right?'

'Actually, it kind of does,' he said. Kaia could see the way his eyes lit up with enthusiasm. 'There are variations in the tooth structure from breed to breed; for instance the Grey Nurse has very different teeth to a Great White. A Nurse eats mainly smaller fish, smaller prey, so the edges are different.'

'Huh. Are there any types of fish that have teeth like that too?'

'Barracuda teeth are actually pretty similar to shark teeth.'

'That's interesting,' she mused, taking a sip of her drink. 'Has anyone been able to train a shark, like, say a killer whale or a dolphin?'

'You're pretty into this stuff, aren't you?'

'Just making conversation.' She shrugged. 'I don't do many blind dates.'

'Right.' He smiled. 'I'm kind of a veteran of the blind date thing. But no, to answer your question: there's a higher level of intelligence in dolphins and killer whales, a family structure. Sharks hunt alone, they're solo predators and they have three main objectives: hunt, feed, breed.'

'So you're saying that the family structure is important, it's what differentiates the more intelligent species from the less intelligent?'

'Definitely. Hey, you know if you wanted to just come by my office and see the animals some time, that would have been okay.'

'What do you mean?'

'You don't really seem …' He coughed. 'Into this. Excluding my immense knowledge on all things aquatic.'

'No, no! I am! I just had a very strange day and—'

He laughed, cutting her short. 'Kaia, it's okay. It's actually refreshing.'

'What is?'

'Meeting a girl who cares more about my work than me.'

'That's not … I—'

'Look, Cabby mentioned that you had been through some stuff and I know some of the specifics.'

'The Gold Coast,' she said, looking at her hands. 'It's a city that still behaves like a small town.'

'If you're not ready to do this, to date or whatever, we can try it another time.'

She sat there for a few moments, taking in his manner and what he had just said. 'You seem strangely okay with that.'

'Of course, I'm a reasonable guy.'

'That's rare for me.'

He laughed again. 'Listen, how about we just have a nice,

causal dinner tonight? Don't think of it as a date. When we leave here, we leave as friends.'

'No strings?'

'No strings. None. You know, if you're not doing anything next week you should come visit my office. I could show you the answers to your questions in person.'

'I would really like that.'

'Let's shake on it,' he said, extending his hand. Kaia shook it, returning his smile.

When Travis and Kaia left The Den an hour later, Storm discreetly following behind, they kept it friendly. He gave her a brief hug when they reached his car and she promised to visit him at work and "sate that curiosity", as he said. When he drove off, she thanked heavens for Cabby who had set her up with someone not only useful but actually lovely. Jumping in her own car with Storm, she knew she had a faint smile on her face.

'Why are you so happy?' he asked. 'It sort of looked like you got blown off.'

'I did, I think.'

'That's what you wanted?'

She looked at her brother, who had an expression of genuine confusion on his face. 'Yeah, I got what I wanted.'

CHAPTER TEN

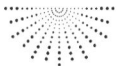

K aia dozed for a few hours, desperately needing to catch up on a bit of sleep, before setting off towards Lake Pelutz. She hadn't bothered to change clothes so her date outfit was crinkled from where she had laid on it and her hair was thrown up in a messy bun. Peddling through the darkness, she did not care a single iota. She was excited to see Amos and when she threw her leg over the side of her bike, cruising to their meeting spot, she spotted a flash of his tail appear above the surface of the water. Dumping her bike on the ground, she slowly jogged to the edge of the lake and jumped in fully clothed. She didn't have to wait long until he appeared. His mouth was open as he was about to speak a greeting, but she cut him off.

'How did you learn about the world?'

He laughed. 'Questions straight away, huh?'

'I think about them all day and then file them away in my mind until they're bubbling up.'

'How did I learn about the world,' Amos repeated, smiling. 'From Father, mostly. He taught me with lessons and then when he couldn't, he would put on documentaries for me to watch.'

'Like when he was away?'

'Yeah, when he had more classes. He didn't want me to get bored or lonely, so he'd set them up and they played back-to-back. When he'd return, he'd ask me questions about what I watched and he'd answer whatever questions I had to ask him.'

'What about music, books, movies—'

'Oh!' Amos smiled, genuinely excited, 'Father loved movies. Every Saturday and Sunday night he'd stay in and pick a different one. He'd never play the same film twice, he told me there was too much to watch.'

That intrigued Kaia, after all, what sort of movies did you program for a merman? *The Little Mermaid*? *Jaws*? *Splash*?

'What kind?' She was genuinely curious as she spun around, treading water while Amos moved around her in a circular motion.

'You mean what's my favourite?'

'Sure.'

'That's easy: *An Affair To Remember*. But *Some Like It Hot* is very funny. *The Maltese Falcon*, *Casablanca*, *Top Hat*, *The Man Who Knew Too Much*—'

'Have you seen anything from this century?'

He thought about it for a moment. 'Documentaries, mainly. They were all modern. But Father liked *classics*, or at least that's what he called them.'

'Man,' Kaia said. 'We need to catch you up on some new movies.'

'That would be great! But how will you ...' As he trailed off, she realised the problem.

'I don't know,' she said honestly. 'Leave it with me. If we can get rid of the beard and get you some decent food, then it can't be too hard to sort this out.'

He seemed to sense the second she was growing tired and he moved forward, offering his back. She took it gratefully and linked her arms around the top of his shoulders and loosely at the base of his neck.

'Thanks.'

'Do you want to see something amazing?'

'Amos, I'm clinging onto the back of a mer— an aquatic humanoid. Your definition of amazing may be a bit out of date.'

Without a full view of his face she couldn't be certain, but Kaia thought he may have just rolled his eyes at her.

'Something *more* amazing.'

'Sure,' she said, with caution. 'But remember I'm not like you, I'm human. If you take me too deep the pressure will make my brain explode.'

Kaia made an exploding gesture with her two hands while trying to do the same with her mouth to emphasise the point.

'I'm not stupid, Kaia,' he said, trying to mock sounding hurt. Yet she could feel the slump of disappointment in his shoulders that implied a trip down into the depths of Lake Pelutz was exactly what he had been planning.

'This is something else, something better. We need more room though.'

In an instant he changed direction and headed towards a far-off end of the lake.

Kaia tightened her grip with the sudden increase in speed and relished the sensation of the water and night air ripping past her. A cool, metallic object brushed against her arm and she looked down to see Amos's chain and the keys attached to it.

'Are you ready?' he asked.

'Sure.' She smiled.

'You'll have to hold on very tight, as tight as you can. Don't worry, you can't hurt me.'

Kaia nodded solemnly.

'And you can't scream.'

'Scream?' She flinched, her levels of concern leaping upwards dramatically at that last comment. 'Why would I scream, Amos?'

'Just promise?'

'Okay, okay,' Kaia whispered, tightening her grip.

'Here we go,' he said, giving her one last look behind. 'Now hold your breath.'

She did as she was told and with a forward jerk they were shooting faster than she thought it was possible for any living creature to move. Her hair tie was whipped out of her bun almost instantly and her locks stretched behind her as they sped beneath the water. There was a final lurch downwards and another back skywards, then they were shooting vertically from the depths of Lake Pelutz and continuing up, up, up. In a rush of cool air, Kaia and Amos were suddenly no longer in the water, but soaring above it. Water fell from their bodies in droplets and Kaia was certain the sight would have looked beautiful if anyone was watching. From her position clinging to Amos's back, she looked down and all the breath sucked out of her lungs as she realised how high they were. And going down.

Their downward arch was just beginning as they started to descend some twenty metres below. *Don't scream*, she thought to herself, *don't scream, don't—*

With a rush of wetness and an exhilarating change in temperature, they had ended their fall back into the water. Amos brought them up slowly to the surface where Kaia swam backwards and let out a shriek of elated laughter.

'OH MY GOD!'

'Ssshhh!' he hushed, coming closer and pressing his hand

over her mouth. He looked around at the homes far off at the edge of the lake, as if he expected lights to start flicking on at any minute.

'Oh my God!' she whispered, wide-eyed. 'That was incredible, you went so fast, it was just – oh my God! We were so high!'

He beamed at her like a co-conspirator.

'Amos, how fast can you go?'

'I don't know. I've never had the space to try anything like this before. That's been one of the few good points about being stuck here – the room to swim.'

'How—?'

'Well,' he started enthusiastically, 'Father said my structure is much like that of a dolphin with one long vertebrae running the length of my body. Except mine is stronger than a dolphin's – which is pretty strong – but my spine is almost reinforced so I can push harder, faster. Plus, I have these.'

He held up his hands in front of Kaia with his fingers extended just like a normal human hand. With a *thwick* sound, a layer of skin appeared between each of his fingers, linking them together.

Kaia jerked back at the sudden shift. 'They're a ... seems—'

'Webbed,' he said proudly, holding them up in front of his own face and examining them. 'Father theorised that I had hands like a human and an ape – opposable thumbs – so that it was possible for my kind to hunt and gather.'

'So you could pry objects free and maybe even make weapons,' she mused. 'Spears or—'

'Yes, precisely. I rarely use my arms when swimming because my tail is enough, but in times when I need acceleration my webbed hands act as a way to increase speed.'

She examined his webbed fingers with her own and marvelled at the evolution.

'Amazing.'

'I can also see better than you,' he continued.

'Like, underwater? I mean, obviously,' Kaia scoffed, laughing at herself.

'Yes, but in the darkness too. My night time doesn't look like yours, neither does my day.'

She glanced up at him, her gaze focused on the unique colouring of his eyes that she had picked up before. Amos blinked, staring right back at her.

'Kaia,' he said, his tone serious. 'Yesterday you asked what the last thing was that Father was working on before he died.'

'Yeah,' she said. 'If he was intentionally murdered, maybe it had something to do with that.'

'Me,' he said, his eyes burning into hers. 'He was working on me. He thought he had finally found a way to get me back to my people.'

'Holy mackerel,' she breathed, her mind trying to catch up to her racing thoughts. If Professor Waldman had discovered where the rest of Amos's kind were – or at least a way that he could get to them – he had officially discovered a whole new species. A discovery like that was momentous, a game changer, and definitely something someone would kill for. Kaia's mind switched back to the current moment as Amos's words rung out.

'Kaia, he died because of me.'

She could see the guilt and pain swimming in his eyes because she had seen the same thing in her own reflection so, so many times before. She knew how helpful the words 'no, it's not your fault' were to her. That is to say, not at all.

'Amos,' she started, trying to choose the next sentence carefully, 'When the Professor decided to keep you all those years ago, he must have known the danger. He would have known there were people out there willing to kill for a discovery like you. He knew that, but he did it anyway. He kept searching.'

'I don't—'

'He loved you,' she said, with urgency. 'It's obvious.'

Riding through the streets of The Lakes an hour later, Kaia's thoughts were preoccupied with darker and deeper ones than previous nights. What she'd said was true: it was clear Professor Waldman had loved Amos enough to risk everything. The aquatic humanoid became his life's work and reuniting Amos with his family was the last thing he was trying to do before he died. And ultimately, it cost him his life. Kaia had made it through high school by the skin of her teeth: her education was good, but no way near the level of people whose world she was suddenly mixing in. She felt the stakes were high, getting higher, and she wondered if she could keep her head above the water.

The idea came to Kaia in the middle of her first ski training session since the attack. She was back with the regular squad, but on the doctor's orders (and her dad's) she was only doing two sessions a day. Part of that was to chart her physical and emotional recovery properly before she returned full throttle. The other part – which no one wanted to talk about – was that fewer sessions made it easier to protect her in case there were any more attacks. Although she knew the Tyler brothers were responsible, and now dead, the police didn't. The two most likely suspects were AWOL and Chris was being closely monitored. She hadn't caught him in the act, but she knew her father had been talking with Sergeant Ferris. The very idea of them coming up with a joint plan amused her, as she couldn't imagine KC and the police officer texting back and forth. Would they use emojis like her and Cabby? There were a few variations on the police emoji, so she figured they might.

Regardless, Kaia had a sneaking suspicion there was some collusion going on between not just Sergeant Ferris and her dad, but also Storm, Cabby and her coaches like BB. Everyone had been briefed and was keeping an eye out for anything unusual. That's why she had her own personal Craig escort to every session. Storm and KC were teaming up. They would either hang out at the surf club, chatting with the locals, or chill in the car. She had moaned about it to Cabby, who had responded by saying it was actually a smart idea. That's what made Kaia think that she was in on it too. That and the fact Cabby stuck close to her throughout most of the session.

'I'm just glad you're back at training,' she said, as they dragged their surf skis to the water's edge. 'It's a sausage fest here as it is.'

'That's the whole sport,' Kaia replied, while Cabby snorted in agreement.

Although she usually kept to herself at ski training and didn't have much to add to the conversation, Kaia enjoyed Cabby's causal asides that she muttered under her breath. The session had been progressing as it usually did, with the squad pushing past the back break in three minute bursts of speed. The wash of two guys in front of Kaia had created a generous channel and she was letting it drag her along when she had a light-bulb moment. It caused her to do something she never did: stop paddling. It had come on so abruptly that Kaia paused just as she had her paddle in the air and was ready to spear the water. She didn't even realise she had stopped until the stragglers came flying past her.

'Kaia, whattaya doing?' Cabby shouted.

She shook her head slightly, blinking the salt water out of her eyes before throwing herself back into motion and accelerating towards the tail of the pack.

Some 45 minutes later on their way back to the house, Kaia asked Storm a question she was sure he would react strongly to.

'Storm, can you pull over in that car park?'

'What car park?'

'The one at the end of that path.'

He knew exactly the one she had been talking about because, naturally, he knew exactly what road they were driving along.

'You want me to stop at Lake Pelutz?'

'Yes, for a moment.'

'Kaia, what—'

'Please, Storm, I need to do this.'

'All right.'

Begrudgingly he pulled off the main street and down the gravel path that led to the main car park of Lake Pelutz. She jumped out of the car before it had even stopped and threw her dry clothes on the bonnet. Sprinting down the path towards the lake edge, she yelled over her shoulder.

'I just need to swim to the other side!'

As she leapt off and into a deep portion of water, she knew Storm would be following her to make sure she didn't start quacking like a duck or behaving in another crazy manner. Kaia started swimming towards the side of the lake that slightly curved around a bend and would be hidden from Storm's view. Hoping Amos would be drawn out by the 'excitement' of someone swimming in his lake, she kept her stroke at a solid pace as she looked for the telltale signs that he was following her. Sure enough, she saw a streak of silver flash past her five, six times before his grinning face slowed down enough for Kaia to catch a proper glimpse of it. Beaming back, she increased her pace until she was in the exact spot and stopped abruptly. It took a few moments for him to realise what she was doing and surface beside her, a cautious look on his face.

'You look like part of the water in that black bathing suit,' he said quietly.

'There's no time for that,' she said, leaping forward and grabbing his shoulders.

He looked around nervously, as if searching for a spectator.

'If anyone's watching from within a house it will just look like two people swimming, they can't see your tail. My brother's on the other side but he can't see us around the bend. Quickly, we don't have long.'

'For what?'

'Amos, I think your father hid whatever those keys open in here.'

'Where?'

'In *here*, in Lake Pelutz.' Kaia could see the cogs in his brain ticking over as he tried to rationalise her theory.

'Think about it,' she continued. 'Why else would your father give the keys to you? He's not gonna give you keys to a safe inside some bank when you can't physically get there yourself. That would be pointless. He assumed you would be alone, so the keys must open something you can get to. Perhaps *only* you.'

His mouth popped open with realisation.

'The riddles, the games we used to play—'

'The camouflage,' she finished.

He swam around Kaia in one quick movement, his mind clearly still working through the possibilities. 'You think he's hidden it here, whatever it is, and disguised it as something else?'

'Amos, I'm almost certain he has.'

'What do you think is in there?'

That's something she didn't have an answer for, no matter how many times she had spun the idea around in her mind.

'Honestly? I don't know. It could be anything.'

Amos looked thoughtful as he glanced down at the keys hanging around his neck, his fingers running along the length of the chain.

'Father said this was the key to everything, right?'

'Right,' Kaia agreed.

'Maybe "everything" meant finding a way to get back to my people.'

'Maybe,' she breathed.

'That makes sense, doesn't it? He gave me the keys the night he was killed, by people who were looking for something. I assumed what they were looking for was me, but maybe that's just part of it. Maybe they needed whatever this unlocks as well.'

She could see just from the outset that his brain was racing, replaying that final night and every moment back inside his head. Kaia felt two things simultaneously: hope, largely hope that Amos was right and everything he needed to get back home was at his fingertips. Selfishly, she also felt a pang of regret. If he was right, that meant he'd be leaving. She had only just discovered him and in the few weeks they had spent together, she already knew that she would deeply feel his absence.

'Listen,' she said, pushing her emotions aside. 'I have to go.'

'Okay,' he said, jerking back to the present. 'I'll have found it by tonight.'

'That's ambitious.' Kaia smiled, as she backstroked.

'It won't be easy to find,' Amos agreed. 'Father was a

clever man and he had to cater for the possibility of someone else discovering where he had hidden it before I did: divers, those men, whoever.'

'You've got this,' she replied, before hurling herself into swimming and heading straight for the shore. She even got a sneaky tow from Amos, which accelerated her already signif-icant pace. When she made it back to the path, she looked up to find the toes of her brother angrily wiggling as they hung over the edge. His arms were crossed and he was furious. He was also waiting with a towel, so Kaia took his spiky mood with a grain of salt.

'Kaia, what the hell do you think you're doing, coming here? This is where you were attacked, nearly killed! You saw a man get pulled under the water and never come back up. Why the hell did you just dive in there?!'

'I needed to see if I could make it to the other side without getting eaten,' she replied, matter-of-factly. It had been a true enough statement when she had first dived into the water and met Amos. Storm's mouth opened and shut with shock as she trotted up the concrete stairs and grabbed the towel from his hands. Kaia buried her face in it and peeked out only to measure his expression.

'Well?' he managed to strangle out, watching her carefully.

'Fine,' she said, extending her limbs in an exaggerated act of inspection. 'Mind you, I wouldn't want to try that at midnight.'

A strangled laugh from Storm was her only reply. She couldn't be certain, but she was almost sure she heard Amos's as well.

'Kaia?'

An uncertain voice attached to an even more uncertain face was sticking out of a doorway and staring in her direction.

'Yes? Oh, hi!'

Pulling herself away from the thousands of thoughts occupying her mind, she thrust her hand out in a dorky greeting. 'Travis! Nice to see you again.'

'You too,' he said, shaking her hand but then doubling down by giving her a kiss on the cheek. 'I'm glad you decided to come by.'

'Figured it would be a shame not to take you up on the offer.'

'Sorry I had to leave you out here waiting so long. Scuttle, one of the 'star' dolphins, is under the weather and they wanted me to have a quick look.'

'Star dolphin, what a title!' She smiled.

'You're telling me,' he replied, gesturing at her to follow him past the reception desk where she had been waiting and down a long, white hallway. 'And just quietly, Scuttle acts completely like a star too.'

'Dolphin groupies?'

He laughed. 'Groupies, a rider, caviar, the whole thing. And here, this is for you.'

Kaia glanced down at the plastic lanyard he handed her, which had her name and photo printed clearly on one side and a barcode on the other.

'It's a temporary security pass so you don't get turned into chum or anything.'

'And here I was thinking those rumours about Sea World were untrue,' she joked. 'Thank you for this.'

'You're welcome. You should keep it for next time you come back.'

'I'll do that,' she said, smiling at the implication she'd be returning for more visits. 'And where did you get this pic of me?'

'Google,' he shrugged.

The pair came to a stop at the end of the hall where the name 'Dr T. Tishop' adorned the door they were about to pass through.

'This is my office,' he said, casually pointing to the label. 'It's basically base camp because we bounce around between specific research labs, different tanks or areas of the park that need—'

'ERMERGHERD! It's her!'

Travis was cut off as an enthusiastic woman in a lab coat burst out of the door and joined them in the hall. She had hair so grey it looked almost silver, with strands breaking loose of her bun and jutting out at odd angles.

'When Travis said you were coming in today, I did *not* believe him!'

Kaia glanced behind herself, just to check the woman was speaking to her and not someone else.

'Uh, Kaia this is my colleague Doctor Sophie Tiu,' Travis said, looking mildly embarrassed. 'She's a bit of a surf sports nut.'

'My niece does nippers at Point Burleigh – she's in Under 13s – and I've taken her to see your races a few times. Your surf skills are incredible. Are you sure your father's not part dolphin?'

The woman let out a breathy laugh at her own joke while Kaia blushed, suddenly very aware of an almost 'part dolphin' that she knew personally.

'I think if Dad could have it his way, he probably would be.'

'I bet.' The woman grinned, silence hanging between the three of them for a moment longer than was comfortable.

'Right, well, sorry to fangirl all over the place. Just wanted to say hi. My niece is going to be in hysterics.'

'That's very sweet of you,' Kaia said. 'Travis has my number, he can pass it on to you and if your niece ever wants to come out for a body surf, I'd be happy to take her.'

She beamed. 'Oh my God, that would be amazing. Ah! I'm sorry, I'll leave you two to it, but I'm going to call her *right* now.'

Kaia laughed. 'Nice meeting you.'

'Bye, bye!' she said, waving enthusiastically as she rushed from the room.

Travis gave Kaia a look. 'Well. Take that, star dolphin.'

'Ha, I've never had that happen before.'

'Sophie is absolutely crazy about that stuff, her whole family are into it. We share an office between the two of us as we have similar lines of work.'

He pushed the blue door open and guided Kaia into the space. As she stepped inside, it felt as if she had been immersed in an underwater universe. One wall was decorated with what looked like a tropical reef mural painted by schoolchildren, with several desks pressed against it and covered in mountains of paper. The mess extended outwards in the space until, almost precisely, the halfway mark. From there across to the other side, the room was pristine and white. Ikea appeared to have branding rights with modern and polished furniture housing a plethora of books and papers in an orderly fashion. Kaia's head swivelled from one side of the office to the other. She didn't even need to ask the question.

'I'm a bit of a neat freak.' He shrugged.

'Me too.'

'I have a few hours to myself,' he said, landing in a chair. 'Whatever it is you want to see just name it and we're off:

sharks, dolphins, starfish, the works. I'm your personal tour guide.'

'Actually,' she said, moving a pile of papers off a chair so she could sit down. 'What I wanted to talk to you about was Professor Viktor Waldman.'

Travis had been rhythmically bouncing backwards on his chair when he came to a stop. 'What?'

'Professor Waldman. You went to Hodgkins, yeah? You must have run into him.'

'I … I mean, sure. I was one of the last graduating classes he taught before he stopped teaching altogether and just focused on research.'

Spinning around in his chair, he began riffling through a series of papers that were kept neatly together in a manila folder.

'Here,' he said, handing Kaia an article cut out of the *Gold Coast Bulletin* from several months earlier. 'This tells you everything you need to know.'

The article was dated a few weeks after the Professor's death and was a full-page story on his funeral. His gruesome, unsolved murder had warranted proper coverage, with various snaps from inside the service and of guests leaving the church. Travis was one of them, Kaia noted, pictured looking away from the camera in a colour headshot. She read the article slowly, the reporter summing up what had been said during the service and who was there. Travis wasn't the only former student in attendance; there was a girl credited as being mentored by Professor Waldman who was quoted in the story.

'I think there's few who can say they truly knew Professor Viktor Waldman personally, but what he did professionally is what people are here to celebrate,' she'd said. 'Everyone came together to commemorate the life of a true scientific visionary, a man who felt the significance of every marine animal – whether that be a mollusc or a blue whale.'

Kaia's eyes moved down the page to a grainy image that was captioned as having been taken from security footage. It showed two men in matching floral shirts standing side-by-side, their faces concealed behind white, plastic masks. The image was in colour, yet it didn't help add any detail to the photo besides the offensive orange shade of their clothing.

'That's the two men who killed him,' Travis said, following the path of her eyes on the page. 'It's the clearest photo they have, but no one has come forth and identified them.'

She looked up at him, intrigued. 'You went to his funeral.'

'It was mostly former students there.' He nodded. 'Actually, quite a lot of people who work at Sea World came up under him at Hodgkins – Sophie too.'

'What was he like?'

'He was a good teacher. Not *Dead Poet's Society*-level or anything, but you could see he was passionate about the work. If you wanted to *really* be in his class, you could get a lot out of it.'

'You sound like a fan.'

'Of his work? Definitely.'

He seemed to hesitate about what he said next, leaning back and taking a sip from a mug that was sitting on his desk.

'You're full of surprises, you know. First I think we're going on a date, then you spend an hour grilling me on marine science. Now I think you're coming here to follow up on *all* those questions you asked by checking out the animals. But really, what you want to know about is Professor Viktor Waldman.'

Truthfully, Kaia had thought about skipping Travis altogether. She had first thought of going directly to Hodgkins

University, but decided against it. It was the only place he had worked in his lifetime and the only place he had done his primary research. Professor Waldman's name was synonymous with Hodgkins and if it *was* his work that had got him killed, then she was betting they had found him through the university. Put simply: she didn't know who could be trusted. What if the university itself had something to do with his death? In a bid to find out more about Professor Waldman and his research, she needed to find someone who knew him and could explain his work to her. Travis was a long shot, but the fact he mentioned going to Hodgkins and studying in the exact same field the Professor was famous in was too good an opportunity to pass up.

'I know it's weird,' she started.

'It's not weird. There are scientists all over the world who want to know about him. He's an enigma. What's weird is that *you* want to know about him. You're an ironwoman who seemingly had no interest in this stuff before. Why do you care now?'

'I … I met someone,' she admitted. 'He was the Professor's nephew.'

'Nephew? I didn't even know he had family. Mind you, there were a lot of people at the funeral, including city counsellors, so it's not a surprise I missed him.'

'He's a pretty private guy,' she said, feeling relief as Travis nodded and indicated that he bought what she was selling him.

'What's his name?'

'Amos. With the case still open, it has given him a lot of pain and for some reason he thinks trying to sort through the Professor's work will help him. I kinda promised that I'd help too.'

'He doesn't want to come in and meet me himself?'

'I'm sure he will,' Kaia said. 'If you're okay with that?'

'Sure, anything to help.'

'Thank you. I know this is all kinda weird, but I've been reading up on the Professor's work – or what I could find of it online – and I'm conscious of how far out of my depth I am. I want to help Amos, but there's questions neither of us can answer.'

'And you think I can?'

'Cabby said you were one of the best in your field.'

'Hmm. She did, huh?'

'The best,' Kaia emphasised.

'Okay,' he said. 'How about we go for a walk around the park and you can pick my brain. I need to get out of here and stretch my legs anyway.'

She followed Travis from his office and down the hall, where he swiped them through a series of security gates. It wasn't long before she walked through a final door and out into the park itself. Even for a weekday in early September, the place was packed. Families wearing dorky dolphin hats rushed by, kids pointed excitedly at a ride far off in the distance, while a toddler awkwardly carried a crocodile toy at least twice her height. It was a sunny day, not too hot, but in the mid-twenties so a singlet top or a loose shirt was comfortable.

'I remember watching the water ski show here as a kid,' she said, gesturing to the large body of water off to their left that sat in front of stadium seating.

'Yeah, it still happens. Every day at 3PM.'

'Ice cream?' she asked, drawing to a stop in front of a confectionary stall.

'Sure.' He shrugged. 'Boysenberry, if they have it.'

Kaia bought them each a cone – mint choc chip for her – and they continued their stroll.

'So,' Travis started, swallowing a mouthful. 'What parts of his work were you interested in? Biodiversity, marine biology, conservation, wildlife management, extinction, climate change, invasive species; those were his specialties.'

She did her best not to choke on a chocolate chip at the influx of scientific terms just thrown her way and think about what areas could be useful.

'Extinction,' she blurted, her mind snagging on a field that screamed of Amos.

'Full of surprises,' he muttered.

'What?'

'Never mind. I thought you'd be more interested in his conservation work. That's what he won the prizes for, the Notre Dame Acknowledgement, the Griffith Award—'

'I'm more keen on what he was doing with marine species: wildlife management and extinction, that kind of thing.'

'Funny.' He smirked. 'Those are the aspects of his research that I find fascinating too. Especially the more recent stuff.'

'Do you know what he was working on? Before he was ...'

'Murdered?'

She nodded.

'No, Viktor was always very private with his work – like his family, I guess. The only time you ever saw it was when he was done. He hardly ever worked at the university itself any more. Mostly he operated out of his home and I never heard of anyone who got inside to see his lab set-up.'

It made sense, Kaia thought. Any breakthroughs that resulted from studying Amos would've had to be kept quiet or he would risk exposing him.

'To be honest, he was kind of an unusual guy. One of the mentors for my PhD worked with him a lot in the nineties and said he was pretty paranoid.'

'About what?'

'Life in general, I think. I could count the number of

times he sent me an email on one hand – said he rarely trusted it unless he was desperate.'

'That does sound paranoid.'

'Maybe,' he said, pointing towards a path that led to the turtle enclosure. 'Actually, I think I have the last one he sent me saved in my inbox.' He pulled out his phone and fiddled with it for a moment. It was a regular model, but it had a special casing around it that Kaia recognised as being water-proof: probably essential for a marine biologist. 'Yeah, here it is. At the end of last year Viktor sent me a message, just out of the blue.'

'Had you been contact?'

'Not really. I saw him at an alumni dinner once, but I think it was because we crossed paths here a few weeks before that he sent me the email. I honestly don't think he remembered me from class, but he seemed interested that I was working here.'

'What was he doing at Sea World?'

'He'd been asked to consult on a type of jellyfish a fish-erman caught in the seaway, it wasn't a big deal. But then he emailed me this paper he had just published and asked what I thought of it.'

Kaia took Travis's phone when he held it out to her, looking at the document there.

'*The Migration Movements of Humpback Whales in a Marine Environment Affected by Climate Change*,' she read. 'That's a mouthful.'

'With a particular focus on the east coast of Australia,' he added.

She began flicking through the PDF, which included maps of the Australian east coast and various arrows outlining the paths humpback whales took annually as they moved to warmer waters.

'Viktor had never taken more than a passing interest in

173

the migration movements of any species before, at least in the published work of his that I could find,' he said. 'At some point towards the end of his life, that changed. What he was working on or how he envisioned this research being used, I'm not sure. There's nothing particularly groundbreaking here, mainly a very comprehensive look at the migration paths over the past 20 years.'

Kaia raised her head with interest. 'That seems like a very specific figure.'

He shrugged. 'I guess, but I gathered there was a reason he decided on that number as a point of origin, some working that wasn't included in these documents.'

It wasn't excluded calculations, she thought. It was Amos's age. She didn't quite understand how, but she felt in her bones that Professor Viktor Waldman's final research had something to do with his creature from the deep.

'Can I email this to myself?' she asked.

'Sure,' he replied, watching as a group of kids ran excitedly around an enclosure that held various species of sea turtle. Some of the turtles were tiny, Kaia noted, while others were so large she almost mistook one for a mossy rock as it sat there, dormant.

'Do you ever think it's cruel?' she asked, her fingers running along the glass. 'Keeping animals here in captivity like this?'

'Some of them, no. We're not like our US counterparts; this is mostly a rehabilitate and release facility. We also do a lot of work trying to improve local marine habitats. The turtles and seals and rays and seabirds, I don't think that's cruel. The smarter animals, like the dolphins—'

'What about the polar bears?' she asked. 'If their habitat is shrinking, they're endangered, is it kindness or cruelty to have them here?'

Travis sighed, his hands slipping into his pockets. 'Honestly, I don't know if there's an answer for that – not an easy one.'

Kaia's gaze turned back to the turtles as she watched them dip below the surface and inch towards the treats at the bottom. They looked happy, but how could she really tell? If she knew they could be happier elsewhere, could she keep them there? Or was she big enough to know when to let them go?

CHAPTER ELEVEN

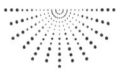

I t took four nights for Amos to find what his keys opened. He'd grown increasingly frustrated each night Kaia visited him and she was beginning to doubt their theory. Eventually he had discovered two metallic boxes just metres apart from each other. One had been neatly disguised among the native foliage, while the other was made to look like it was part of an underwater pipe. When Kaia arrived the night of his discovery, Amos had her swim over to the reeded area of Lake Pelutz to open the boxes, paranoid that someone would see.

'If I get bitten by an eel it's all your fault,' Kaia grumbled, eyeing a nearby ripple nervously as she made her way towards where he had hidden the boxes.

'They stay away from wherever I am.'

He gave her a grin that highlighted the major differences in their teeth: his were all slightly jagged, serrated formations. He had the two boxes resting on the edge of the bank, which was cloaked by the reeds where they extended up from the water and to the perimeter of the walking path. Kaia jumped, feeling a wet and silky 'thing' wrap around her ankle, only to realise it was a clump of reeds. Amos took in her startled expression and in one movement pulled Kaia onto his back and swam forward closer to the boxes.

'The eels are as far away from us as they can be,' he said softly.

She could hear the smirk in his voice. Sliding from his shoulders, Kaia curled up at the edge and tucked her long legs under herself, trying to avoid contact with as much of the environment as possible. Amos lifted the key chain over his head and held the keys ready in anticipation. He looked at her, eyebrows raised.

'Do it.' She nodded.

Key one went into the lock like a knife in warm butter. The first box – army green in colour – popped open with a puff of air as a few final remnants of water dripped from its corners and onto the contents. A clear, plastic box sat inside and Kaia watched eagerly as Amos lifted it out and fumbled with the release. It protected a series of documents: all maintained in pristine condition within an airtight laminate. There were no headings, no subtitles, no sections bolded or coloured in. It was just text. Eight pages, covered front and back in text. The ninth page was a clear sheet of laminate. Amos was so consumed in reading the other pages that Kaia slipped out the clear one for closer inspection. She frowned at it, wondering what its purpose was. It was a moonless night so there was no light from above, but she thought she could almost make out a symbol on the sheet. Holding it up in front of her face, she could see there were patterns but she couldn't quite make them out with the lack of illumination. She ran her index finger over them and could feel the raised surface where they were.

'What is it?'

Amos had stopped reading the papers and was watching her.

'I don't know. There are symbols on here, but the rest of the sheet is clear. It's too dark to see. What about you?'

He looked just as confused. 'It's three case studies of humpback whales. Two calves and then a general study on species migration along the east coast of Australia.'

'Just like the last paper he sent to Travis.'

'Exactly. I don't see how—'

'The other box,' Kaia blurted. 'Open it.'

She hoped the contents of the final box may hold the answer. It didn't. What it did hold was a USB.

'What's that?' asked Amos, confused by the tiny object as he rolled it over in his hand.

'It stores information. It can only be read by a computer.'

'Why would he give that to me? He knows I wouldn't have access to a computer.'

'Maybe this wasn't intended for you. Maybe he just needed to put it somewhere—'

'Safe?'

She shrugged. 'Maybe. I guess it all depends what's on it.'

'Can you find out?'

'Of course, it's just ... do you trust me with this?'

Amos gave her a confused expression. 'You know I do.'

'Whatever is on here is obviously very important. You're okay with me taking this out into the world?'

Amos leaned forward to cross any remaining distance between them. His face was inches from Kaia's and she felt something jump her throat as her heartbeat increased. He placed a cool, wet hand on her cheek and she found herself drawn to the strange blueness of his eyes.

'I trust you,' he whispered.

They were such simple, calm words. The response they ignited in Kaia was anything but. They stayed like that for some time, both of them staring at each other and not saying anything more. Suddenly the moment was gone and the closeness was almost awkward. He slunk back.

'This Travis Tishop, can *he* be trusted?'

She thought about that. In reality, she didn't know a whole lot about him. Sure, she had been out with him on a date, but how much could you truly learn from a person in one sitting? Yet after visiting Sea World, she saw how much Travis truly respected Professor Waldman's work and the man himself. He admired him and considered him a personal hero of his. You just didn't murder your heroes. Or betray them, even after death.

'Yes,' she answered, finally.

'Show him this,' said Amos, shuffling the plastic documents together and handing them to her. 'See what he can make of it.'

'Are you sure? What if it exposes you?'

'Nothing in these sheets will. None of it even makes sense out of context. The only thing that could might be what's on that USB.'

She clenched the device tighter at the very mention of its contents. 'I'll go to him with the documents first. See how that goes, then we can decide what to do with whatever information your father put on the USB.'

Amos gave her a tentative smile and reached across once more, interlinking his fingers in hers.

'I'm glad I'm not alone in this.'

———

'What am I looking at?'

'Uh, I'm not quite sure.'

'And how did you come across it?'

'Well ... I, er, can't tell you.'

Travis was giving Kaia a look she truly deserved as she

handed him the clear sheets with Professor Waldman's research. As he began reading at his desk, she sat there nervously and watched, fidgeting. After about 20 minutes he looked up at her, thoughtful.

'I printed off his paper after the last time we spoke so I could go over it again,' Travis said, reaching into a drawer and pulling out a small stack of documents. As he began flipping through, he cast her another look.

'This is Viktor's work,' he stated.

'Yes.'

'How did you get it, Kaia? The nephew?'

'If I tell you, it can't leave this room. Okay?'

'All right.'

'Swear on Scuttle, your star dolphin.'

'I *swear*.'

'These documents were left to Amos, but he only found them recently. He's a nice guy but he wants to stay off the radar. Especially after what happened.'

Her explanation seemed to settle a question in Travis's eyes as he nodded.

'I could understand that. Does he – what's his name again?'

'Amos.'

'Does Amos study within the field as well?'

'He knows a little, but that's mainly from being associated with someone like the Professor. Science isn't really his thing.'

'Hmmm ...'

'What? What is it?'

'The documents break down like this: three summaries of case studies on humpback whales and their migration. It ties in perfectly with the last material he sent me, meaning all of this came from the same research pool. One of the studies looks at a specimen we dealt with here that was caught in the shark nets and had to be rehabilitated before being released back into the wild.'

'What does that have to do with the migration?'

'The Professor was examining how well the specimen integrated back into the wild. It did, along with some of the other examples he looked at. The calves rejoined their old herd and continued to migrate each year for the next five or so that he has recorded.'

Travis was silent again as he re-read several sections of the papers. Kaia picked at the pockets of her jeans, feeling exposed. He hadn't remarked about the strangeness of the documents being covered in plastic, but he must have been wondering about it. She had caught Travis just before he left the office for the day and she had rushed to make it in time from board training. Because of that, her hair was still wet and dripping down her back. The green singlet she was wearing was sticking to her skin in the places that were still damp. Travis was in what she had dubbed his usual attire – slacks and a polo shirt – and he looked up at her again and leaned back in his chair. What he was looking for, she didn't know. She sensed that he was on the edge of saying something.

'Essentially, Kaia, what Viktor was looking at was the likelihood of reintroducing a specimen into the wild after it had been separated from its herd for a long period of time.'

She stopped breathing in that moment, realising what that meant. The Professor was trying to work out if Amos could ever return home and exactly where that 'home' might be.

'Some of this research is so specific,' Travis continued. 'I'm betting it relates to a specific creature. Since his specimens were the property of the university and reacquired when he died, I know roughly what he had in the tanks at his home laboratory. But none of the information he has gathered here is applicable to those creatures.'

Kaia was so lost in what Travis had found out about the research and what this could mean for Amos, she had stopped listening to him. He reached across, placing a hand on her forearm to get her attention. She was immediately jerked back into the conversation. He was looking at her with a serious stare that seemed to highlight the age difference between them. Kaia felt strangely like a child about to be scolded.

'I have to ask you this,' he started, voice low but urgent. 'Are you and Viktor's nephew keeping one of his specimens alive? Do you have it hidden somewhere?'

'I... uh—'

'I know it's hard when you get particularly attached to an animal, but you can't keep something like that secret,' he continued, understanding lining his tone as if he was speaking from personal experience. 'It's property of the university and – as this research demonstrates – it probably contains valuable information you don't know how to access.'

Staring at the deeply sombre look on his face, Kaia couldn't help the eruption of laughter that escaped her lips. Oh, one of his creatures was still alive all right. Except Amos could think, speak and swim for himself. She was sure he had all kinds of designs for his life that didn't involve being poked and prodded in a university laboratory. The harder she tried to stop the laughter, the worse it got. Travis was rightly staring at her like she was a crazy person by the end of the outburst. If only he knew.

'No,' she wheezed. 'We're not hiding any secret creatures. All we have is what's in your hands right now.'

She neglected to mention the USB. Half an hour later when she headed for the Sea World car park, Kaia pondered why the Professor had chosen to use humpback whales in the case studies. How did they relate to Amos and how he could get back to his people? For all the answers the Professor had left them, Kaia was beginning to feel he had left more questions.

KC had a handful of his mates from the surfing label around for a brainstorming session and dinner. Apparently there was a gnarly low-pressure system forming off the coast of New Zealand and they were trying to decide if they should fly over. The discussion went late into the night as they inspected various surf cams and called contacts at the Bureau of Meteorology. Kaia had to wait until they were long gone and she was sure her dad and Storm were in bed before she could make her escape. The wait was agonising and she was impatient to see Amos. Whether it was because she was eager for his company or because she wanted to impart the information she had learned, Kaia was uncertain. She was, however, certain that she didn't want to think about it too much. It was well past 2AM when she finally arrived at Lake Pelutz. Hiding her bike in the usual section of bush, she picked up her pace into a slow jog as she trotted down the decline to the edge where Amos and she met. His grinning face emerged from the water and Kaia returned the beaming smile. She was almost at the edge of the footpath when she heard a twig snap behind her. Kaia's smile dropped immediately and she spun towards the sound.

'I knew it, I knew you were up to something,' came Storm's voice as he appeared from the shadows.

Her body must have blocked his view of Amos initially and Kaia hoped he had the sense to duck back under the water now.

'Storm, what a—'

'What am *I* doing here? I think the question is more what are *you* doing here, Kaia? Why have you been sneaking out the past two nights to come here? You were attacked here, it's dangerous! What the fuck is going on?'

'It's not what you think.'

'I have no idea what to think because I have no idea why my little sister would be coming back to this spot after Dad and I have been doing everything we can to keep you safe.'

There was another rustle in the bushes and Cabby appeared behind Storm, batting away a series of leaves that had tried to embed themselves in her hair.

'*Cabby*?' she hissed. 'Oh, now I get it. You didn't exactly follow me, did you, Storm?'

'I had to tell him,' Cabby said, apologetically. 'We're worried about you, Kaia. Its been a month since I came here with you. What are you doing back at Lake Pelutz?'

Kaia crossed her arms, determined not to say another word.

'So?' Storm snapped, throwing his hands out in an exasperated gesture. 'You got nothing to say? And don't blame Cabby for this, either. I spent years sneaking out of the house under Dad's nose, you didn't think I would notice when you started doing the same?'

She opened her mouth to reply when they all heard a car door slamming nearby. It sounded close, almost as if it had come from the car park. No sooner had Kaia thought that, the light of a torch flickered on at the top of the hill near the entranceway.

'Who's out there? Come on, it's much too late to be playing funny buggers in the dark. This is the police.'

'Crap!' she whispered. Without a second thought, she threw her backpack into a nearby bush.

'Kaia, what are you doing?' Cabby said, dropping her voice low.

'Be quiet, we can't be caught here!'

'No shit,' Storm snapped.

That was obvious. For the victim of a physical assault to be found at the spot where it occurred at 2AM *with* her brother and her good friend … well, that would be majorly weird. The police officer was still at the top of the incline and she thanked God for the overcast evening that made everything a touch darker than it would usually be. There were no lights on the path, nothing to illuminate Storm, Cabby and herself, so the officer hadn't spotted them. Yet. She watched the movement of his flashlight with horror as the illumination began to slowly move its way over the grass and in their direction. They could all outrun him, she guessed, but how long would they have to stay hidden before they could return for their stuff? What if it reached daylight while they were still out and about on the streets of The Lakes? As she was thinking over all of this, the light was inching closer and closer.

'Kaia.'

Amos's soft and worried voice came from behind her and she turned to him with a panicked expression on her face. She only needed to look at him for an instant to know what she had to do.

'Who the—' Storm started.

She cut him off as she took a leap forward and grabbed him by the shoulders, throwing him off the edge of the path and into the lake below. Cabby stood there shocked at what had just happened. It gave Kaia the element of surprise as she shoved her friend in the lake as well. She just hoped Amos was ready. Before the officer had a chance to turn his flashlight in the direction of the splashing sounds, Kaia took off at a sprint in the opposite direction. She shouted as she ran, trying to make the strangest and most unusual sounds she could to draw his attention away from the lake. Glancing over her shoulder, she saw it had worked as the light was bouncing with the officer's movements as he ran after her. He hadn't seen who she was and as she grunted and growled, she hoped he wouldn't even suspect it was a woman. Better yet, maybe he'd think she was a neighbourhood dog who had got loose.

Kaia was extending her lead on the cop, whose seeming lack of fitness she was grateful for. She ran harder still, streaking through the dark and along the path she knew so well at this point. When she had increased her lead to 100 metres, she came to a dead halt. Crouching down and stepping off the ledge into the water as soundlessly as she could, she tried to calm her breathing. *Don't panic*, she told herself, slowly pushing off from the bottom as she let her body float further and further away from the shore. The officer's light was close now, less than twenty metres, and Kaia worried that her very breathing would alert him to her presence. She couldn't afford to make any strokes with her body, as the noise would draw him to the lake. Instead, she gently moved her legs backwards and forwards together in a butterfly kick to propel herself even deeper. At this point, even if he thought someone was in the lake, his torchlight wouldn't reach that far.

She watched anxiously as the officer neared where she had leapt off the path and then kept going, his flashlight pointed directly in front of him as he continued to chase after the source of a noise that was no longer there. She let out a nervous breath, increasing her kick enough now that she could afford to make the smallest sound. Her eyes tracked the flashlight as she moved, never once looking away as it followed the path up and onto one of the back streets of The Lakes. Kaia nearly let out a shriek, choking on the water around her as a hand snaked around her waist. It was Amos, of course, and she spun to see his eager face waiting for her. They remained silent, not needing to communicate as she wrapped her hands around his shoulders and he swam her to the quietest and most private part of Lake Pelutz. It was around the bend where she had swum to speak to him during daylight a week ago, with no path and minimal houses to prevent any chance of discovery. As they drew closer to the shallow end, Cabby and Storm came into view and Kaia let out another sigh of relief. They were safe. They were out of sight. They were out of danger. As she unlinked herself from Amos's back and walked towards them, her brother met her gaze with a deadly stare. Perhaps they weren't out of danger yet.

'WH—'

'*Sssshhh!*'

She held a finger to her lips and motioned to the other side of the lake and the distant houses. From the way his eyes kept darting from her to Amos and back again, keeping quiet was not what he was taking issue with. Cabby was hugging herself, standing in the shallowest part of the lake she possibly could. With the water coming up to her waist, she was shivering but she was quiet as she stared at Amos in shock. Storm shook his head angrily and took a deep breath.

'What just happened, Kaia? And who the heck is this? How did he get here?' he whispered.

'This is Amos,' she said quietly, walking closer to her brother with her hands extended in front of her. 'There was a police officer and none of us can be caught here, so I pushed you both into the lake hoping that he could take you somewhere safe while I created a distraction.'

'*How?!*'

Kaia spun around to face Amos, who was hanging back in deeper water. She gave him her best 'What have we got to lose?' type of expression and he nodded. The surface of the water rippled as Amos slowly lifted his tail out of the lake and in front of Storm and Cabby's faces. Her brother's blond hair was dripping and stuck to the front of his forehead as he gaped at the silver, scaled entity. He looked from the tail to Kaia, back to the tail, then to Amos, and back to the tail again.

'*Mama wata*,' Cabby whispered, sinking down.

By the second time he looked back at Amos, Kaia knew what Storm was going to do and threw herself in front of her brother as he tried to rush at the aquatic humanoid. She had no idea what Storm thought he could do if he reached Amos – *will* him to be a normal person? – or if he thought Kaia would float idly by, but she spliced herself perfectly between the two of them.

'STO— Kaia, let me at him!'

'Really, Storm? What can th—'

'Just le—'

'No!'

'Wh—'

Storm tried to nudge her out of the way, but Kaia used all of the strength she had to push him as hard as she could. He stumbled backwards, his eyes wide as he lost his footing and landed with a splash on his butt. As siblings, they had wrestled with each other their whole lives. But Amos had probably never seen anything like it with his diet of documentaries and classic Hollywood movies. Kaia felt his arm wrap around her stomach as he yanked her backwards and away from Storm. When they were a good fifteen metres away he stopped moving and negotiated with her physicality until she was behind him once more. Storm looked dumbfounded as he clutched at the water where Kaia had been not a moment earlier. He blinked, wiping the hair off his face as he took in their distance from him. Within seconds he was swimming towards them and, testament to his speed, he nearly got there before Amos whipped her out of his path again. The rush of water swept Kaia's hair over her cheek as Amos brought her closer to the shore and towards Cabby. Her friend's shaking hand reached out for her and Kaia slid over to her, gripping her arm for comfort.

'Amos,' Kaia begged. 'It's okay, Storm won't hurt anyone. This is just how he works things out. We need to give him some space.'

He gave Kaia a look that said he believed her about as much as he believed in Santa Claus. Storm, who had been watching this transaction with a mixture of fascination and disgust, suddenly swam towards him again. Amos diverted once more, ducking away in a flash.

'Really?' Cabby moaned. 'You're gonna try and drown a merman, Storm? I know you're pretty but I didn't think you were dumb as well.'

She sounded beyond frustrated and Kaia didn't blame her.

'Quit acting like an idiot,' Kaia scolded. 'Storm, stop moving and be quiet. Amos, stay where you are.'

The two men fell silent at Kaia and Cabby's harsh tones. Reluctantly, Storm surged forward and swam slowly to the shore until he was alongside the girls.

Cabby turned to face him, still clutching Kaia. 'Learn to control your bloody masculinity, will you?'

'I'm sorry,' he huffed. 'This has kind of taken me by *surprise*, Cabby.'

'Oh and I'm handling this perfectly?'

'You seem pretty okay about it.'

'I thought she was having a mental breakdown when she brought me here, mate! I was trying to help her through it! I didn't think she was actually right.'

Kaia gulped, watching her brother and friend come to

terms with something she'd had time to digest. Cabby turned to her, face apologetic.

'You were right, Kaia. There was something down there.'

'I know,' she whispered. 'And thank you for not making me feel like I was completely crazy, even though you thought I was.'

She shrugged. 'Hey, we're standing here uneaten by a sea creature. Let's call it even.'

Kaia chuckled, feeling immediately better as the gesture helped relieve some of the tension she had been feeling. Her brother, however, still looked pissed.

'Why are you so mad?' she asked, genuinely interested.

'Because ... you, he – you lied, Kaia! You lied to the police about what you saw!'

'That's what you're going with?' she snorted. 'Mister "I don't know how Dad's car ended up wrapped around the pole, officer, I was at home in bed".'

'I was sixteen!'

'You were twenty!'

'Whatever,' he snapped, falling silent and looking off into the distance.

'She didn't actually lie,' came Amos's soft voice.

Kaia's brother jerked around to glare at him, as if he had just said the most atrocious thing in the world.

'She didn't. Kaia had no idea what I was, what was in here, when I saved her from those brothers. It wasn't until af—'

'Brothers?' Cabby asked.

'It was the Tyler brothers who attacked me,' Kaia said.

'And you knew this?' Storm questioned.

'No. I mean, I figured as much from their accents and physical type—'

'You never told the police any of this, Kaia,' he said. 'They could have had them in custody by now.'

'What was she supposed to do, Storm?' Cabby sighed.

'You wanted me to tell the police that the only two children remaining in the family whose life I destroyed attacked me?' Kaia asked. 'That not only was I responsible for the death of their daughter, but now I'd be responsible for taking the freedom of their sons as well?'

'Okay, first thing,' Storm said, raising a finger. 'Bree Tyler's death was *never* your fault. Never. I know it, Dad knows it, the court proved it and everyone on the beach knows it, despite whatever rumours or nasty gossip they want to spread. Her parents were looking for someone to blame and they settled on you. After that, they tried to sue Stingray Surf Craft. They were desperate for a target. It was never your fault and you need to accept that. I know it's been hard, Kaia, the last six months especially, but none of it was your fault.'

She was quiet as he spoke, Storm drawing himself up to his full six foot three height.

'Second thing: it's *also* not your fault that Bree Tyler's brothers attacked you. The fact they thought they were delivering some demented form of justice is on them and them alone. You protecting them by not going to the police isn't helping anyone. They need to be punished, publically, and the sooner that happens the better.'

Somewhere during the last few sentences of her brother's speech, Kaia had grown teary and exceedingly fond of him. She dashed across the distance between them and dived into a hug. Storm was startled at first, but he relaxed into it and returned the gesture. After a long moment, she untangled herself. He gave her a sympathetic smile.

'Where are the Tyler brothers hiding, do you think?' His question had been asked innocently. He legitimately thought she knew where they were and that she was protecting their location. In a way, he was right. She shared a look with

Amos, whose expression showed no sign of guilt or remorse.

'Holy shit,' whispered Cabby, making the leap a second before Kaia's brother did.

'They're dead,' Amos said, speaking up. 'I drowned the both of them so Kaia could escape and their bodies are at the bottom of the inlet over there.'

He gestured in the direction of the underwater graveyard as her brother gaped at him.

'So you *did* save Kaia that night?'

'Yes.'

'And she had no idea you were here?'

'Not until I drowned the brothers.'

Storm turned to her. 'Then how did you find him?'

'I started coming here at night looking for answers, I guess. I found Amos.'

'Amos,' Cabby repeated, rolling the name around in her mouth like it was a lozenge.

'Amos,' Storm whispered. 'A mermaid called Amos? What the fuck?'

'Technically that's merman,' Kaia murmured. 'And he prefers the term aquatic humanoid.'

Amos swam closer, sensing the conversation had flowed into safer territory.

'Amos means "born by God" in Hebrew,' he said. Kaia looked at him, surprised.

'My father was Jewish.'

'I didn't know that,' she replied, genuinely curious.

'Wait, your dad lives here too?' Cabby asked.

'No,' Kaia cut in. 'Not his real dad. I mean, no offence, Amos. He was caught in a net during a research expedition by this man, Professor Viktor Waldman. He worked for Hodgkins University and lived at that house over there. He was murdered months ago, we think by people who had discovered Amos's existence and wanted him for themselves. Before he was shot, the Professor emptied Amos's pool into the lake and this is where he has been living ever since.'

It was a lot to take in. Cabby nodded as Kaia spoke and she could almost see the cogs in her brother's brain as he processed everything. He turned and looked at Amos more carefully.

'Who else knows about this?'

'No one,' she answered.

'Just Kaia,' Amos replied. 'I never revealed myself to anyone until …'

The silence of the night grew around the four of them as they waited there, Amos the merman and the humans all dripping wet and fully clothed.

'Do you want to see his gills?' Kaia asked suddenly, trying to break the mood.

'No,' replied Storm, wrinkling his nose.

She sighed, giving Amos a look. He smiled at her, moving his shoulders into the smallest shrug visible. Kaia fought the urge to laugh at the ridiculous scenario she had found herself in.

'Kaia, we need to go home.'

She glanced at her brother and the serious expression on his face. She knew she had to concede this demand.

'Okay.'

'Good,' Cabby whispered. 'I'm freezing.'

'How *did* you get here by the way?' she asked

'I was waiting out the front of your place, down the street,' her friend replied. 'When I saw you leave, I texted Storm and we drove over here.'

'I didn't even notice your car,' Kaia whispered, scolding herself for not being more careful. 'You didn't park in the car park, did you?'

'Please, I'm not stupid – I worried you might see us drive down. I'm around the corner, near the primary school.'

'Phew,' Kaia breathed, thinking about how much worse the situation could have been if her car was visible enough for the cop to run Cabby's plates. All of this hiding would have been for nothing. Amos swam forward, as if offering the others a lift. Storm quickly put his hands out and shook his head.

'We'll swim, thanks.'

'Head to the reeds,' Kaia said. 'Just in case. It's the spot that offers the most concealment.'

Storm nodded, but didn't say anything to her as he and Cabby pushed off and started swimming for the opposite end of the shore. It was a long swim, and they were taking it slow just in case the cop reappeared or their splashing drew some extra attention. But the night was quiet – no flashlight or inquiring minds in sight – as they all carefully breast-stroked their way forward. Kaia hung behind them, giving Storm and Cabby as much space as she could. She watched her brother's head bobbing in front of her, thoughtful, as Amos stuck by her side.

'We should talk more tomorrow,' she said, turning to face him as she swam. 'But what I came to tell you tonight is that we have confirmation your dad was close to discovering a way back to your people.'

'Really?' he said, his eyes lighting up. The hope there was unmistakable.

'What was in that box was part of a plan to return you home, I just don't how all the pieces fit yet.'

'And the stick?'

'I haven't had time to look at what's on the USB yet, but I will. If it doesn't expose you, I might be able to go to Travis with it too.'

She drew quiet as her brother turned around, looking

back at where Amos and Kaia swam over his shoulder. When his eyes returned to the front, she continued.

'Tomorrow,' she whispered.

'Tomorrow,' Amos replied.

When Kaia made it to the shore, Storm was waiting there – glowering – while Cabby jumped up and down on the spot to stay warm. Grabbing her bike and backpack from where she had hidden them, Kaia threw Amos a small wave as they began to walk away from the lake. It took them longer than it should have to get to Cabby's parked car, with the trio cutting through several public parks and sticking to the backstreets so they wouldn't be seen. Sure, it was *very* late and the likelihood of anyone they knew driving home at this hour was small. Yet if they were spotted – even by a stranger – it would look incredibly suspicious. The night was quiet as they walked, just the slaps of their feet against the pavement the only real sound.

'You can't tell anyone about this,' Kaia mumbled, breaking the silence.

'Kaia—'

'No, Storm. You have to promise me. You too, Cabby.'

Cabby threw her hands up in the air. 'Hey, who would believe me? I didn't believe you.'

'I think someone would believe you,' she remarked. 'I think someone would pay a lot of money, *kill*, to know what you both do now.'

'Kai, this is out of your league,' Storm breathed. 'All of our leagues. We have to tell—'

'An adult?' Kaia offered. 'We're all legally adults. And in case you missed it, Amos's dad is dead. I'm pretty sure whoever killed him wanted Amos too. I don't trust anyone except the two of you standing here with me right now.'

Storm sighed, nodding his head. 'Fine. I promise.'

'Cabby?'

'Like I said … yeah, I promise too.'

'Good,' Kaia said, feeling relieved. 'Thank you.'

'I remember,' Storm said.

'Remember what?' Cabby asked.

'When my biggest problem was worrying about how I would get girls out of the house in the morning.'

Cabby laughed, drawing her keys from inside her soggy jeans pocket as they turned the corner to find her car – a Suzuki Jimny – waiting there patiently for them.

CHAPTER TWELVE

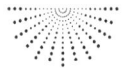

W hen Kaia woke, it was to the sound of her dad and brother fighting. For either of them to get worked up enough to raise their voices was significant and she stumbled into the kitchen in a daze.

'Now hang on, it wasn't like—'

'YOU LEFT, DAD! YOU LEFT WHEN SHE NEEDED YOU!'

'HEY! That's not what happened, Storm!'

'How would you explain it then? You gave a quote and got her lawyered up and then fucked off overseas!'

'You both know I have contractual obligations to the brand, I always have!'

'Obligations that you've broken now that Kaia got beaten up! She didn't need a high-powered lawyer, Dad, she needed you! Just like she didn't need hours out in the surf with you, she needed a mum! Maybe if she'd had a female role model she wouldn't be hanging out with—'

'HEY,' Kaia shouted, making both men jump like busted schoolboys. 'That is *enough.*'

She glanced at each of them, taking in the expressions on their faces and the reddened pallor of her dad's skin.

'What's going on?' She asked the question calmly and quietly, hoping to bring a sense of rationale to the argument.

'Ask him,' her father huffed, gesturing at Storm. 'I came down to see if you kids wanted to go knee-boarding and then suddenly I was the *bad guy* getting yelled at.'

'You're not the bad guy, Dad,' Storm groaned. 'But before Kaia was attacked, did you even see how she was doing? Did you even care about what she was going through?'

'Of course I cared, how dare you? I've spoken with BB on the phone every week and, you know, besides being a bit distant he told me she was going well at training. Participating and—'

'That's not the same as *being* there!'

'Storm, just stop!' Kaia yelled.

He turned his back to her in agitation and paced to the end of the kitchen. KC was still looking surprised by the whole thing. Storm generally wasn't an angry guy, but when he felt strongly about something he *really* felt strongly about something. He was mad, Kaia got that, but he was angry with her and not with their dad. The things he was saying were hurting the wrong person.

'Dad,' she said, laying a hand on his shoulder, 'he's mad at something that has nothing to do with you, okay? This is all my fault.'

That unintentionally got Storm's attention. 'No, don't you go blaming yourself for this too, Kaia. Not everything in the world is your fault.'

'Oh and what? I suppose the remainder of stuff *is* Dad's fault then?'

'I'm out,' exclaimed KC, tossing his hands up in the air in a gesture almost identical to one Storm had used earlier. Their father didn't like confrontation, which had been a problem in his marriage, and he grabbed his car keys off the bench.

'Great. Do what you always do when it gets tough, Dad, leave.'

'STORM! That's not fair and not true!' Kaia screamed.

A slamming door signalled KC's exit and she whirled on her brother.

'What the hell? I understand you're mad at for me lying to you, but why take it out on him? You know he has always done the best he could for us, which is a thousand times better than most fathers.'

'You can't tell me it didn't hurt when he left more often this year, especially after the accident.'

'No, I can't tell you that. Of course it did, but I understood. It was hard for him to be blamed, to see me blamed, even inadvertently. KC's never been on people's bad side before, so I understood.'

'That's not good enough, Kaia. He should have stayed.'

'I know,' she pleaded, glancing down at her body and realising for the first time she was still in her pyjamas. 'But he didn't. There's no point going over and over it and rubbing it in his face when it can't be changed. He's here now.'

Storm let out a long, deep exhale as he placed both hands on the kitchen bench to steel himself. Kaia could see him mentally calming his mind as he took another series of breaths.

'Shit,' he said, 'I lost it, didn't I?'

'You've been doing that a lot, lately.'

He nodded. 'I owe Dad an apology, that's for sure.'

'Now, I'm here and we're alone. Say what you need to say to me about this whole Amos thing.'

Storm poured himself a glass of water and drank it slowly as he looked out at the ocean in the distance. Placing the empty glass on the counter top, he turned his whole body to face her.

'How did you get involved with this fish?'

'Aquatic humanoid,' she corrected.

'You said his dad got murdered over him and now you're practically dating the guy?'

'Whoa. WHOA. I am *not* dating Amos. That's not even possible, given how he *lives in a lake* and all that. Slight oversight.'

'You've visited him every night for how long now?'

'A month, a bit over, which is not the same as dating someone.'

'I've seen the way he protects you. For Christ's sake, Kaia, he was shielding you from me last night.'

'You were acting crazy—'

'He's in love with you!'

'He saved my life, Storm! I'm the only friend he's ever had besides his father, who was murdered seconds after leaving him in a lake without any answers or any hope. You take issue with Dad going away for a few weeks? At least he comes back. Amos's father was killed and he's never return-ing. He has no one. He's scared and alone. Where is your humanity?'

Storm had the sense to look vaguely ashamed of himself. They stood there in silence for several long moments as the full extent of Kaia's words washed over him.

'I never thought about it like that,' he said quietly.

'I know. I also know it's hard having this thrust on you out of nowhere. It's—'

'Epic.'

'Yeah.'

'So what are you going to do?'

'What can I do? I like him, Storm. He's a nice person who's alone and needs help. The very least I can do is try and find the answers his father left him. There might be a way back to his people.'

'You mean there's *more* out there like him?'

'There has to be. Everything has parents. Amos has vague memories of swimming with others before he was caught in the net and the Professor, his dad, was certainly hell-bent on the idea of there being others out there like him in the ocean.'

'Other mermaids …' he whispered, trailing off.

'I know,' Kaia said with understanding. She knew exactly what he was feeling in that moment: it was a lot.

'It's like a fairy tale.'

'But sad.'

She began telling Storm everything Amos had told her about his life, from when he was first accidentally caught to living inside a tank and a pool. She told him about how the only time he got to experience open water had been brief, limited stints in Lake Pelutz when his father could manage it. Kaia even explained how his only human interaction came from his dad, Professor Viktor Waldman, who wasn't even his own blood but had been the lone person he knew. From learning about the world through documentaries and studying life through classic movies, she didn't hold back. She offloaded all of Amos's story on her brother, trying to get him to understand. It felt glorious for Kaia to be able to share it with someone, this secret that had been pent up inside of her. By the end of it, the siblings were sitting side-by-side on the kitchen counter.

'I think I probably owe him an apology too,' Storm said.

'On account of how you wanted to drown him? Nah, I wouldn't mention it. It's not as if you would have been successful anyway. Drowning an aquatic humanoid may be too much, even for your talents.'

'Hey,' he laughed. 'Far as we know, we're the only three people in the world who know mermaids exist.'

'I doubt it.'

'Why? Who else knows about him?'

'Of *all* the people in the world and *all* the coastal communities out there, there's bound to be other humans who've interacted with them at some point.'

'Maybe. Maybe they ended up like the Tyler brothers.'

They were both silent at that comment.

'Plus,' he continued, 'we don't know how many merthings there are out there. Maybe we are the only people.'

'Doubtful. I did some research at the library with Cabby – when she was still trying to placate me – and there are hundreds of stories over time. Most people just wrote them off, but now I'm beginning to believe all those people weren't crazy. Not every sighting could have been a hoax.'

'Either way,' Storm said. 'It doesn't really matter. We can't start a support group about it or anything.'

Sliding off the bench, Storm gave Kaia a quick hug.

'I'm proud of you. I'm proud of what you're doing and I'm proud of you being brave enough to help him.'

'Er, thanks,' she said, her words jumbled through being squished against his shoulder.

'Whatever you need to get him home, let me know.'

'Okay.'

'And I'm coming with you when you go and visit him.'

'Sto—'

'No ifs or buts. This is dangerous and don't try and tell me it's not. Someone got killed because of this, maybe.'

He was right, of course. Kaia begrudgingly agreed.

'Now,' Storm sighed. 'I need to go and find Dad.'

'Yes, go do that, will ya? I'm gonna call Cabby.'

He was almost at the front door when he paused, looking back his sister. 'Kaia?'

'Yeah?'

'With everything you're doing for him and the time you're spending together—'

'Yes?'

'Just remember: you're not the same species.'

Her brother ducked out of the front door immediately after those words, leaving Kaia in an empty house with the gravity of that statement. Huh. As if she could ever forget.

'You both really didn't have to come with me,' Kaia whined.

Cabby made a clicking sound with her tongue to show how much she disagreed with that statement.

'I told you,' Storm said. 'You're not going to do this stuff alone any more.'

'I'm going to see Travis at Sea World. It's not exactly going to a lake by myself in the middle of the night.'

'No, but he did call you at 8PM on a Thursday and I don't want you going solo. I'll even wait outside the office so I don't hear what you're talking about.'

She slumped back in her seat, crossing her arms in a huff.

'Looks like a grumpy toddler, doesn't she?' Cabby remarked, as she glanced up at Kaia in the rear-view mirror.

'She does that when she's mad,' Storm chuckled, turning around to flash her a smile where she sat in the back seat.

'Think of us as, like, the three musketeers now,' Cabby said, pulling into the empty Sea World car park.

'There were four of them,' Kaia grumbled.

'Fine,' Cabby chirped. 'Amos can be our fourth.'

'You coming in?' Storm asked as she brought the car to a stop.

'Nope, I'll wait here. It's a bit weird since I'm not only dating his little sister but I set him up on a fake date.'

'Fair enough,' he replied, holding the back door open for

Kaia as she scrambled out. 'And this guy doesn't know that Amos exists?'

'NO,' Kaia said. 'He's never met Amos, but he thinks he's the Professor's long-lost nephew who I'm trying to help sort through some of his work.'

'Kaia,' Cabby remarked. 'That's a good lie.'

'Thank you.' She smiled. 'I'm trying to get better. See you soon.'

Scanning the now shut-down park at night, Kaia had to admit it was nice having Storm and Cabby with her on this. It's just she hadn't thought they would be so proactive when they both said they'd be looking out for her from now on. Storm had cooked Kaia and her dad a big apology dinner that evening, which Cabby was also invited to, so when she'd received a call from Travis midway through dessert saying that he had "big news" she finally had people to share it with. She took the phone to her room when she saw who it was, telling Travis she could be there first thing in the morning when Sea World opened up. There was something in the tone of his voice that she put down to excitement. He said she should come straight away, it was that important. When Kaia returned to the dinner table, she waited until her dad had taken the dishes to the kitchen before leaning in and sharing the information with Storm and Cabby. In under a minute, the trio decided they would head to Sea World first, see Travis, then stop by at Lake Pelutz to check on Amos all in the one round trip.

'You have your own pass?' Storm said, as Kaia flashed it to enter through the staff entrance.

'It's a temporary pass,' she replied, the scanner beeping as it read her I.D and the door clicked open. 'It only lasts four weeks at a time but you can have it extended.'

'And this Travis guy hooked it up for you?'

'Uh-huh.'

'So you've been here a bit, yeah?'

Storm was clearly impressed by her familiarity with the layout, as she cut through the pool of now-empty public relations desks, heading towards the maintenance door that led to the scientists' offices.

'A couple of times.'

'Travis is cool with you guys being "just friends"?'

'Yes, Storm,' she said, rolling her eyes. 'More importantly, he was friends with Amos's father, kind of, before he was murdered. I went to him because he was familiar with Professor Waldman's work and I thought it was safer than going to people at the university.'

Her brother's silence was concerning her and she threw him a look. 'He's a good guy, Storm.'

'Okay, okay. I was just—'

'What?'

'Impressed. With you, with everything you've done.'

'Pfft. Besides feeding Amos and some Googling, I haven't done anything yet.'

'Still.'

They were a few doors from Travis's office when she stopped. 'The blue door on the left is where I'm headed. You're okay to wait here?'

'You don't want me coming in with you?'

'Honestly? No. Also, I don't know how Travis would feel about me bringing a stranger into his office late at night.'

Storm agreed and she left him behind – he already looked bored as his lanky frame stretched along the white walls.

It turned out Travis felt just fine about strangers in his office late at night, as there were two of them standing on either side of the door as Kaia entered the room. Both were tall, probably around her height, and muscular. The younger of the pair was bald and his head shined in the well-lit office space. The older man's hair looked like oil – slick and black – and it was fashioned into a tight ponytail at the base of his neck. They were dressed in the uniforms of Sea World cleaning staff and both were aiming guns squarely at Kaia's chest. Travis looked as if he'd had his hands raised in the air for a while and sweat was forming at his temples. His glasses looked a few degrees away from fogging up.

'Shit,' she whispered, coming to an immediate halt as the door closed behind her.

'Now, now,' said the older man. 'No need to get carried away, Miss Craig. We just want to have a talk.'

His voice was so quiet Kaia would have had to strain to hear him in normal circumstances. But these weren't normal circumstances. He gestured with the gun for her to move until she was standing next to Travis, who was still sitting frozen in his chair. She wondered how his legs would go in the event of standing up. Positioned between the chaos that was Sophie's desk and the doctor himself, Kaia tried to sneak a glance to see if there was anything she could use as a weapon. The closest she came was a small, circular fish bowl that held some kind of sea snake or eel. It looked precarious enough balancing on a stack of papers as the occupant swilled around inside the tank.

'Where's the creature?'

This time it was the bald thug who spoke up. He didn't smile, but he was trying very hard to project a sense of reasonableness. Kaia found it hard to focus on his words as she kept glancing at the guns. She had never even seen one in real life before, let alone two, *let alone* being pointed at her.

His voice was steady and calm as he repeated the question. 'I will say it again, Miss Craig: where is the creature?'

She looked from the men to Travis and back again. He looked as genuinely befuddled as she hoped she did.

'What creature?' Kaia replied, attempting to sound earnest.

The man with the ponytail showed a vague sign of irritation as he scratched his forehead with the tip of his weapon.

'Miss Craig,' he whispered. 'There is no point playing dumb with us. You saw how well that ended for Professor Waldman.'

She gulped as Travis rose from his chair, hands shaking as he lowered them from above his head.

'Y-You killed him?' he said. 'You're the monsters who did that?'

They didn't even try to look offended.

'No need to get your panties in a knot, Doctor. All we want to know is where in the park you're keeping the creature?'

Kaia tried to keep her face neutral, tried to keep everything that she was projecting a blank slate. They thought Amos was here. It made sense, she supposed. Somehow they must have tracked down Travis and found out she was working with him. Naturally they would think they were keeping Amos here: it was one of the best equipped marine facilities in the world. It was a strange sensation she felt: relief while still being held hostage at the end of gun.

'I don't know what you're talking about,' Kaia repeated.

'Neither of us do!' Travis pleaded. 'I don't know what creature you mean, you won't even say! We certainly don't have any of Professor Waldman's specimens here, so you'd better just go before I call the police.'

'Travis,' Kaia cautioned, her eyes still glued to the men. 'They're not going anywhere. You think they would have told us they killed the Professor if they were going to let us live?'

Horror flashed in his eyes as he realised what Kaia meant. At least the two men didn't deny it.

'Yes, we intend to kill you,' said the calm one. 'But the question is, how long will that take? We can make it very slow. Like the Professor, for instance, who received an extremely painful bullet to the kneecap before we ended his life.'

The muscles in Kaia's neck tightened as she watched the malice pouring from the bald man's face as he described the murder. She was genuinely scared.

'Alternatively, just tell us what we need to know and it will be over quick. Almost painless.'

'Do you know what this is?' his colleague asked, jerking his wrist to indicate the gun in his a hand. 'The Walther PPQ, loaded with 9mm rounds. Some might say it's a poor man's Glock, but me? I like the impact it has when the bullet connects with flesh.'

Kaia thought about Storm, waiting in the hallway and just metres away from the door. She was supposed to have come alone and far as they knew, she had.

'Why do you need to kill us?' she asked, raising her voice and trying to pass it off as panic. 'We don't know what you're talking about or where this creature thing is, so just let us go. I never even knew Professor Waldman! I never met the guy in my life!'

'It's funny then,' started the ponytailed man, 'that you have taken such an interest in his research. Why is that, Kaia Craig?'

He had her there. She fell silent.

'Dr Tishop at least has some excuse, given they were colleagues. But you ... well, Travis here says you only knew him for a few weeks before you started taking an interest in the Professor and his research papers.'

'Now that's only because she knows his nephew,' Travis

spoke up, leaping to her defence. 'There's nothing strange about that. They were discussing research papers he'd inherited and she brought them to me to better understand them.'

Kaia closed her eyes and silently cursed him. He saw her do so and looked over, uncertain as to why the two men were smiling at each other.

'Professor Viktor Waldman never had a nephew,' said the bald man. 'Never even had a sibling. He was a bachelor through and through, which begs the question: where did you get the research papers?'

'We wouldn't mind having a look at those too. Where are they, Miss Craig?'

'You know,' Kaia said, slowly. 'I seem to have misplaced them. If—'

She never got to finish what she was saying because at that very moment the entrance to the office burst open as her brother flew in, having thrown his whole body weight behind the door from outside. The door pinned and squished the man with the ponytail behind it. As he fought to get his way free, Storm threw himself back against the wood again and again until the man's grunts eventually stopped. His bald colleague was ready to jump to his aid but, seizing the distraction, Kaia picked up the fish bowl from the desk and hurled it at him. He spun around at the last minute, copping the full impact as the bowl shattered on his face. She watched, frozen in shock, as the occupant of the bowl sprang to life and began biting the man. He screamed, his finger reflexively pulling the gun's trigger and letting off a shot. Storm, Kaia and Travis dove to the floor, cowering as the bullet ricocheted around thc room. When the noise eventually stopped, the three of them straightened up cautiously. Kaia's hands flew to her mouth as she watched the bald man feebly trying to fight off the tiny snake, continually striking blows to his own face. The bites on his cheeks and neck were already swelling as he tried to pull the creature off, his movements growing slower. Eventually the snake retreated of its own accord. The trio watched it cautiously as it slithered into the darkness under Travis's desk.

'What was in that fish bowl?' Kaia strangled out.

'Belcher's Sea Snake,' Travis replied. 'I was transferring it back to its tank after analysis when they arrived.'

'*Man*,' Storm whispered.

'They're usually very docile, unless—'

'Provoked?' she offered.

He nodded. Kaia guessed having your home thrown at someone while you were still inside it was provocation enough. She felt a hand reach around her own as Storm pulled her into a sideways hug. She hugged him back, eyes still fixed as she looked at the twitching body of the man on the ground.

'Is he—'

'He's not going to make it,' Travis said, cutting her off. 'Not every bite is full of venom, but the way his body is reacting ...'

As if on cue, the man let out a deep groan. His eyes had now swollen shut entirely. Storm separated himself from Kaia, carefully pulling back the door to inspect the condition of their other attacker.

'How is he?' Travis asked, stepping carefully over the bitten man. 'And who are you, by the way?'

'My bad,' Kaia apologised. 'Travis, this is my brother, Storm. Storm, Travis etcetera.'

'Hey.' Storm nodded. 'And this guy's fine. Small cut on his head, but I think I only knocked him out.'

'We need to get out of here now,' Kaia said, glancing around at the carnage of Travis's office. 'In case there are others coming.'

Storm nodded, pushing the door back to cover the guy with the ponytail. 'Who were they?'

Kaia looked at Travis, hoping he would have the answer. He shook his head.

'I have no idea. They burst in here just after 7PM and held me at gunpoint the entire time. They searched the office for the research you brought, but I told them you would never leave it behind. That's why they got me to call you, figuring you would bring it.'

'I did, but it's in the car, thankfully.'

A cough from behind the door interrupted the conversation.

'Let's make a move,' ordered Storm. 'We should tie him up.'

'With what?' Kaia snapped, 'Another errant sea snake? We don't have the time, lets just get out of here.'

'I'm with you sis.'

'Travis – grab any of your research you think they might be after. Don't leave it here. We can call the police from the road.'

He snatched his laptop and slipped a folder out from an almost-invisible space wedged between two tanks. Kaia raised an eyebrow at him, impressed with the hiding place. He leapt over the body of the sea snake victim and the three of them set off down the hallway at a run.

'What was the research they were after?' Storm called.

'The material they wanted was to do with whale migration,' Travis replied.

Kaia glanced at him, before turning to her brother. 'That's the same thing covered in the papers I have as well. All of it is from Professor Waldman.'

'The fish's dad?'

'Don't call him that!'

They slowed to a walk as soon as they were out of the building and in the Sea World car park.

'Hold on,' Travis said, grabbing Kaia tightly by the arm. 'What's this business about the Professor not having a nephew? I thought that's where you said you got his unpublished research from?'

'I did, it's only—'

'And what was this creature they kept talking about? They were convinced I had it at the park, some final specimen that Viktor kept hidden.'

'Uh ...'

'You know where it is, don't you?'

'It's so much an "it" as it is a "he".'

'A male specimen?'

'In a manner of speaking.'

'Sis, you need to tell him,' interrupted Storm.

'I will, but right now we need to get back to Amos before they find him.'

'The nephew?'

Storm let out a growl of frustration and he grabbed Travis by both of his shoulders. 'His name is Amos, he's a merman, and this Professor guy was keeping him as his pet until he got killed by those nutters. My sister has been hanging out with him and is the only one who knows he's alive and where he is. Besides me. And Cabby.'

Kaia slapped her hands to her face, unable to look at the mix of emotions playing out as Travis processed the blur of previous sentences. At first there was a tiny smirk, followed by disbelief, and then shock. Heavy doses of shock.

Finally, after a long pause, he said: 'I guess that makes sense.'

'I ... it does?'

'Yes,' he said, regaining his composure. 'All of this research was setting out to achieve something. It was relating to a specific case, but without knowing what that was – or who that was – we could never really understand it. Now it makes much more sense.'

The honk of a car horn made all three of them jump, followed by the screech of tyres as Cabby pulled up alongside them. Sliding down the window, she hung half her body out the door.

'What the hell are you guys doing? And what's Travis doing here?' She threw up her head in acknowledgment of his presence and he returned the gesture with a small wave.

'He's coming with us,' Kaia said, making a snap decision as they all piled into Cabby's now very cramped jeep. 'Storm will fill you in as we drive.'

Accelerating towards Lake Pelutz, Travis called the police from his mobile and told them about a break-in at his office. Storm had just finished recounting the story of the two armed men when the doctor hung up.

'You need to turn that off,' Storm said, swivelling in his seat to face Kaia and Travis.

'What? My phone?'

'Yeah. In case they try to track us.'

'Who?' Cabby snorted. 'The police?'

'The police, the government, whoever those two pricks work for.'

'Insert faceless organisation here,' Kaia muttered, nervously glancing out the window. She cast a look behind them to make sure they weren't being followed.

'And keep the speed down, Cabby,' her brother continued. 'The last thing we need is to be pulled over.'

'What else do you want from me?' she snapped at him.

'Safe bloody passage?' he replied.

'Are we going to the creature?' Travis asked with unbridled enthusiasm.

'Okay,' Kaia started. 'First of all, he's not a "creature". His name is Amos and he's nearly twenty years old. He's also kind of shy around strangers, so don't frighten him.'

Travis opened his mouth to talk but she cut him off as she launched into a rushed explanation of how Professor Waldman came across Amos and where he had been living.

'The conservation breakthroughs, the sudden change in direction to species extinction, it all connects with the timeline,' he said breathlessly.

'Yeah, that's great,' she said. 'But I'm hoping you can make sense of this.'

She handed him the USB as Cabby mounted the narrow road that led to the deserted car park of Lake Pelutz. She switched her lights off so as to keep a low profile, slowing to almost a crawl.

'What's on it?' Travis asked, fiddling with the device as he inserted it into his laptop.

'I don't know,' Kaia admitted. 'I'm no scientist or doctor. I only had time to glance at it once, briefly. It looked like there were years of documents on there. It was hidden in a box with the research papers I showed you in the clear plastic, so it must be important. Now that you know everything, I'm hoping you can decipher it.'

Travis's eyes darted from hers to his laptop screen and she saw the digital documents illuminated in his glasses as they appeared in front of him. His mouth opened with a small pop and she sensed he was going to be there a while. The car came to a sudden stop, Kaia jerked forward and lightly whacked her head against the seat in front of her. A collection of debris slid off the seats and to the floor, along with the research papers.

'Sorrrrreeee,' Cabby said. 'I nearly drove into the car park barrier without my lights. Everyone okay?'

'I'm fine,' Kaia replied, scrambling to pick up everything that had been thrown around. She cursed as she noticed that a water bottle had split with the impact and its contents were flooding over her feet. The documents had spilled out of their folder and were being covered in the fluid.

'Damn it, this—'

She paused, fascinated by what was happening in front of her. As the water made contact with the clear film of one of the pages, there seemed to be a chemical reaction. The page wasn't clear any more, it was glowing. Shapes began to form and she laughed as they slowly began to resemble arrows.

'Look at this!' she said, holding up the one clear page that had been among them. It wasn't blank after all.

'What the?' Storm asked, glancing out the corner of his eye.

It looked like it took everything Travis had to pull himself away from the laptop but he raised his eyebrows at the documents in astonishment. 'He hid it.'

'Hid what?'

'Arrows,' he murmured, barely audible as his fingers traced the raised lines like she had that night in the lake. 'But to where? I'm not sure yet.'

He frowned as the shapes began to fade with the drying of the page.

'I need to look closer at his,' he said, glancing back at the screen.

'Are you okay to stay with him?' Kaia asked Storm.

'Sure. Where are you going?'

'I want to see Amos and keep him updated on what's going on.'

'What *is* going on?'

'I don't know, but I have a feeling we're going to have to get him out of here soon.'

'How? And take him where?'

She bit her lip, frowning. 'I don't know. I don't know. I'm

hoping whatever Travis is gawking at now will give us some answers.'

'I'll come with you,' Cabby offered, hopping out of the car. She tossed Storm the keys, telling him to lock the doors behind them just in case.

As the two women walked down the grassy slope that led to the lake, Kaia pulled her singlet top over her head, revealing her full piece swimsuit underneath. Kicking off her shoes and wiggling out of her jeans at the water's edge, she was suddenly aching to see Amos. She *needed* to see him, she *needed* to check that he was still there and still okay.

'You coming in?' she asked, turning to Cabby.

'Meh,' she replied, her friend's face twitching with reluctance. 'That's more your thing. I'd rather stay on land and keep… dry.'

'I won't be long,' Kaia said, before diving into the water. Shutting her eyes, she let the cool liquid take her breath away and rush all over her body until she could feel that she wasn't alone any more. She looked up to see the shining silver of Amos's tail and shot to the surface, searching for his face. When he burst up next to Kaia, she nearly dunked him back under the water with how quickly she dived on him. Wrapping her arms around his neck, she pulled herself close to him in an embrace. She savoured his shock and the immediate physical contact. Slowly, a hand found its way to the back of her head where he smoothed the damp hair there.

'Hello,' he said, 'Are you okay? What happened?'

'Everything.'

Her voice was muffled as her face pressed into the skin against Amos's neck. Kaia was reluctant to move from this position, comfortable in his closeness and the protectiveness of the gesture. Eventually, she had to though. As she pulled herself back to face him, her nose just inches from the tip of his, she realised that Storm was more on the money than she had given him credit for. She did have feelings for Amos.

'What happened?' he asked, forehead crinkling in concern.

'The men who killed your father, they found us.'

His hands tightened at the mention of Professor Waldman's murderers and his gaze swept over her.

'But you...' he started, brushing a hand down her face, 'You seem okay. They didn't hurt you?'

She let out a soft, unamused laugh. 'They were going to kill Travis and me, but Storm knocked one of them unconscious and I threw a sea snake at the other.'

Amos smiled at her, half in disbelief. 'You did?'

She nodded. 'I think he's dead.'

'That's great!' He beamed. 'You killed one of my father's killers and made it back to me safely!'

Her mouth had been curling up into a smile, but she felt it drop with the realisation. Amos watched the movement carefully.

'What? What is it, Kaia?'

'I... you …'

The harder she tried to get the words out, the more impossible it became. Her lips moved as she attempted to form the sentence, albeit rather fruitlessly. She looked at Amos, examining every detail of his face. He had clearly shaved that same day as his jaw line was smooth, like a boy's, and his head gave the appearance of almost-baldness. He extended a hand to her face, wiping a finger under the hollow of her eye and catching the tear there. Light reflected from a droplet of liquid and Kaia tried to ignore the salt that stung at the corners of her eyes. He was staring at his finger in fascination, as if he had never seen anyone cry before in his life. Maybe he hadn't. A breath of air escaped his lips as he realised what it meant. Amos's head jerked upright and his blue, piercing gaze met her own.

'We have to get you home,' Kaia whispered.

'Tonight?' His voice was barely audible. She heard the pain there.

'As soon as possible. The longer you stay, the more dangerous it is for you.'

'But ...' His hand traced her jaw until it came to her lips, where Amos slowly traced the shape of them.

'*Unbelievable.*'

Travis's voice broke through the night air like a stone smashing into a glass window. Kaia's head snapped in the direction of his words and to where he was standing in awe at the edge of the lake path. Cabby had graciously turned her back, giving them some semblance of privacy. Kaia didn't disentangle herself from Amos, but when she returned her gaze to his, he was still looking at her, having never even glanced in the direction of the voice.

'Amos,' she started. 'This is Dr Travis Tishop.'

It was only when she gestured at the man watching them that Amos finally turned his head.

'Hello.'

By instinct, she slid onto Amos's back and linked her arms around his neck as he swam them towards the shore.

'He talks.'

Travis was down on all fours now and seemed just about ready to dive into the water if it wasn't for the laptop he seemed reluctant to abandon.

'Of course he talks,' said Storm, still walking down the hill from behind the doctor.

Flipping off his thongs, he flopped down onto the grass and dipped his feet into the lake water. Kaia swallowed any comment that this time last night Storm hadn't been acting so blasé when Amos talked to him.

'Yes, I can talk,' replied Amos. 'I can rationalise and analyse and hypothesise. I can read and write if I have to. I can add and subtract and divide. I can think and I can feel.'

Amos looked at Kaia when he said that last word and she felt herself blushing under the gaze of her brother.

'Amos, is it?'

'Yes.'

'Amos, you are a miracle.'

'A miracle that we need to keep away from the wrong people,' Cabby said, bending down to sit next to Storm.

'Yes, we – uh ...'

Travis seemed unwilling to remove his gaze from Amos but, with great effort, he did so as he returned to the computer screen.

'We seem to have had a breakthrough in that regard.'

'What is it?' asked Amos.

Kaia removed herself from his back so Amos could swim as far forward as the shallows would allow, eager to see what Travis was trying to show him on the screen.

'The USB your father left you has everything. It has every piece of data Viktor recorded on you, from when you were a boy right up until now. It has the results of tests he conducted and the extent of your various abilities: speed, strength and problem-solving, that kind of thing. Scientifically speaking, it's information to kill for. It's the discovery and exclusive study of an entirely new species.'

'Damn,' exclaimed Storm.

'Well, not "new",' Travis said, correcting himself. 'I don't have time to go through everything, but Viktor theorises that your kind – aquatic humanoids – are as old as humans. Perhaps older.' Travis was hunched over and he leaned back suddenly, resting his hand on his chin. 'Who knows? Maybe we evolved from you. Could you imagine?'

'Go on,' Cabby said, glancing at Kaia as she tried to get

him back on track. All of this was interesting, sure, but what they needed was information on how to save Amos.

'Hmm? Oh, yes. Sorry. It's just something like this ... it happens once in a generation, a breakthrough of this magnitude.'

Under the surface of the water, Amos linked his hand with Kaia's. He gave her a comforting smile and she willed herself to be patient.

'When viewed in its entirety, Viktor's recent interest in humpback whales makes a lot more sense. All of this information together, here like this, it logically connects the pieces Kaia and I had but couldn't quite make sense of. He didn't think you were the only one of your kind. He theorised there are hundreds out there like you.'

'Hundreds?' asked Amos, wonder in his voice.

'Possibly thousands.'

'What does that have to do with the humpbacks?' asked Storm.

'Humpback whales know the route of their annual migration and follow that exact same path along the east coast of Australia for decades, never changing, much in the same way geese do. There has been some debate as to whether that's a natural-born instinct or something that is taught by the rest of the herd. Viktor basically proved the theory – through his research and three case studies – that it's nature, not nurture, that sets the whales on their path.'

'English, please,' pressed Cabby.

'He theorised that when released into the wild you would instinctively know where to go and how to get back home.'

Kaia let out a shaky breath as she turned to Amos, who remained completely still. 'Just like the humpbacks. In the same way they know where to go for migration, you would know how to get back home.'

'That's what Viktor believed,' said Travis, 'And quite adamantly, might I add.'

'Could you call out to them like a whale? You know, like *waaaaawooooo*.'

Storm's attempt to make a whale sound made Cabby wince and Kaia splashed him quickly to shut him up.

'Stop it, will you!' she hissed. 'That's ridiculous.'

'Not entirely.' Travis pushed past Storm's joke. 'You can make a cry underwater that would be inaudible to most creatures, except your own kind. Much like sonar. Although there isn't much detail on how specifically that works or what—'

'SEE!' Storm said, excitedly punching Cabby in the shoulder and nearly knocking her into the lake.

'Also,' said Travis, kicking off his shoes and jumping into the water until it was up to his ankles. 'Do you mind if I have a look at your tail?'

'Sure.'

Amos only appeared uncertain for a second and Kaia reminded herself that he was used to a lifetime of poking and prodding. She felt sad at the thought. Travis ran his hands down the length of Amos's tail with fascination as he waded deeper and deeper until he was at the end flippers.

'Could you lift it up a touch?'

Amos raised the end of his tail out of the water and into the air so the dolphin-esque quality was exposed. Kaia turned to see a grimace frozen on her brother's face and she quietly nudged him. He didn't change his expression. Travis was almost pressing his glasses to the flesh of the tail as he examined something there.

'Kaia, come here.'

She splashed over to him and looked at where he was running his hands. On the smooth surface where the scales faded to hard skin, there were distinctive patterns curling in and around themselves. Just like the outline of silver scales on his human skin, these were almost invisible until you ran your hands over them. They were beautiful, swirling and curving and twisting like some kind of elaborate Celtic design.

'It's incredible,' she said, looking up at Travis's adoring expression and turning to Amos. 'Your tail is covered in patterns.'

'I know,' he said, shrugging. 'So?'

'This is how you will find your family,' said Travis. 'Those who are directly related to you will have similar markings. It's the same with humpbacks: they identify each other by the designs on their tails. Each are unique, like a finger print, but through them you're able to recognise parents and siblings.'

'I-I'll be able to find my family?'

Kaia laughed, suddenly forgetting the pain of Amos's imminent departure. Everything he had ever dreamed, everything he had ever hoped for was going to come true. She laughed again and grinned at him, the smile reaching down deep into her very soul. He beamed back at her. With a splash of water and a yelp from Travis, Amos sprung from his position and grabbed Kaia in his arms. He thrashed under the surface and they shot threw the water at remarkable sped. As soon as he dipped and arched upwards, she knew what was happening. They shot out of the water and into the air in a glorious fountain of spray and cheerful 'whoops' from Amos. They'd barely crashed back down before they were up again. Kaia joined in his triumphant cries and enjoyed the exhilarating sensation of being airborne. She had a choice and in that moment? She was choosing to stay happy.

CHAPTER THIRTEEN

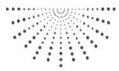

'What are we looking for exactly?' Kaia whispered.
'Anything that looks useful for, you know.'
'Keeping a pet aquatic humanoid?'
'Exactly,' answered Travis.

They had to get Amos to the ocean as soon as possible
and by any means necessary. The 'how' part of the plan was
less clear. So there they were: Travis and Kaia treading
through Professor Viktor Waldman's home in the hopes of
finding something to move Amos in. Travis said there was
equipment back at Sea World for transporting injured
dolphins that would have been perfect. But they couldn't risk
going back there, especially not tonight. It was too
dangerous.

Storm and Cabby had gone off in search of a ute, which
would make the physical relocation a little bit easier. Her
brother had a friend in construction who lived a few suburbs
away and he was heading there to see if he could borrow his
ride temporarily. While Travis and Kaia waited, Amos had
swum them over to his old home so they could enter quietly
through the back. In all honesty, Kaia didn't like being there.

This was where a man had been murdered. This was where he had sacrificed everything to save ... was Amos his son or his experiment? Or his pet? Their relationship was murkier than Lake Pelutz after a heavy rain.

She sighed with frustration as she looked around the bare lab. It was filled with empty tanks and empty desks. In fact, there was an overwhelming sense of emptiness throughout the whole place. She paused when she came to the edge of the indoor pool that was part of Amos's home for over a decade. It was small, too small for anyone to live in. She shuddered at the thought of growing up in such a confined space. It would have been like being raised in a prison cell. No wonder he had survived living in Lake Pelutz on his own. Sure, he had been lonely and scared, but he'd had more space to swim and explore than he'd had in his whole life.

It had long been drained of water and Kaia frowned as she carefully lowered herself into the pool. Her footsteps echoed as she walked along the bottom, looking for the drain Amos that had mentioned would suck him out to Lake Pelutz every time the professor had taken him swimming there. She had envisioned it like a huge funnel that zipped him down to a much bigger playground, yet there was nothing. She crouched down at the centre of the pool, her fingertips trailing the smooth concrete as she looked for any sign of what could have been his escape route. Professor Waldman had proven himself adept at hiding things. Straightening up, Kaia thought about his tendency to disguise certain objects as another to test Amos's capabilities. Walking the pool's perimeter, she gently kicked the discarded filter with her toe as she inspected a series of knobs and buttons built into the edge.

'What are you doing?' Travis asked, leaning over the side to watch her.

'Nothing,' she sighed, fiddling with one of three air buttons. 'Just – '

Her sentence disappeared as the button sunk down flat against the surface of the pool, accompanied by a mechanical *whirring* sound. Spinning around, her eyes widened as she drank in the sight of an enormous hole now at the centre of the floor.

'Oh my God,' she said, inching towards it. Looking down into its depths, she jumped as the edges of the hole begin to close inch-by-inch of their own accord.

'That's how he got out,' Travis whispered, sounding impressed.

Kaia looked back at the button, which had popped back into position seamlessly. It looked identical to the ones surrounding it, so identical that she began to question which knob she had actually pressed.

'How the hell did he get him back up into the house every time he took him for a swim?' she wondered. 'He was an old guy, I can't exactly see him throwing Amos over his shoulder like he's on roids and lugging him up the embankment.'

'There's a hundred different ways to do,' Travis replied. 'A winch, maybe. Or the edge of the lake is no more than fifteen metres from this pool. If you laid down a slick, wet surface he could pull himself up from one to the other.'

'A slide, Travis? Are you saying an aquatic humanoid used a slide in reverse to get himself back in here every time?'

'It's more likely than a theory about the Professor flushing him down the drain like a dead goldfish every time he wanted to give him space to swim around. And yet … '

The scientist hit the button Kaia had pressed just seconds earlier, opening up the hole at the centre of the pool again to demonstrate his point.

'Touché,' she muttered.

'Hmm, this could be useful,' Travis pondered, moving

towards a massive tank situated nearby.

'Yeah, only problem is getting it to the car,' Kaia said over her shoulder, as she headed towards Professor Waldman's desk area.

Some papers had been removed for evidence, but it was still a lot cleaner than the working conditions of Travis's colleague. There were various tidal charts and maps pinned on the walls and Kaia scanned them with mild interest. She was about to turn away when one caught her eye. It was a close-up of the North Queensland coastline near the Great Barrier Reef. It was only in A4, which made it an odd-shaped map: it cut off huge portions of geography she thought would have been useful. And then she saw it. Sketched in the corner of the map in pencil so fine it was barely visible was a pattern. It looked just like the designs on Amos's tail. She examined the map more closely.

'Travis, do you have the plastic sheets with you?'

'Huh? Yeah, sure.'

Travis pulled out the documents, which had been rolled into a cylinder and shoved deep within the back pocket of his pants. He walked over to Kaia and flattened them out.

'The clear one, I need the clear one.'

'Here we go.'

He slid out the sheet and tried to wipe the water droplets from it, but she stopped him.

'Leave it,' she said, watching as the glow of dark shapes began to form once again when liquid made contact. Quickly, she snatched it from his hand and headed for the wall to press the plastic over the A4 map of the North Queensland coast. She lined the sides up and looked at the map again, which was illuminated with the glowing arrows that pointed east from the reef. They went off in two directions that ended in the same place, marked with a small circle.

'Is that—'

'Yup,' she said, 'I think that's Amos's home.'

They stood there and admired the alignment for a moment. It wasn't long before the glow on the arrows started to fade. Before it was too late, Kaia made Travis take a photo with his phone.

'How did you know that would work?' he asked her.

'I didn't. When the page lit up in the car, I remembered that I could almost feel something on it, like indentations. Then this map just seemed like a strange shape when that cut off most of the locations. Unless it wasn't the landmarks you were wanting to chart.'

'It was the ocean.'

Kaia nodded.

'I also saw this,' she said, tapping the small pencil sketch at the corner of the map. 'It looks like Amos's tail, don't you think?'

Travis leaned in close to see the marking. He looked back at Kaia, amused.

'If our search for a tank was futile, at least we've left with something.'

Thankfully Storm and Cabby had better luck. Kaia watched nervously as Cabby reversed the ute as close to the lake's edge as she could, Storm and Travis directing her from outside of the vehicle.

'Whoa, stop there,' Storm ordered, bringing her to a halt. It was as near as Cabby was going to get, given they'd had to do all of this without headlights to make sure what they were up to remained secret. They were so close now, they couldn't afford to get sprung.

'This is the Great Barrier Reef here,' said Travis, crouching down to show Amos the picture he had taken on his phone, zooming in on the image. 'The arrows take two separate paths until they both end in the same spot, somewhere about 100 kilometres, maybe 120 kilometres east of the reef.'

Amos was concentrating hard on the image, as if trying to memorise it. 'So even if I'm not able to use my natural instinct to remember how to get home, now I know where I'm going?'

'Yes! You just follow the coastline up into the warmer water and once you find the reef, head east.'

'And all of that's worst case scenario,' Amos added.

'Exactly.' Travis smiled. 'Once you're in open water, you should know what to do even without this.'

Amos was smiling at the news, but the wide curve of his lips slowly faded as he looked up over the edge of Lake Pelutz and towards Kaia. She was staring back at him, but couldn't hold his gaze. She glanced away, moving off to help her friend.

'Great,' Cabby said, jumping out of the ute. 'Without a tank, now what do we do?'

Storm walked around the car, seemingly hoping a thought would come to him as he paced. It did.

'Why don't we just put him in the tray?'

Kaia looked at her brother for a long moment to see it he was joking. He wasn't.

'You don't think other motorists might notice a half-man, half-fish in the back of the car?' Cabby asked sarcastically.

'Yeah, I know *that*. But it's nearly midnight, there's not gonna be that many people on the road. We fill up the tray with water and—'

He dug into the back seat for something she couldn't see. He reemerged with blue tarpaulin.

'We put this over the top and no one will be able to see what's inside. They'll think it's sand or wood chips or something.'

'I don't need to be completely submerged,' Amos piped

up. 'I can breathe through my mouth until we get to open water.'

'We'd just need to make sure it's damp enough so he's comfortable,' Travis agreed. 'We can put a few bucket loads of water in the tray now to keep him wet and top it up along the way if we need to.'

'How are we gonna get him *in* from the lake to the ute?' Cabby asked, pointing at the distance for further emphasis.

'Awkwardly?' Storm shrugged.

'What if we get stopped while driving?' asked Kaia.

They all looked at each other with nervous glances.

'Then we floor it,' answered Cabby.

———

The strategy was rough, at best. They intended to drive Amos as far north as possible, thereby giving him the best chance of finding his people easily. Maybe if they had been less ambitious, they would have made it further. As it was, they didn't even make it out of the Gold Coast before they were stopped. And not by the police, mind you. It was by *them*. Storm and Travis were squished together in the front cabin of the ute as Cabby drove, while Kaia had awkwardly shoved herself in the space behind the seats so she could keep checking on Amos.

'How's he doing back there?' asked Travis.

'Good,' Kaia replied. 'It looks bloody uncomfortable, but at least there's plenty of water.'

'I'm trying to take the corners as slowly as I can,' Cabby noted.

'You're doing good, hun.'

She patted Cabby on the arm affectionately as her friend kept her eyes on the road. Kaia had been switching her gaze from the ute's tray to other cars around them, which were few given the time of night. None of them owned this car, so she hoped that gave them an advantage if someone was tracking their usual rides. But she was still nervous. Kaia couldn't quite shake the hornet's nest that felt like it was about to burst through her stomach at any moment.

'How did they find us?'

'What?' asked Travis.

'How did they find us?' she repeated. 'One of the reasons I went to you, besides our date, was because you weren't affiliated with the university. Sure, you had studied there, but you weren't one of their researchers and you weren't staff. I figured Hodgkins is how they found the Professor in the first place and if I started asking questions there, then they'd most likely find me too.'

'Oh. *Oh no*,' Travis breathed.

'What?' Storm snapped. '"Oh no" what?'

'I didn't know, I—'

Kaia's pulse quickened. 'Travis, what is it?'

'I called Hodgkins University today to enquire about the specimens they took from Viktor's home. I was trying to see if any of them were compatible with the kind of research we were looking at.'

'Damn it,' muttered Storm.

'I'm sorry, it's completely my fault.'

Kaia sighed. 'No, it's really not. It's my fault. I should have been honest with you from the start, but I wasn't sure if you could be trusted. If you'd known what I was hiding then you wouldn't have had to call the university.'

'I trust them, though,' he said, slowly unravelling something in his mind. 'I've known the researchers there whole career. The Head of Department is an exceptional thinker. I don't believe any of them would have something to do with this or Viktor's murder.'

'Fine, so it's not them,' said Storm bluntly.

'Let's not clear them so easily,' Cabby replied.

'Couldn't those guys – whoever they work for – be monitoring the university somehow?' Kaia asked. 'Maybe they were waiting to see if anything popped up and when you called asking questions—'

'I gave us away,' finished Travis. A loaded silence filled the stuffy cabin of the ute. Kaia asked Storm to wind down the window.

'Who do you think they are?' Cabby questioned, glancing at Travis.

'I've been wondering about that. My first thought was government.'

'Why?'

'While I was waiting for you at Sea World, one of the men had his weapon pointed on me while the other was fidgeting with a gun that's a very technologically advanced piece of machinery.'

Storm straightened. 'A bazooka?'

'Brother,' Kaia scoffed. 'This isn't a Dolph Lundgren movie. You don't think you might have noticed if he was carrying a bazooka?'

'It's a make of tranquilliser that has been repurposed,' said Travis. 'The prototype only came on the market last year. We were looking at getting some for the park because when fired they inject the subject with a harmless and invisible chemical that can be tracked, similar to GPS. They were too expensive for us to warrant buying even one. The man with the ponytail was prepping it, as if he was expecting to use it on whatever we had hidden. He put it away before you arrived and went back to his regular gun.'

Cabby crinkled her nose. 'That's what made you think they were government?'

'Yes, but now it makes me think they weren't.'

'Come on, Travis,' Storm sighed. 'Pick a poison.'

'Our government isn't exactly known for their generous contributions to the scientific community,' he started. 'They wouldn't pay $500,000 for a device like that and then hand it out to bottom-feeding thugs willy-nilly.'

'Then who?' pushed Kaia, getting annoyed.

'If there's some aspect of Amos, some sort of property that can be utilised for medical purposes, then I'd bet a pharmaceutical company. That's my guess.'

'They were planning to use that tracker on him,' she stated, her voice sounding far off and distant.

'I'd say injecting Amos with the chemical would be the first goal these people have. That way, no matter what happened, they'd be able to track him.'

She blinked, fully understanding. 'They could trace him back to his people.'

'Sure. Although I don't think they'd be keen to release him into the wild.'

'Corner!' Cabby shouted, nearing a roundabout.

'Corner,' Kaia repeated, turning to shout back at Amos just in case he hadn't heard them. The tarpaulin was strapped down tight over the tray of the ute except for the part closest to the cabin window, which was where Amos stuck a thumbs-up to express his thank you.

'I feel it should be said,' continued Travis, 'that since you all seem rather attached to Amos, you need to be aware of what will happen to him if he's caught.'

'I know,' Kaia replied, voice tight. Her mind had been running over the horrible possibilities non-stop since they left Sea World. 'He'll be locked up in some lab for the rest of his life, poked and prodded.'

She could feel her brother's discomfort as she outlined Amos's fate. He might act as if he didn't like 'the fish', but at the end of the day Storm was putting a lot on the line to help him reach freedom.

'No. I mean, yes, he will be experimented on, but I suspect not for very long. The only way to perform a conclusive analysis and study is with a post-mortem.'

Cabby swerved the car ever so slightly at that. 'They'll ... kill him?'

'Most definitely.'

Kaia said nothing. Suddenly she felt sick as she thought about Amos laying on some cold slab, uncaring strangers dissecting him like an ibis picking over a discarded fishbone. She closed her eyes.

'We won't let it come to that,' she said through gritted teeth.

Kaia opened her eyes to see the incoming rise that marked the start of Darrell Watson Bridge ahead of them and felt a sense of relief. They'd been taking the back streets as a precaution, but the bridge was the last hurdle out of town before they could cut back to the highway. The final section of upper Coomera River ran underneath the bridge before it joined the massive expanse of water that was the Southport Seaway: a nautical freeway used by fishing boats heading out to sea. Kaia peered out the window to look over the water as it sparkled with the reflections of various street and house lights.

'SHIT!'

Cabby's shout was followed by the screeching of brakes as she slammed her foot down on the pedal. Travis and Storm threw out their hands to stop themselves flying through the windscreen while Kaia rolled into the back of the seats in front of her. There was a heavy thud as Travis's head connected with the glass and when he leaned back, there was blood forming at a cut on his forehead. Amos hit the tray as the ute came to a shuddering halt and Kaia scrambled upright to see if he was okay.

'I'm fine,' he said, head emerging from under the plastic. 'What happened?'

Jerking around to answer that question, it felt like the bottom of Kaia's heart fell out of her chest as she took in the sight. Three slick, black SUVs were parked across the width of the bridge. They were completely blocking the road. To add to that, half a dozen men and women in grey suits were standing next to the vehicles with guns raised at the car.

'We're screwed,' breathed Storm.

Standing at the centre of the collection of cars and people was a man dressed in the uniform of a Sea World maintenance worker. It was the ponytailed thug. Red and blue lights had been stuck to the top of the cars to make the situation look official to any passing spectators. But these guys weren't cops. They were less than fifteen metres away from the ute and Kaia saw the smirk forming on the ponytailed man as he raised a megaphone to his lips. He maintained eye contact with them the entire time. Kaia did the same, never looking away from his face as she cautiously felt around in the back for her phone. She barely needed to look at the screen to know which buttons she needed to press, switching it to silent and turning the phone on. She hit the address book icon and began typing letters, sparing one tiny glance before she hit call. She was grateful Sergeant Ferris had given her his number, in case she might need it. Putting the phone on speaker, she placed it in the drink holder in the middle of the ute's interior. She could hear the vague mumble as he answered.

'Sergeant Ferris, we need your help,' she said quietly, her lips barely moving. 'Fake cops at Darrell Watson Bridge.'

'Calling the real cops doesn't make me feel any safer,' Cabby hissed.

The words were barely from her month when the man in the Sea World uniform began speaking.

'To the occupants of the car: this is the Gold Coast police. We know you have a fugitive with you. We ask you to get out of the vehicle and raise your hands slowly above your heads. There's no need for anyone to get hurt if you just do as we ask.'

The four of them shared a look. Yeah, right.

'You're not the police,' called Storm out the window.

'If you don't remove yourself from the vehicle immediately, we will be forced to fire.'

'What other choice have we got?' Travis whispered.

Storm and Cabby both opened the doors to the car slowly, stepping out of the car with caution.

'Stay behind the doors, just in case,' Kaia mumbled, as she began wriggling into the front seat with Travis.

'Why are there fourteen of you?' called Storm. 'Seems a bit excessive.'

Kaia knew what he was trying to do: he was trying to give Sergeant Ferris as much information possible, if the policeman was still listening. She hoped he got Storm's message, because their attackers certainly did. The man with the ponytail frowned at Storm's question and Kaia paused, halfway out of the car as she watched him react. He looked around for a second, before a flash of understanding crossed his face. Turning to his cohorts, he shouted for the benefit of the two night fishermen who had been standing at the edge of the bridge watching the whole ordeal.

'THEY HAVE A GUN! FIRE!'

A barrage of bullets descended on the ute and Kaia dashed forward, yanking Cabby back into the car with her. They pressed themselves flat against the seats as the windscreen exploded into tiny shards above their heads. The sound was deafening as the bullets thunked into the bonnet of the car in an endless shower of noise. She saw Travis dive under the vehicle and hoped he could find some shelter there. Storm had run around to the back of the tray and was taking cover in the most protected spot. Well, not the most protected.

'AMOS, STAY DOWN!' Kaia screamed.

She hoped that as long as he stayed within the safety of the tray, he wouldn't be hit by any stray bullets. The gunfire continued for what felt like a lifetime. Tiny pieces of glass were cutting into her hands as she attempted to protect her head. Kaia scrunched her eyes up as tight as she could, Cabby gripping her shoulders for dear life. Then it stopped all at once. She raised her head from under her hands, but not enough that she would be exposed over the dashboard. Travis must have tried to emerge from under the car as they heard him shout and the sound of a bullet hitting the ground near where he had been. Kaia hoped he had scuttled back under the car. Cabby's eyes were wide as she too glanced up, cautiously. Shaking her head gently loosened small pieces of glass from her hair. Kaia watched as her friend reached back towards the steering wheel, fiddling blindly until she felt the handle that controlled the lights. Cabby gave Kaia a smirk, before switching it on as far as it would go in the hopes the high beam would momentarily blind anyone trying to make their way towards them. A frustrated murmur ran through the group of people who had just been firing at them.

'Go,' Cabby whispered. 'Go go.'

Kaia nodded, sliding out of the seat backwards and on to the ground as she watched Cabby roll down onto the floor below. The last image she had of her friend was Cabby trying to cover herself in whatever debris had been laying at their feet. Kaia sprinted to the back of the vehicle. She screamed when she saw Storm laid out on the concrete, unmoving. She dived to his body and looked for the blood, but she couldn't see any. There was a massive lump on the side of his temple that was swelling quickly. Her shaking fingers felt for a pulse and she let out a relieved sob when she connected with the steady throbbing coming through the skin of his wrist. He'd been knocked unconscious and Kaia glanced up just in time to see the culprit ripping back the tarpaulin to reveal Amos underneath. The guy with the greasy, gross ponytail had used the gunfire as a distraction to sneak behind the ute and take out her brother. He must have been out of bullets.

'Incredible,' he whispered, the words slithering out of his mouth as he stared at Amos in complete and utter amazement.

Swivelling around to face him, Amos didn't look afraid: merely surprised at the man's sudden appearance. What happened next felt like it did so in slow motion. The man cocked a second weapon at his belt. A light went from red to orange on a digital display, before a charging sound began beeping from it. The light turned green and the man took four steps back to get a clear shot as he aimed for the middle of Amos's tail.

'KAIA!' Travis shouted from his position under the car. 'That's the tracker!'

She leapt up from her brother's body and sprinted towards Amos, covering the distance between them just as the man fired. The tracker hit Kaia right in the stomach, the impact knocking her back against the corner of the ute's tray. It was so sharp it pierced the material of her hoodie and tore through her swimsuit like it was tissue paper. She glanced down and could see the small knob that was sticking out of her stomach. Doubling over with pain, she groaned and tried to stay steady on her feet. There was hardly any blood. After all, the tracker wasn't designed to hurt the target: it was designed to infect them. She yanked it out of her stomach with a grunt and let the plastic casing fall to the ground, watching as it bounced along the road with a hollow clunk. Kaia felt Amos's hands on her shoulders, helping to keep her upright as he splashed to the edge of the tray to see the damage.

'YOU STUPID GIRL!'

The ponytail man was furious and he stormed towards her, discarding the device and reaching for another weapon. She had been wrong about him being out of bullets. He pressed the gun under Kaia's chin, but before he could pull the trigger he was yanked up and into the tray.

'Wha— WAIT!'

Kaia drowned out his cries as she stumbled forward, still clutching her stomach. A metallic taste was filling her mouth and she was sure it was due to the chemicals spreading through her body. She spat onto the concrete, but the taste remained on her salvia. Water was splashing from the back of the ute and the man's cries were dying off. Peeking closer, she saw glimpses of red spreading through the water and quickly shut her eyes.

'DEREK? SIR? DO WE PROCEED?'

An uncertain female voice belonging to one of the shooters came across the loud speaker. Derek. That was the name of the killer with the ponytail. He was most certainly dead now, lying lifeless in the back of the ute as blood slowly spread from a head wound. Amos was panting with the effort of the fight and he leaned against the metal at the far side of the tray. The headlights had worked better than they could have hoped, with their pursuers oblivious to what had just taken place. They didn't know if everyone was dead, if the creature had been found or if 'Derek' had the situation under control. Amos met Kaia's eyes, his chest still rising and falling. Travis finally scrambled out from under the car. Besides his head wound from earlier and a few minor scratches, miraculously he seemed to be okay. The sound of sirens rang out in the night air and broke the tension that was running through the group. Kaia turned and saw the red and blue flashing lights of *real* police cars speeding in their direction. They would mount the bridge behind them in a matter of seconds. This was both good and bad.

'What do we do?' asked Travis, who was looking between Amos and her.

As much as the arrival of the police had saved them, it would ultimately be the end for Amos. If they got one peek at him, it was over.

'Look after my brother, will you?' she asked, marching back towards the driver's seat.

'Where are you going?'

Not pausing for a second, she glanced at Amos who had moved to the edge of the tray and was dangling his arms over it. She saw the complete and utter trust in his eyes.

'We're going over the bridge,' she told him.

He didn't even look frightened. He nodded at Kaia with a determined stare.

'The *bridge*?' said Cabby, her head emerging from her place curled up on the floor. 'You've gotta be crazy!'

'I've gotta be out of time,' Kaia responded, helping pull her friend up and out of the car. 'Help Travis with Storm, if you can.'

Cabby was about to say something, her eyes glassy as she stared at Kaia. Pressing her lips together, her friend steeled herself and headed after the guys. Jumping into the driver's seat, Kaia started the engine and prayed the car would still turn on after everything it had just endured. It took two goes, but she revved the engine just enough to hear it splutter to life as she clicked on her seatbelt. She could see the people in front of her milling about in confusion. Some still had their weapons pointed forward, their eyes squinting as they waited for a command telling them what to do. Others had reacted to the incoming police presence and were dashing towards their cars, doors slamming as they dived inside.

'Hold on,' she called back to Amos.

Slamming the gear into reverse, Kaia accelerated back as far as she could across the width of the bridge. Revving the motor as she switched into gear, the remaining shooters finally realised what she intended to do. By the time they started firing, it was too late. Kaia hit the railing of Darrell Watson Bridge at close to 50kmph, which was as fast as she could get to with the short run of road she had left. She ducked the bullets as they pinged around the hull of the vehicle and the ute shot off the top of the bridge and into the air. She felt like they hung in space for the tiniest of fractions before the ute started to plummet some thirty metres. Kaia had the seat belt done up tight around her chest and she braced herself for the impact. They landed in the water about as gracefully as a hippo. Given most of the windows of the ute had been shot out, water from the river began pouring in instantly.

Kaia tried to stay calm as the liquid rose around her, pouring in through the holes in the windscreen and shattered windows. There was no point trying to escape from the vehicle while this was happening, the water pressure would be too strong for her to get free. She'd end up wasting energy and probably trapping herself. No, she knew she had to wait until the ute was completely submerged before she'd be able to swim to safety. Kaia just hoped Amos was free and okay. As the water rose around her face, the last thing she heard before it covered her ears were the shouts of people on the bridge and fading gunfire. And then she was under.

Everything was better underwater. It was calm there. Quiet. She could just make out a few metres ahead of her as the headlights projected into the depths. Bubbles were emerging from everywhere as the last pockets of air disappeared. It was time to go. Kaia reached down to undo her seat belt and pulled. The latch was stuck. Yanking at it with all the force she could muster, she tried not to panic and release much-needed air. Then suddenly a hand was wrapping around the clasp. With one incredibly strong pull, the plastic broke apart.

She looked up to see Amos softly smiling at her. Kaia tried to return the expression, but it was difficult when her cheeks were puffed up with air. He reached his hands out to grab her body and she tightened her grip around his as he delicately removed her from the cabin. He looked at Kaia with a question in his eyes and she nodded, signalling that she was okay to stay underwater for a while longer. She pointed in the direction of the Southport Seaway and he took off.

Each second that he swam, he seemed to get faster and faster. Amos didn't have the perimeters of a lake to worry about any more. There was only an endless path stretching out before him that led to an ocean. When Kaia thought she couldn't hold her breath any longer, she squeezed his arm. They came to the surface instantly and she sucked in several big gulps of air. Blinking the water out of her eyes, she looked around. They were at the end of the sea-wall that marked the final stretch of the seaway and the beginning of the ocean. She turned to face Amos, panting slightly. He was grinning at Kaia as he held her tightly in his arms.

'We did it!'

She laughed at the tone in his voice. It was one she had never heard before. It was more than hope or anticipation. It was the voice of someone who had a future. It was the voice of someone who was free. It was also, she realised, the voice of someone who had to leave her. Kaia's smile slowly began to fade and as hers inched away, his did too.

'Come with me,' he said, leaning in to emphasise his words. 'We can live off the coast as I make my way north and when we—'

'Amos,' Kaia interrupted. She moved his hand to the flat surface of her stomach and to the tear in the fabric of her swimsuit where the tracker had ripped through. 'I can't. Wherever I go, they'll know.'

His face dropped with disappointment. He was quiet for a long while, finally coming to the realisation that this was it: this was the end.

'Whoever these people are, they will never stop watching me to get to you.'

'Then I'll stay,' he said, resolute. 'You live on the beach, right? I can stay off-shore and we can see each other every—'

'*Amos*,' she said again, closing her eyes. 'We didn't fight this hard for your freedom so that you'd be trapped with me. All of the answers you've been looking for, your family, they're right there.' She extended her hand over his shoulder as she pointed out towards the sea. It was rising and falling gently with the rhythmic movements of the tide.

'But …' His words trailed off as he stroked the skin on her cheek.

Kaia felt the sting of salt as tears began to form. She leaned forward so that their foreheads pressed against each other.

'I love you,' he said.

Kaia jerked back, her mouth falling open in shock. Before she could think about it any further, before she could question herself, she leaned forward and kissed him. It was nothing more than a slow, tentative peck at first. Yet as their lips connected, something happened: something internal. Amos grabbed her face and pulled her closer to him as he returned the kiss. Kaia poured everything into that physical act, every fear and every emotion that had been building came pouring out. Bobbing in the ocean, with their arms wrapped around each other, she kissed Amos deeply and with all that she had. Every other set of lips she had touched in her lifetime seemed insignificant compared to his. They felt as if they were built to match perfectly with hers. She had no idea how long they stayed like that, lost in the motions of each other as they kissed and kissed and kissed. When they pulled apart, she wouldn't have been surprised to see the sun peeking over the horizon. But no, it was still dark and only the faintest glow of the moon was visible across the surface of the water. Taking a shuddering breath, she couldn't untangle herself from him quite yet.

'Don't forget me,' she whispered, staring into his big, wide eyes. 'Wherever you go, whatever you see and whoever you meet, don't forget me, Amos.'

'How could I ever?' he replied, watching her every expression.

With a sigh, she pushed herself gently backwards and away from him. The second she was treading water by herself, it felt like she was going to plummet straight to the bottom of the ocean.

'You need to go,' she said. 'They could be tracking me already.'

He didn't want to leave, she could see the reluctance in every inch of his features. Slowly, Amos lifted the chain of keys over his head and hung them around Kaia's neck. She looked down and fingered the metal where it fell into the groove between her breasts. Amos leaned in one last time and pecked her gently on the lips, sweet and quick.

'Goodbye,' he said.

With that, he was gone. Ducking under the surface of the sea and towards his destiny. Kaia trod water for a few moments longer. She was desperate for one last look at him. Just when she had almost given up, a figure burst from the ocean far off in the distance. The long, black shape arched above the surface and plummeted back into the water. It was a leap of faith. To Kaia, it looked like a leap of freedom.

EPILOGUE

The surf was flat. It was also swelteringly hot. The lycra of the full body suits designed to protect athletes from stingers and deadly jellyfish didn't help. Kaia could feel sweat clinging to the fabric as she shook her limbs out on the starting line. Given what had happened in rough conditions at the last Australian Titles, this year the event had moved to Emu Park in North Queensland. It was excellent in theory. The location was protected by the Great Barrier Reef some kilometres off-shore so calm conditions were guaranteed. It was also ideal for Cabby, it being closest to her natural habitat of the pool. She had won the open women's swim race by almost twenty-five metres that morning, making her officially an Australian champ. It was perfect for officials too – and the nippers. It was, however, terrible for Kaia.

'Woo! Let's go, Kaia, let's go!'

She looked behind her to see Storm's goofy grin next to a figure who looked like a dwarf in comparison: her father, waving madly. They were standing side-by-side at the corner of the marshalling tent and beaming at her with complete faith. Further back, there were other familiar faces. Cabby was smiling with her arm casually slung over Imogen Tishop's shoulder. Her girlfriend was chatting animatedly to her brother, Travis, who spared Kaia a quick smirk. Her very own personal cheer squad.

Even Sergeant Ferris had said he wanted to be there, but he couldn't wrangle the time off work. The veteran cop had looked after Storm, Travis, Cabby and Kaia with incredible care following the shoot-out on Darrell Watson Bridge. Every single member of the enemy had escaped, despite leaving police a somewhat solid trail that they were still tracking. The net was closing on whatever organisation had been responsible for what the four of them claimed was a "bizarre" and "completely random" attack. The only fatality from the whole incident was the mysterious Derek, who had suffered a severe head injury after taking Kaia hostage and driving off the bridge. Somehow Kaia had managed to escape, but was washed out to the Southport Seaway where she was spotted climbing over the rocks by night-time fishermen an hour later. It was a remarkable story and the press loved it. Trouble, it seemed, followed the Craig family wherever they went.

Only the four of them knew the truth. In a bid to protect themselves, they made sure that everyone knew they were 'survivors' of some violent case of mistaken identity in the cutthroat world of corporate espionage. It had started with Professor Viktor Waldman, Travis's former teacher, and it had carried over to them like a toxic virus. They did newspaper interviews, radio interviews, television interviews: anyone who wanted to speak to them, they gave access to as KC's publicist managed the aftermath. Travis's theory was that the more people who knew their story, the better. He had called it insurance. And it was. The public profile had guaranteed their safety to some degree. But after a few unexplained and unsuccessful break-ins at Travis's office and the

Craigs' beachfront home, they had resolved to destroy the USB and the remaining papers for good. They lit a chemically enhanced bonfire one evening and said goodbye to it all, guaranteeing Amos's safety forever.

Amos. There had been a huge hole in all of their lives since he left, none more so than Kaia's. She couldn't go back to Lake Pelutz, the emotions were too raw. Instead she often found herself sitting on her dad's balcony and looking out over the ocean at night, imagining what he was doing and the things he was seeing. She only took off the key chain he gave her when she had to train, which was what she had poured her energy into since. Suddenly she had a lot more free time on her hands and needed a way to keep her mind busy. Training it was.

The months of hard work had led her back to where so much of her life started to spin out of control: the Open Ironwoman Australian Title. As Kaia crouched down in anticipation of the starter's gun, she told herself that she needed to get her head in the game. Forget that these weren't her ideal conditions. Sure, she wouldn't have the advantage of a wave going out or coming in. And yeah, there was nothing to separate the tug and tumble of the pack except speed. But Kaia was the best and she wanted this title more than anything. As the gun fired, she launched herself down the sand and into the water. The ocean was so warm she doubted even her home shower was this hot. Kaia tried putting her discomfort to the side as she waded to the front of the pack with three other girls. They launched themselves into deeper water with gusto and began throwing their arms forward for the swim leg.

Of the three disciplines, the random draw had seen the ironwoman event start with her weakest. She wasn't used to competing in conditions this hot and already she could feel her heartbeat pulsing at the points where her silicon bathing cap tightened around her scalp. Kaia took a breath of sticky, humid air and almost wished she hadn't. Her pace was slacking and she was falling behind the two other girls who had pulled to the lead. She could see their toes in front of her through the green water and the lens of her goggles. And then she saw something else that made her jolt like she had been touched with a cattle prod. A flash of silver streaked past her eyes, lightning-fast and gone in an instant.

Had she imagined it? Was she hallucinating in the heat? No, there it was again! The unmistakable silver of a tail that belonged to something of legend came into view once more, baiting Kaia. She felt herself grinning underwater and saw a grin of equal enthusiasm reflected back at her. Suddenly Kaia found a source of untapped energy as she accelerated forward, pushing herself through the water. The warm current sped past her as she swam, harder and faster towards victory.

ACKNOWLEDGMENTS

It Came From The Deep was never meant to exist as a physical book. But as I've learned with mermen, they so rarely do what you tell them. This was supposed to my e-baby, but since the digital version was first released on my favourite day of the year – Halloween – in 2017, I was overwhelmed and, frankly, surprised with the response. People wanted this as a physical book: they wanted to hold it in their hands and see that glorious cover in the flesh. The demand was high and coming from all angles: over social media, face-to-face at pop culture conventions, phrased as a question at writers festivals and even from the barista at my local coffee shop. So because you wanted it, it now exists.

I knew jack shit about self-publishing, so a colossal thank you has to go to the living legend that is Keri Arthur who – along with Ineke Prochazka – hustled me into the position of finally, nervously, pushing this through the printing process. Without the two of you ladies giving me advice, responding to my questions and just generally being baller It Came From The Deep would still solely be swimming around on the net.

I'd also like to thank IRL ironwoman and legit Australian champ, Courtney Hancock, for being an inspo and ye olde training buddy. In fact, the whole Hancock brood deserve cheers here: Bonnie, Indi, Georgia, Richard and Julie. Because so much of this book is embedded in the world of surf life saving, of which I spent more than 12 years being a part of, the late Pat O'Keefe also needs a thank you even though I'm pretty sure he'd be as weirded out by me writing a merman book as he was about me writing werewolf ones. Merci merci to Flora 'Frenchie' Manciet, thanks for the language lessons and for being the only person I know crazy enough to paddle on a board from Canada to fucking France. Everyone's favourite fighting French man Lafayette ain't got nothing on you.

Kudos to my patient tech saviour Sam Spettigue, best of husbands and best of men. Everything is a dumpster fire without you. Sup to your goldfish, editor enchantress Abigail Nathan whose words remain bothersome and whose eyes and supervision remain sharp as ever. Cheers to Trevor Long at Sea World on the Gold Coast for being an excellent source all these years.

Thanks to the awesome network of writers including (but not limited to) Angela Slatter, Alan Baxter, Jodi McAlister, Justin Woolley, Marlee Ward, Lynette Noni, Ann and Patrica Briggs, Caris Bizzaca, Alison Goodman, bodyguard Tom Taylor, Kim Wilkins, Ryan 'cleverest man' Griffen, Debbie Moon and Nicola Scott. Massive smooth handshake to my boi BossLogic for coming up with such killer Amos art and Allison Tyree, master baker, master map drawer and master locator of ancient sea charts.

Cheers to friends who go above and beyond selling my shit better than I ever could, namely Greek God Greg Vekiarellis and Crime Night members Jeanne Kidd and Ramona Sen Gupta. Also Caitlin Jinks, Sophie Ly, Blake Howard and the barrage of book bloggers who helped raise It Came From The Deep's profile. Snaps to Cat aka Little Book Owl for helping launch the news of this novel to the world when I was sweaty and anxious about it. Tilting a llama in recognition to my agent, Ed Wilson, who's as fascinated by the sex organs of aquatic humanoids as I am.

Cheers to Detective Thomas Lewis, Blue Crush's biggest fan Teresa and my mum, Tania, for years of getting up early and driving me to training. Arrroooooo to the ever-loyal wolf-packers for following me from full moons to aquatic adventures. Thanks again to the Supanova fam, as always, for being the launch pad for my career as both a journalist and an author.

Finally, although this book is set on the Gold Coast and I have used real locations, I have taken liberties with some of the key set pieces. So if you go looking for Lake Pelutz, you'll find that it doesn't exist. But hey, while you're there … Lake Hugh Muntz is pretty close.

ABOUT THE AUTHOR

Maria Lewis is a journalist, screenwriter and author based in Sydney, Australia. Getting her start as a police reporter at the Gold Coast Bulletin, her writing on pop culture has appeared in publications such as the New York Post, Guardian, Penthouse, The Daily Mail, Empire Magazine, Huffington Post, The Daily and Sunday Telegraph, Film Ink and many more. Seen as a presenter on SBS Viceland's nightly news program The Feed and as the host of Cleverfan on ABC, she has been a journalist for over 13 years. Her critically acclaimed debut novel Who Afraid? was published in 2016, followed by its sequel Who's Afraid Too? in 2017. Who's Afraid? is being developed for television by the Emmy and BAFTA award-winning Hoodlum Entertainment.

You can visit Maria Lewis at marialewis.com.au and find her on social media at:

Twitter: @MovieMazz
Facebook: MariaLewisWriter
Instagram: @MovieMazz

Lightning Source UK Ltd.
Milton Keynes UK
UKHW022348061218
333617UK00007B/34/P